THE QUEST

A Western Trio

MAX BRAND®

CENTER POINT LARGE PRINT
THORNDIKE, MAINE

2017

ISBN: 978-1-62899-980-8 (hardcover)
ISBN: 978-1-62899-984-6 (paperback)

Library of Congress Cataloging-in-Publication Data

Names: Brand, Max, 1892–1944, author. | Brand, Max, 1892–1944.
Paradise Al. | Brand, Max, 1892–1944. Paradise Al's Confession. |
Brand, Max, 1892–1944. Quest.
Title: The quest : a western trio / Max Brand.
Description: Center Point Large Print edition. | Thorndike, Maine :
Center Point Large Print, 2016. | ©2009
Identifiers: LCCN 2016008257| ISBN 9781628999808
   (hardcover : alk. paper) | ISBN 9781628999846 (pbk. : alk. paper)
Subjects: LCSH: Large type books.
Classification: LCC PS3511.A87 A6 2016b | DDC 813/.52—dc23
LC record available at http://lccn.loc.gov/2016008257

Printed and bound in Great Britain
by TJ International Ltd, Padstow, Cornwall

MIX
Paper from
responsible sources
FSC® C013056

Also by Max Brand® and available from Center Point Large Print:

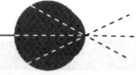

Table of Contents

PARADISE AL

The year 1932 saw the publication of twenty-three short novels and fourteen serials by Frederick Faust. All but two of these appeared in Street & Smith's *Western Story Magazine*, Faust's primary market beginning in 1921 and lasting through the mid-'Thirties. "Paradise Al", the first of a duo of stories, appeared in the June 4th issue under the David Manning byline. In it Faust deftly wove a number of plot elements including a long-standing feud between two families, an unbroken wild horse, and an Eastern criminal on the lam who takes on a false identity.

I

The first pinch of autumn was in the air that morning, and the cold filled the blue mist that lay in the hollows around Jumping Creek; all the lower flanks of the mountains were dimmed by the same exhalations, although their tops gloried in the clear upper air, far above timberline.

Paradise Al, looking out from the blind baggage of the passenger train as it stormed up the grade toward the wide railroad yards of Jumping Creek, noted all of these features, and he saw, furthermore, how the leaves of the bushes along the hills were stained with yellows and reds and purples, some of them already brown and crisp. The wind, as he leaned out, cut sharply against his thin, handsome face and threatened to freeze his fingers to the handrail that he so firmly gripped. However, he was not perturbed by this. Legs were what counted, in the maneuver that was to follow, so he squatted half a dozen times and rose again quickly in order to make sure that his running muscles were in perfect trim. Then he slipped down the steps, clinging with both hands, his feet resting on the lowest step, and his body bent far outward in a bow, and finally let go with his right hand so that his body swung rapidly out. Just as he faced into the wind of the train's passage, he dropped clear.

His feet began to run in the empty air, swiftly, and, as he struck the grade beside the track, which seemed to be shooting backward with hurricane speed, he was sprinting with all his might.

Even so, the forward impetus threatened to hurl him on his face. When he forced back his head and shoulders with an effort, the added weight made his knees sag, and he staggered a bit from side to side, but by the time the last car of the train had shot by, leaving a whirl of dust to curl about him, Paradise Al was in control of the situation.

He dropped to a jog, and then to a walk. After that, he paused and dusted himself with care, took off his coat, shook it out, examined it with a minute inspection in the search for grease stains and, finding none, smiled with pleasure.

He was half into his coat again when two men stepped out from behind a pile of ties; one of them had empty hands, but the other carried a Colt revolver of a formidable length.

"I told you, Jay," said the man with the gun, "that the tramp royals and all the fast boys climb off down the track a way . . . but I didn't know that they got off clear down here. You don't need to get all the way into that coat, brother."

The last was addressed to Paradise Al, and the latter made no further effort to get into the coat, the sleeves of it manacling him perfectly.

"Fan him, Jay," said the man of the gun.

Jay, accordingly, went through the pockets of

the tramp. The latter said: "This is an outrage. If you men pretend to represent law and order in this town . . ."

"Oh, can that," said he of the gun. "Shut up and be reasonable. You're Paradise Alley, ain't you?"

"Al," corrected Jay. "Paradise Al is the moniker he wears. Always in Paradise because he never does no work. This is all that he's got on him." He straightened from turning the last pocket inside out. In his hands he held a wallet, a small clasp knife, a pencil, and two handkerchiefs, together with a small, well-worn notebook.

"Is that all?" asked the man with the gun.

"That's all, Tucker," said his assistant.

The railroad detective took the plunder into his hands. "There's four hundred and eighty-two bucks here. How you come by that much money, Paradise?" he asked.

"Me? Work, brother," said Paradise Al. "That's the way to make money. Speculation lets you down in the long run. Work is what pays. Hard, hard work!"

Harry Tucker looked down at the slender hands of the other. "What sort of work have you ever done, Paradise?" he asked.

"Lots and lots of different kinds of jobs," said Paradise Al. "I've spieled in a circus for the side-shows, and I've dealt cards many a month, partner."

"General all-around bum and crooked gambler, eh?" asked Tucker, but without heat.

"Never crooked when the rest of the boys want to go straight," declared the tramp. "Never, never. Now, with you and your friend, here, I could play seven-up or poker all day long, and there'd be nothing but luck and the fall of the cards to make one of us lose."

"Maybe," answered Tucker. "But we're not sitting down with you to a little game of cards just yet. We're standing here for a little talk. Understand?"

"So it appears," said Paradise Al.

"And we're talking turkey, eh?"

"Glad to do that," said the tramp.

"Where did you get all this coin? Come across, now."

"Dealing. And taking a slice out of the races, now and then."

"Where?"

"Denver."

"Working for whom?"

"Tiger Mullins."

"I know Tiger."

"He's worth knowing."

"Why'd you leave Denver?"

"I wanted a change."

"Why'd you leave Denver?"

"I was tired of the town. Denver's too far east for me, Tucker."

"All right. Let that go. While you were in Denver, how many times did you see Stuffy Miller?"

"Who?" asked Paradise Al.

"Stuffy Miller."

"I don't think I know him."

"Come on, kid. Stuffy Miller? You don't know him?"

"Oh, Stuff! You mean Stuff, do you?"

"Who else would I mean?"

"There's a lot of Stuffys in the world, but there's only one Stuff. We always called him Stuff, not Stuffy."

"Quit playing for time. How many times did you see Miller?"

"Oh, just now and then."

"Where?"

"He came into Mullins's joint, now and then. I used to see him other places, too."

"What was he doing the last time you saw him?"

"Saying good bye."

"Good bye?"

"Yes."

"Where was he going?"

"New Orleans."

"That's a lie," said Jay Winchell.

"How come?" asked Tucker of his companion.

"Stuff Miller never told nobody where he was going. That was never his way."

"I knew the fellow was lying all right. I just wanted to lead him on a while," said Harry Tucker. "If he says that Stuffy was going to New

Orleans, it probably means that Miller is up in Butte, or some place up there, by this time." Then he shook his fist under the chin of the young man. "Are you gonna shake it up and talk?" he asked.

"I've been talking," said the tramp, his brown eyes calmly meeting the glare of the detective.

"You've been talking, have you? Well, now you start in and talk on the other side of your face, will you?" demanded Harry Tucker. Suddenly drawing back his fist, he jerked it against the chin of the young man. Or, rather, it seemed that was where he drove home the punch. But the detective's arm shot over the shoulder of the tramp, who had moved his head just enough to one side.

"That was neat," said Jay Winchell. "The fellow can handle himself, I guess."

"He's gonna need to handle himself better than that, if he don't loosen up and talk a little," declared Tucker. "Now, damn you, I won't miss you the second shot. Will you talk?"

"I've been talking," said the tramp. "Stuff Miller was barging away for New Orleans. That's the fact. He was flush, and he was barging for New Orleans . . . he wanted to get down some of his coin on a good time. It's a long time since he's blown himself the way that he likes to do. He wanted me to come along."

"You wouldn't go, eh?"

"No, Stuff steps out too fast for me."

14

"Where did he get himself so flush?"

"He ran into a big poker game right there in Denver. Everybody was wise, but Stuff was by far the wisest of the lot. He grabbed the dough."

Tucker, without warning, struck again, and again he missed that slightly moving but elusive target. However, he quickly crossed over his left, and this time the punch went home. The head of Paradise Al flicked back and he fell in a heap.

"That's kind of rough," said Jay Winchell, yawning.

"It ain't any too rough," replied the other detective, looking down curiously at the knuckles of his left hand. "Fast with his head, ain't he?"

"Yeah, he's fast, all right," said Jay Winchell.

Tucker stirred the prostrate heap with his foot. Paradise Al rose again to his feet and, with calm, brown eyes, looked upon his tormenter.

"Now, do you talk?" asked Tucker.

"I've talked already," calmly replied Al.

Tucker snarled and cursed, smashing with all his might against the head again. This time Paradise Al made no attempt to dodge. The blow went home with terrific impact, the tramp spun about and pitched over on his face.

The two detectives looked down at him.

"Maybe you better quit," suggested Winchell.

"He didn't go and move his head," said Tucker. "Maybe I've cracked his skull for him. Well, that'll be resisting arrest, eh?"

"Sure," said Winchell. "But lay off him a while, will you?"

"Yeah. We'll just take and slam him in the hoosegow. That's all."

II

They put him in the jail of Jumping Creek, which took its name from the waterfall that leaped the cliff just north of the town and kept its voice booming heavily all through the year, except when the white winter froze the water in full leap and left it as a gigantic icicle until the spring returned.

The limp body did not recover life until Paradise Al was stretched on the prison cot with irons on his hands.

Both of the detectives were with him when he opened his eyes.

"Hello, fellow," said Harry Tucker.

"Hello, Tucker," said a calm but rather small voice.

"Are you gonna talk to me now?"

"What do you want me to talk to you about?"

"About Stuff Miller. You know what he done, and so do we. And believe me, you're gonna turn Stuff up for us, too."

"Am I?"

"Yeah, you are."

"Tell me what Stuff did, then?" asked Paradise Al.

"You don't know? Oh, he don't know, Jay," said Tucker, sneering. He thrust forward his thick, muscular shoulders as he spoke. "You don't know that Stuffy Miller stuck up the Q and R Express and cracked the safe and got a couple of hundred thousand, eh? No, I guess that's all news to you, eh?"

"Two hundred thousand is a lot of thousands," said the tramp mildly.

"Take and stand him up again, Jay," said the elder detective. "I'm gonna make him talk or third-degree him to death, the rotten bum."

Jay Winchell shrugged his shoulders, as one disapproving but not greatly interested one way or another. He took the young man underneath the arms and lifted the slight body easily. For that matter, Paradise Al helped, and now stood erect before his persecutor with his head high and his eye as calm as ever.

"Look," said Harry Tucker, balling his fist.

"I see your fist," said the tramp.

"I'm gonna beat your face to pieces, if you don't talk," declared Tucker.

"No, you won't do that," replied the tramp.

"Hey, won't I?" asked the detective.

"No, you won't," said the other gently.

"You go and tell me what'll keep me from it?" asked Tucker, furious, but inquisitive.

"You'll keep yourself," answered the tramp. "You're beginning to be afraid."

"Afraid? Me afraid? What am I afraid of? You?"

"Yes, you're afraid of me," said Al.

Tucker's laughter, following hard on this reply, was more a snarl than a sound of mirth. He swayed back, balanced himself for the punch, and lurched forward to deliver it, but he stopped himself in the middle of the blow, staggered on tiptoe, righted himself.

"I'm gonna bash your face in," he said. "Only, first I wanna know why should I be afraid of you?"

"You ask yourself that," answered Al. "You know better than I do. I don't know why you should be so afraid of me. You're a lot bigger man than I am. Besides, you've got me in jail, and you've got the law behind you." His way of saying the word *law* would be impossible to reproduce or even to describe.

Tucker dropped his head a little and scowled. "You tryin' to bluff me, fellow?" he asked.

"That's done already," answered the tramp. "Even your friend, here, can see it. He's not the brightest thug in the world, but he can see that you're paralyzed with fear. He's looking at you and laughing at you."

Tucker whirled about. "You handing me the hah-hah?" he demanded of Jay Winchell.

"*Aw,* shut up and don't be a fool, Harry,"

answered the other. "This here bum is just trying to get us in wrong with each other. What for would I laugh at you on account of a bum like this? Will you tell me that?"

"You can't kid me, Winchell, that's all I wanna say," Tucker replied sourly.

"*Aw,* who's kidding you?" asked Jay Winchell. "Come to life and look at things the way they are, will you?"

"I'm gonna knock in his face," said Tucker savagely.

"Go on and do it, then," answered Winchell. "I don't care what you do to him."

"You do, though," said the tramp.

"Do I?" asked Winchell.

"Listen at him," said Harry Tucker, grinning. "He thinks that he's got us hypnotized or something. Maybe Winchell, here, is afraid of you, too?"

"Yes," answered Paradise Al. "Neither of you will ever put a hand on me again."

"Now will you listen to the fool asking for it?" demanded Harry Tucker. He took a half step forward, with a swing of his body in readiness to drive home the punishing blow, but again he halted himself on tiptoes, staggering.

Paradise Al laughed in his face very softly. "You see?" he said.

"Why, he really believes it," said Harry Tucker. "He thinks that he's got me buffaloed."

"I have you buffaloed, you four-flushing bounder. You're only a rat," said Paradise Al. "You've dressed yourself up like a man, but I saw through you in the first moment. I ought to have taken your guns away from the pair of you, when we met, and kicked you off the railroad. I was a fool not to do that. The next time . . ."

"Go on," said Tucker, blind with rage. "What'll happen the next time?"

"The next time will take care of itself," said Paradise Al, and he smiled upon them gently.

"Back up and gimme room, Jay," requested Tucker. "Now I'm gonna let him have it." He was swinging his arms a little to loosen his shoulder muscles.

"Hold on a minute," said Winchell loudly and suddenly.

"Well, what?" asked Tucker.

"Come here a minute." He drew the angry detective to the door of the cell.

"You can't get me out of here. I'm gonna kill him," said Tucker.

The other caught him by the shoulder and whispered in his ear: "Listen, you fool. I know why he's so cocky. I see it in his face."

"What?" muttered Tucker.

"Look at him again. He's a Pendleton, is what he is. And you're going to catch hell in this town for roughing a Pendleton."

"Him a Pendleton?" muttered Harry Tucker. His

wrath was cast off like a garment. He turned and gaped at the tramp. "You're right," he muttered. "Why didn't you see that before, you fool? Why didn't you . . . ?"

He backed up to the door of the cell, glared again at the young man, more in fear than in rage, now, and suddenly both he and his fellow detective were hurrying down the passage between the cells.

"Suppose that he's a Pendleton?" said Tucker gloomily as they stood in the jailer's office.

"Yeah, suppose," muttered the other.

The jailer exclaimed: "Suppose that who's a Pendleton?"

"*Aw,* nobody," replied Harry Tucker roughly. And he turned his broad, heavy face toward the jailer, his features wrinkled with disgust, fear, and suspicion.

He and Jay Winchell left the room, and the jailer remained there, apparently quiet, but gripping the edges of his desk. There were two names to conjure with in Jumping Creek. One was that of the old Pendleton family, which for three generations had been spreading its name and its acres over the range. The other was that of the rival clan, the Draytons. Although the Draytons were now on top and had, in fact, supplied Jumping Creek with both a mayor and a sheriff, at the next election this situation might easily be reversed.

At any time, no matter which faction was in

power, it was very bad business, indeed, to tamper with the men of the Pendleton faction. They were people capable of action, and, when they acted, it was all as one body.

There was need, therefore, that the jailer should grip the edges of his desk and wonder what unlucky devil had prompted the two railroad detectives to pick up this man. The jailer, scanning the features of the prisoner with his mind's eye, readily remembered the face. And it was true that he seemed a Pendleton in every detail. He was much smaller than the majority of the clan, to be sure. He was not only smaller, but he appeared more finely made. He had the same cast of face, however, and his dark-olive skin and deep brown eyes were the same, also.

A Pendleton?

Yes, it must be so, and what would the town say? Why, that the sheriff was using the powers of his office to persecute the opposing faction. Whatever happened, he must find the sheriff at once. He put on his coat, hurried out of the building, and left eleven prisoners to take care of themselves while he strode off, bent on discovering the whereabouts of Timothy Drayton, present sheriff of Jumping Creek.

Rumor already had preceded him. Whispers had been passing up and down the street until they came to a great giant of a man with silvered hair, but with a swarthy skin and deep-brown eyes.

He had been standing in front of the post office, about to climb into his buckboard, but, when he heard the whisper, he turned suddenly about and faced toward the jail.

His face darkened—his brows beetled—suddenly he strode forward with a long and ponderous step. His left hand was gripped into a fist, his right hand worked nervously at his side. He was Thomas J. Pendleton, the senior member of the clan, and the most influential member of the entire body.

III

When Thomas J. Pendleton reached the jail he found Gresham, the jailer, just returned and panting from his excursion into the town. Gresham, in the meantime, had encountered one of the Drayton cowpunchers on the loose in Jumping Creek and had promptly commissioned him to find Timothy Drayton, the sheriff. For his own part, Gresham would have been very glad to have turned loose from the jail, at once, any member of the distinguished Pendleton family, but he had to wait for authorization from the head of the Drayton clan.

He was a saddened man when he saw the tall form of Thomas J. Pendleton standing in the door of the jail, frowning. Pendleton's long, silvery hair was worn in the fashion that was familiar in the days when this range had been part of the great frontier. He had shaggy gray eyebrows, also, and a commanding presence. His voice was low and his manner had about it a grim gentility that frightened lesser spirits like Gresham.

"There is in this place a prisoner arrested for vagrancy, or some such charge," said Pendleton, "and the name under which he passes is Paradise Al, I believe. May I see the man?"

The jailer would rather have lost a pair of his eyeteeth than permit the interview, but he felt helpless before the great man. Therefore, he submitted and guided the visitor to the cell.

There Pendleton saw a slender form, lying flat on his face on the cot. Instantly Thomas J. Pendleton sighed with relief and shook his head, for no member of his family or clan, of the male sex, had ever been as small as five feet and eight inches.

"Hey, Paradise," said Jailer Gresham. "Wake up. Here's a visitor for you."

Paradise Al stretched and yawned while he was still lying flat on his face, and Thomas J. Pendleton shook his head disapprovingly, but with relief, again. No member of the Pendleton family ever had been guilty of such lack of dignity, to say nothing of bad manners.

Then Paradise turned as a cat might turn and sat up.

Thomas J. Pendleton was taken aback. There was the swarthy skin and the deep-brown eyes of his people. If the features were chiseled a little more carefully, well, that would go with the generally small scale on which the man was built. Close to the bars stood Pendleton, and stared down at the prisoner.

"My name," he said, "is Thomas Pendleton."

He waited. Nothing happened. The brown eyes stared calmly at him.

Again he sighed with relief. The name, it appeared, meant nothing to the young fellow, who steadily, nervelessly regarded the visitor.

"District attorney, eh?" said Paradise Al.

Pendleton shrugged his shoulders. Gresham, even more relieved than his guest, grinned broadly. "I can leave him alone with you here, Mister Pendleton?" he said.

"I suppose you can safely do that," said Pendleton dryly.

Gresham withdrew, and Paradise Al was saying: "Not the district attorney, eh? You sort of had the look."

Pendleton smiled. He felt that it was safe for him to withdraw at once, but, having been introduced, he was obliged to make some few remarks before going.

The quiet, calm glance of the prisoner was traveling steadily over the other. He noted the tall body, the large head; he also noted the silver hair and eyebrows, but, most of all, his attention was attracted to the swarthy skin and to the deep-brown eyes. An air of interest began to pervade the scrutiny of Paradise Al.

"I am simply a citizen of the town," said the visitor, "and naturally I take an interest in the doings of the police department. We wish to treat strangers well in Jumping Creek, you see."

"Do you?" murmured the tramp. He stood up, stretched, yawned, and sat down again. He said nothing, but watched and waited.

"You understand," said the guest, a little embarrassed, "that we in Jumping Creek are interested in seeing that everybody secures a square deal. Have you anything to complain about?"

"I've nothing to complain about," said the tramp. "I came in on the bum, jumped off a train, and they copped me. That's all. They slammed me a couple of times, took my money away, and dumped me in here."

"They . . . *er* . . . they struck you, eh?" said Pendleton, the blood of a freeborn Westerner mantling in his face.

"That's nothing," said the tramp. "Nothing at all."

"If you have nothing to complain about," said Pendleton, "then I suppose that I may as well leave you."

"You didn't come here to ask about my complaints," said Paradise Al.

The other started. "Then why did I come?" asked Pendleton.

The tramp paused. Something, very distinctly, was on the mind of his visitor. What? The mind of Paradise Al turned over several thousand times a minute, in times of need, and it began to turn with some such liveliness just now. But he could arrive at nothing. What had brought this imposing-looking man to the jail to speak to him? He decided that he would begin to throw cards on the table and see which one registered some shock in the eyes of this Thomas J. Pendleton.

"Why did you come?" said Paradise Al, feeling his way. "Well, I suppose this isn't the best place to talk about it."

Pendleton took a long stride forward that brought him against the bars of the cell. He gripped one of those bars with a big, brown hand. Then, lowering his voice, he said: "Why isn't this a proper place?"

Paradise Al threw another card into the dark. "If you don't know that, you don't want to know anything," he said. And he pretended to be about to turn away.

"Wait a moment!" exclaimed Pendleton, and there was much emotion in his voice. "Who are you?"

"Paradise Al," said the tramp promptly, but he allowed a faint smile to appear and disappear on his lips.

Pendleton frowned. "Why can't you talk frankly to me?" he said.

"Why can't you talk frankly to me?" asked Paradise Al, thus casting out another card.

He was greatly rewarded by seeing another convulsive start move the big man.

Pendleton retained and freshened his grip upon the bar of the cell. "Do you think," he said, "that you have any claim on me?"

A thrill passed through the young fellow. What claim could this stranger possibly think that he, Paradise Al, citizen of the underworld of many nations, could possibly have upon him? He made another vague gesture, saying coldly: "There's one thing you have to admit. I haven't asked you for anything, have I?"

"No," said Pendleton. "That's perfectly true. And why . . . ?"

He was about to ask what right the young man would have had to ask for help, when the tramp continued, with an air of disdain: "I didn't even let you know that I'd come to town."

All the while he was wondering eagerly to himself what possible claim he might have on the tall man, for it was now sufficiently clear that the other suspected that such a claim might exist. What was he, Paradise Al, to Thomas J. Pendleton? He knew that something was wrong in the mind of the other; he must play delicately to take advantage of every fall of the cards.

"You didn't let me know," said Pendleton. "But why should you have let me know?"

Paradise Al adopted an air of lofty superiority and pride. "That's for you to decide," he said very shortly. He moved again, as though to turn away, although he now expected the voice that eagerly called him back.

"Young man," said Pendleton, "I want to be of help to you. What should you be to any Pendleton?"

It was a straight question, a facer, and the tramp saw that he would have to make some sort of a decisive play at this point. He remembered the mutterings of the two detectives and exclaimed suddenly: "What should I be? Use your eyes for yourself, and see!"

It was very effective, that remark. It was as effective as an exploding bomb.

"Albert," said Pendleton, "if that's your name, are you one of us?"

"I'm claiming nothing," replied Paradise Al. But he watched like a cat from his lowered eyes. *One of them? One of whom? Of the Pendletons?* The mere suggestion was enough to start his heart hammering. So far as he knew, he belonged to no family at all. He was simply a waif, who had cut a path through the difficult jungle of the world by the keenly tempered steel edge of his wit. *A Pendleton? Was that what the big man meant?*

"You claim nothing," said Thomas J. Pendleton.

29

"It's not a matter wherein you need to make any claims. We are all willing to take you for whatever you may be. I'm asking you to tell me, frankly, if you belong to the Pendleton family."

Again it was a facer, and the young fellow, cornered, played another card, one of his highest aces. He stood up, straight and tall. He folded his manacled arms as well as he could and replied in quiet tones: "No Pendleton talks about himself in jail."

Thomas J. of that name went backward a full step. "That's the true spirit, the real spirit, or my name is not what it is," he muttered. Suddenly the visitor exclaimed very loudly: "You must be Rory Pendleton's son! You are the image of Rory in the small!"

The brown eyes of the tramp never wavered. "Remember this one thing," he said solemnly, meeting the burning glance of the big man steadily. "I never claimed to be his son."

"Claimed it?" cried the big man. "What do you think Pendleton blood is made of? Water? You don't need to claim it. I see the spirit of poor Rory shining in your eyes!"

IV

Things began to happen with wonderful speed. Big Thomas Pendleton in a stride was upon the jailer, Gresham. Before Gresham was able to speak, however, Timothy Drayton came in, sweating with haste. Like all the Draytons, he was built rather close to the ground, very wide and massive in his proportions. Like all the Draytons, he was a man of less grace than the Pendletons, but of more muscle. They were Greeks to the Roman of the Draytons, so to speak.

Timothy Drayton was not silver, like Thomas Pendleton. He was rather a beaver-gray; he looked not old, but hardened, and now he was perspiring with haste and with fear. He was in fear because he dreaded lest an actual Pendleton had been thrown into the jail. It was not that he feared the Pendletons. He hated them heartily, like all of his clan, without fearing them at all. But he dreaded, like all Americans, the weight of public opinion, and it now seemed certain that he, Timothy Drayton, would be accused of having taken cowardly advantage of his position as sheriff to prosecute his private enemies. At that moment, he sincerely wished that the two railroad detectives were in the bottomless pit. He was ready to throw them there.

When he saw Pendleton, he flushed to the roots of his hair. Drawing himself up with a clumsy dignity far different from that of the Pendletons, with their natural grace, he said: "Good day, Thomas. I'm glad to see you. I heard there was some kind of a mistake. I came along here to put it right."

"Mistake?" said Pendleton. "I don't know what you mean."

"About a Pendleton being jailed for vagrancy," said Drayton, flushing again.

Thomas J. Pendleton smiled coldly. "The law is the law," he said.

"The law be damned," said the sheriff, not altogether convincingly. "I hope you won't think that I've been behind this, Pendleton?"

"I dare say not," said Thomas Pendleton. "I know nothing about it, except that my nephew is lying in the town jail." It was his turn to flush, a slow color that gradually spread over his face.

"Your nephew?" exclaimed the other. "You mean that that's Rory's son? Did Rory have a son? Is that fellow his son?"

Pendleton cleared his throat. He merely repeated: "My nephew is still in the jail for vagrancy."

"Vagrancy be damned. I got nothin' but fools workin' for me!" exclaimed the sheriff. "We'll have him out right now. Gresham!"

Gresham, pale as sun-faded grass, came in, trembling.

"You gone and arrested a tramp by the name of Pendleton," said Drayton, his voice quivering. "Mind going now and turning him loose? No . . . I'll go and do it myself."

He grabbed the keys from the jailer and strode before the others toward the indicated cell, while Pendleton followed next, grimly gratified by this turn of affairs.

The sheriff himself unlocked the door. The sheriff himself grasped the steel handcuffs that bound together the arms of the young man and exclaimed to the shrinking jailer: "Irons, too, eh?"

"You see, Mister Drayton," said Gresham, "he was considered kind of dangerous and . . ."

Drayton unlocked the manacles, exclaiming: "Dangerous? Wasn't that a proof that he's a Pendleton? Was there ever a Pendleton that wasn't dangerous? Damn it, Gresham, you gone and got me into a lot of trouble." Perspiration poured down the face of the sheriff. His color was changing from red to purple.

Now he leaned forward and stared at the face of the young man who was before him. "Where'd you get the welts on your face?" he demanded, looking along the finely made jaw of the prisoner.

"Accident," said Paradise Al, speaking for the first time.

At the soft, the almost feminine sound of his voice, the sheriff started. All of the Pendletons were educated, all of them spoke rather quietly for such a community as Jumping Creek.

"Accident, eh?" repeated the sheriff. He turned sharply on the frightened jailer and stretched out his arm. "You do that?" he demanded.

Gresham turned to water, to icy water. "You know, Sheriff," he whined, "a railroad detective is kind of hard. It was a pair of them that turned up this fellow. They kind of handled him rough, I guess."

Drayton could not speak. He dared not glance toward the great leader of the rival clan. He dared only to say: "Young man, how'd they handle you?"

"They were all right," said Paradise Al.

"All right?" exclaimed the sheriff. "Did they beat you up?"

"I don't know anything about that," said Paradise Al.

"You don't know anything about it?"

"No," he said. "I only know that I have their names."

An expression of singular satisfaction spread across the face of Thomas J. Pendleton, as though he had received, at that moment, a benediction of peculiar grace and power.

Timothy Drayton, also, suddenly stiffened his back a little and a faint smile came over his face. "You're all right, son," he said. "I reckon you know that the Draytons and the Pendletons, they don't set down peaceful in the same room together, but I've always said . . . and I always will say . . . a Pendleton is a Pendleton, and I'm glad to meet one of the true breed. Son, I'm glad to get you out of this, and I'm sorry that I've got a flock of fools working around this town. Jumping Creek, it's gone and growed too much to be watched by any one man. You're free, young man. I didn't get your name correctly?"

"Albert Pendleton," said Paradise Al slowly.

"Albert?" exclaimed Thomas J. Pendleton. "I thought that Rory had you baptized Alfred?"

Paradise Al turned without confusion on his supposed uncle and merely said: "You know how it is, Uncle. What father wanted was one thing. What mother wanted was the opposite. He called me Alfred, but mother always called me Albert, and that's the name I've come to use."

"A bad idea," said his "uncle" sharply. "The baptismal name . . . However . . ."—he broke off, controlling his feeling on the subject—"however, let that be as it may. I'm glad to have you with us, Albert."

They went into the office of the jail.

"Here's the money," said the tremulous Gresham. "You count it, Mister Pendleton."

Paradise Al took it and stuffed the wallet carelessly into his inside coat pocket. "That's quite all right, I'm sure," he said carelessly.

Again the face of his "uncle" flushed with pleasure.

Paradise Al received back his other few possessions.

"No luggage?" asked the elder Pendleton.

"I was making a fast trip . . . without tickets," said the young fellow, smiling.

Thomas J. Pendleton looked up and down the lines of the brown suit. They were very neat. The trousers were sufficiently well pressed. There was nothing about the get-up to suggest a professional tramp.

"Very well," he said. "Very well, indeed. It's the proper spirit, also, that takes a young man across the continent to see his relations."

He fairly distended his chest with his pride in this accomplishment. Even the sheriff nodded.

"Blood will out," said the sheriff, smiling and nodding at Thomas Pendleton.

"Thank you," said the other very coldly and briefly. Then he added: "Weapons, perhaps, my dear fellow?"

"Only this pocket knife," said Paradise Al.

"Pocket knife!" exclaimed Pendleton, amazed.

The sheriff grinned. "Concealed weapons, you know, Pendleton," he said.

"Concealed damnation!" exclaimed the rancher, much irritated. "What use would a pocket knife be in a brawl, I'd like to know?"

"Only in a pinch, and then it would be useful," said Al. "If you'll excuse me, Sheriff. . . ."
Pointing to the side of the room, he added: "The

window sill, for instance." Suddenly the knife flashed in a long streak of light from his hand, and that streak of light went out, and left the pocket knife buried to the handle in the soft wood of the sill.

Paradise Al stepped to it and tugged it forth. "In a pinch, it's useful," he said, "and it doesn't weigh as much as a gun."

They were impressed. The sheriff stepped to the scar the knife had left, and traced a forefinger over it.

"Damned good shot," he muttered. "If some of my boys could do as much with a gun . . ." He left off, and faced around upon the others. "Pendleton," he said, "I don't have to tell you again, how sorry I am that this thing's gone and happened. I reckon you know that, don't you?"

Thomas J. Pendleton pocketed some of his surplus dignity, then stepped forward and said: "Timothy, there never was a time, even in the midst of our disagreements, when I have not been willing to admit that every Drayton is a man, and a real man, above petty meanness. I'd like to shake your hand on it at this moment, sir."

The sheriff flushed again, although he blinked with surprise, almost with bewilderment. Then he reached out hastily, as though afraid that the opportunity might disappear, and gripped the hand of the other heartily.

"I hope, Thomas," he said, "that there'll be some

good come out of this here. There was a time when we thought different, but maybe there's room enough on the range for all of us, and we can get along like other folks. We been following a habit of crossing each other. I'm willing and more'n willing to forget that there habit."

Pendleton dropped his liberated hand on the shoulder of the sheriff. "Perhaps," he said, "this may be a bright day in the history of our families, Drayton."

V

When they left the jail, a brown-faced girl with blue eyes, and hair sun-faded almost to white at the outer fringes, got out of a buckboard and waved to the sheriff.

"Waiting, Father!" she called.

Young Paradise Al looked at her swiftly, but with care. She was not, he told himself, the type of woman who made any great appeal to him. He preferred girls who had a certain flair for gaiety; he preferred a little coloring in the cheeks, a touch of rose on the fingernails, and a trace of darkening about the eyes. Mother Nature was all very well, but Nature could be improved upon, he felt. Then he felt that women with any pretensions to looks ought to be dressed up to their pretensions in full. Silks, colored silks—

that was his idea, and high heels, something, on the whole, precious and useless, that might be forgotten tomorrow, perhaps, but that made an instant impression when it was seen.

He decided that this was a dowdy one. And that was a pity. With such a body, such a carriage, such eyes, she could have been made into almost anything. Instead, she preferred to dress like a man. The old sombrero on her head was largely battered out of shape, and its wide brim dipped down over eyes that should not, under any consideration, have been covered. Her clothes were simply khaki, neither well fitted nor, for that matter, overly clean. He could see the saddle and sweat stains on her divided skirts.

So he saw her, appraised her, and dismissed her from his mind. He was ready to yawn about the subject, as they reached the sidewalk.

"Molly," the sheriff was saying, "this is Paradise Al. He's Alfred Pendleton. Albert his mother calls him."

"Oh, a Pendleton, is he?" said the girl, with what seemed to Paradise Al endless effrontery. "Hello, Alfred. Glad to meet you." She came forward and stripped from her brown right hand a gauntlet glove and grasped his much paler fingers.

"Thanks," said Paradise Al. "Glad to see you in Jumping Creek."

"That's where you'll find most of the Draytons," she said.

He felt that she was looking him up and down with a lack of interest that even exceeded his indifference to her. And this was an offense. No man ever reached a stage of existence or a place in society or an age, when he feels that he is really unattractive to the opposite sex. That the girl should venture to look him over and obviously dismiss him from her mind in this manner was a distinct shock to him. His lip curled a little. There were certain things about him that, if she were told, would make her eyes open suddenly, and very widely, too. This rather grim satisfaction he hugged to his heart. Then he looked at her again, with a retort on his lips, but swallowed the remark, for already she was turning away from him, and from this angle he saw her in full profile, with her head lifted as she looked up to her father and spoke to him.

These two things may be very strange, but they are very true. In the first place, every woman's face is best seen, for her beauty, when it is viewed from below. Thackeray knew it, and that was why he had Esmond see Beatrix for the first time on his return from the wars as she was coming down the stairs—that moment when the great novelist put his mind to its full stretch and described the girl who had grown to be a most dazzling beauty.

So Paradise Al, young in years only, looked at the girl, and, seeing her face uptilted, he saw in it such beauty that he was hushed, because beauty in a woman is to every man, no matter how degraded, a holy thing.

Furthermore, he was seeing her now in profile, and the blue Western sky was her background, and she seemed to Paradise Al as lovely as something cut from Grecian marble, a brown old marble, but now flushed with life and, therefore, all the more pricelessly desirable.

He balled one hand into a fist. He straightway forgot all about Jumping Creek, his "uncle" Pendleton, and the rôle that he was playing. Like a child at the theater, he believed what he saw as thoroughly as though he had been drawn up upon the stage. And nothing existed for him, in that moment, except Molly Drayton.

Why waste words about it? It was the oldest disease to which the mind of man succumbs. It was love. Love at first sight has been doubted, but there have always been fools who could not believe in it. All that had happened before, on this rather crowded day, appeared as nothing to the mind of Paradise Al. His very existence seemed to him to begin at this moment.

So, like a man, he said nothing, but stood, still and silent, and turned very pale. The girl was chattering something to her father about affairs on the Drayton Ranch. And now, at his side, he saw the tall form of Pendleton, mounting a horse and pointing to another with an inviting gesture.

"Ride Ginger," said Pendleton. "He needs some

riding, but every Pendleton can ride a little, I suppose, and I don't expect that Rory's son will be found to be behind the rest in that."

Ginger was a blue roan. It is never a pretty color, and Ginger, besides, was built like a mule, heavy in the body, thin in the legs, and large in the head, with a back that promised mischief to any understanding eye.

But Paradise Al lacked an understanding eye, so far as horses were concerned. He could read off the mind of a man like a printed page, he knew something about women, also, according to the dark ways of his kind, but, when it came to riding, he was more familiar with the rods under a freight car or, above all, the blind baggage, than with the back of a horse.

If he had been completely himself, he would have taken in what his "uncle" had just said and refused a dangerous mount without shame, for you must understand at once that Paradise Al was a very practical fellow, who never risked his neck to make a show. When he stirred his hands, it was because he was sure of the work that they could perform. He was as coldly logical as a mathematician, when it came to living—hence, his nickname. He was known, among what he would have called the craft, as a man who makes happy days easy, because he never did reckless things. When he handled a knife or a gun, for instance, it was not recklessness at all. It was simply the master working well inside the heart of his craft.

So Paradise Al, in a dream about Molly Drayton, climbed onto the back of Ginger with a clumsiness that brought a frown of wonder and surprise to the face of his "uncle", Thomas J. Pendleton.

A moment later, Paradise was brought out of his dream as smartly as though fingers had been snapped under his nose, for Ginger, realizing that his rider was not proficient and being always desirous of bringing to the earth as much hell as possible, left the earth and soared toward the sky. When he came down again on stiffened forelegs, it just happened that Paradise managed to keep in the saddle.

In other words, his balance, by sheerest chance, was perfect. He almost wished that it had not been so, for he took the whole shock of that abrupt landing on the base of his spinal column, and a great wave of darkness suddenly swept over his brain.

His wits were not entirely obscured, however. Through the dim cloud he heard a peal of delighted laughter, and, staring in the direction of the sound, he saw Molly Drayton convulsed with mirth that bowed her over and made her hold her sides with both arms. She even stamped upon the ground with her high-heeled boots in the excess of her pleasure. Another sound penetrated upon his mind—the happy yelling of a child, who was crying: "Ride him, cowboy!" Then there was the stentorian voice of his "uncle", which shouted something about getting the head of the horse up and riding "like a man". Paradise Al, however, cared nothing for riding like a man. He only knew that he was in great distress, and he felt sure, if he were thrown from the saddle, he would certainly break himself to pieces on the hard roadway.

So Paradise Al did what had never been done before in Jumping Creek, not even by the veriest of tenderfeet—he yelled loudly for help and frantically gripped the saddle, fore and aft.

The mirth of Molly Drayton mastered her completely. Even the grim sheriff began to roar. After all, this was a Pendleton, as he supposed, and he could not help being amused when he saw a member of the famous clan disgraced.

"Ten thousand damnations!" roared Thomas J. Pendleton. "Get his head up. Stick your spurs into him! Ride him like a man!"

"Ride him, cowboy!" screeched the child in the street.

For the roan gelding, having measured his rider with a precise nicety worthy of so great an artist, now did a whirling side-step that the veriest tyro of a cowpuncher that ever rode on the range could easily have warded against. But it was all new to Paradise Al. It dawned upon his brain, that trick, at the same moment that his body left the saddle and was hurled sidewise, straight at the form of the prancing child.

The latter managed to avoid the whirling, spread-eagled body of the rider, but Paradise Al could not dodge the broad, hard face of the road at which he was thrown.

He hit it screeching like a tomcat. Luckily for him, he fell at such an angle that he rolled head over heels, and the rolling broke some of the jar that would have resulted from a sheer, solid impact of man against the ground.

When he staggered to his feet, he looked down to see that he was white as a sheeted ghost with dust, and the whole of Jumping Creek seemed to have gathered to witness his downfall. There was one vast uproar, one volcano of laughter, all pouring forth in waves and all aimed at him.

Why, he might have been killed by the beast, but there was the girl, quite helpless with her mirth, tears of pleasure streaming down her face.

He looked sourly at Pendleton and was amazed to see that even from him he received no sympathy. No, upon the face of that old veteran of the range, there was only a look of the profoundest disappointment, the profoundest disgust.

VI

Probably no human being in the world could have been subjected to so much scorn, mirth, and disapproval and have remained so little affected by it as young Paradise Al. He had his own points of pride, to be sure, and on these points he was a stickler. But such a matter as riding a horse or yelling for help when the horse was about to buck him off was not listed among them. If it were a human antagonist, well, that was a different matter. Or, if it had been a deal of cards, he would almost as soon have cut off his right hand as to permit the crookedness of the deal to be seen.

He was an artist, and, therefore, he was his own best critic and audience; very severe was he in his judgments pronounced upon himself, but, as he stood now in the street and observed the torrents of derision that were flowing his way, he was totally unmoved except by surprise—unmoved, that is to say, except for one thing, the laughter of Molly Drayton.

There was the sword with the poisoned point, and that poison instantly was flowing into him. Why was he ridiculous in her eyes? As for the stony face of his "uncle", that made very little difference, indeed, to the tramp.

Straightway young Paradise Al offended all

Western standards even more than he had done before. For he walked straight up to Molly Drayton, knocking off the dust from his clothes, and said to her: "Why such a big laugh, Miss Drayton? Never saw a man fall off before?"

"I never heard a man yell so much before," she said.

"I always yell when I'm scared," said Paradise Al.

"Then you'll probably make a lot of noise in Jumpin' Creek," she said, "because it's an awfully scary town."

He heard his "uncle" calling him, and turned back. Tall Thomas J. Pendleton was dismounting from his horse and preparing to take Ginger; he waved the boy to the saddle that he had just vacated.

"There's a gentler horse," he said stiffly. "I'll try Ginger."

"Will you?" commented Paradise Al. "Good luck to you, then. I'd just as soon try to ride a rock python that imitates a whiplash. I never could tell whether the sky was over my head or under Ginger's feet while I was on him."

"You weren't on him long enough to make up your mind," Pendleton was heard to say. And there was a stir of grim laughter from all who heard this remark.

However, Paradise Al was eventually in the saddle on the quieter horse, and there he sat and watched Ginger make one more frantic effort to snap a human burden from his back. It was a vain effort, however. Thomas Pendleton might be rather brittle with age, but he was supple with experience, and he easily sat out the efforts of the mustang. Presently he was jogging down the street, waving to Paradise Al to come on.

So they left Jumping Creek and rode out through the brilliant sunshine toward the Pendleton Ranch.

The head of the clan found it possible to converse after a time. "Where is your father now, Alfred?" he asked.

"Uncle Tom," answered the young man, "the fact is . . . my job while I'm out here with you is not to answer questions. I'm sorry, but you can imagine why it is."

Pendleton shook his head. "Rory never did anything that he needed to be ashamed of. His father had ideas that were not like Rory's. He couldn't understand how any man would want to give up his life to painting pictures, when he might be raising cows on the range."

Paradise Al nodded. He was reaching far out to get together enough facts to enable him to guess at the life of his supposed "father".

"And he's still painting, I suppose," said the rancher.

"You know how it is," said Al. "When a man starts that sort of a business, it's hard to give it up. He still paints. Yes."

"Do anything with the stuff?" asked Pendleton.

"Yes, fills attics with it, but there I am talking!" exclaimed Paradise Al. "I'm sorry. But you can imagine. I'm not supposed to talk at all, if you'll forgive me."

"I understand that," said Pendleton. "Poor Rory. He was full of the Pendleton pride. Full of it. He swore that he'd never speak or write to me again . . . and he's kept his word. I suppose he's told you that he felt I'd helped to make trouble between him and our father?"

Paradise Al reflected. Then he said truthfully: "As a matter of fact, my father never mentioned your name."

"Never mentioned my name?" murmured Pendleton. After that, he rode on for a considerable distance without saying a word, but with his face set in bitter lines.

At length, he sighed. "Well, I suppose that he's right to keep his pride. How are his business affairs?"

"There aren't any," said Paradise Al.

"Hold on. What . . . all the money gone?"

"You know that it's hard to paint even bad pictures and have any time left over for looking after the money affairs?"

Pendleton nodded his head. "I know that," he said. "I thought at first that he was getting much the best of the deal, when he got his half of the property in hard cash, and I got nothing but land

and cows weighed down with mortgages. After that there were the bad years, when the whole country seemed to be going broke."

"My father's talked to me about that time," said the young man.

"I was sure that I'd have to sell off everything for a song," said Pendleton. "But I weathered through the hard times, and then affairs grew better and better."

He sighed. Perhaps he was glad to get his mind off the nephew who had just disgraced the family name before the whole town of Jumping Creek. At any rate, he went on with his own history in brief.

"Your aunt was a tremendous help," he said. "She worked in the kitchen while I rode the range. She lived in calico. In her small body there's the greatest heart in the world."

"But then everything went better, I understand," said Paradise Al.

"Yes, your father would have heard about that," Pendleton replied, nodding his head. "The bad times ended. There was a jump in prices. We had a number of good grass years. And the mortgages were paid off by magic. I managed to put money behind us, and, when the next hard times came, we were able to buy land and cattle cheap. That was the end of trouble for us. Things have gone on very well. My family will be provided for, I trust. And you, Alfred?"

Paradise Al shrugged his shoulders. "I've got four hundred dollars and something over. It's in my wallet now. I never expect to get a penny more from my father."

Nothing could be truer than this, of course. Pendleton shook his head and sighed again.

"The place for our whole family is out here on the range," he declared. "We're Westerners. Look at you, Alfred, a grown man . . . and not able to sit on the back of a horse that . . ."

He bit his lip with shame, but Paradise Al merely smiled.

"I could learn the trick, maybe," he said.

"Yes"—Pendleton sighed—"but already . . ."

He did not finish the sentence and he did not need to do so, for the young fellow could understand. Already, he, the tramp, had sufficiently disgraced the family name. The fact that a man made noise when he was on the back of a murderous beast of a horse seemed to be a lasting disgrace.

Paradise Al shrugged his shoulders. He was not shamed, himself. He was merely amused. These people had a different code of manners and different standards of manhood. It would be interesting to delve into them.

They came in view of the ranch house. It was a prepossessing view. The building stood halfway up an easy slope that sheltered it against the north wind, and the irregular roof line lifted, here and there, above the tops of the grove of trees that surrounded it. It looked like a house where happiness and great domestic content might be gathered; it looked, in short, like a home. His glance, running from the house over the sweep of rolling ground that extended about it, young Paradise Al was struck, first of all, by the small number of fences that ran gleaming over the hills.

"How far does your land go, Uncle Tom?" he asked.

"My land?" said Pendleton. "Oh, it runs as far as your eye reaches from this spot. On the other side of that range of hills it goes down to the land of Jim Pendleton, in part, and in part it joins onto the land of your cousin, Hal Smythe. Over there to the south is Harry Pendleton's place, and Samuel Pendleton has a ranch to the north of us. Sam is getting old now. But I suppose that your father used to tell you what a wild fellow he was as a boy."

"My father," said Paradise Al truthfully again, "used the name Pendleton just as seldom as he could."

This produced another conversational silence that lasted until they had ridden through the grove of trees and had come to the house itself and the wide pasture that was fenced in behind it.

There they dismounted, unsaddled, and turned the mustangs loose. Then they went toward the back of the house. They were on the rear porch when they heard a door slam in the front of the house, and the powerful voice of a man shouting: "Mother, Mother! Where are you?"

"Here, Dick," said a woman's voice. "What's the matter, dear?"

"Uncle Rory's boy, Al, has turned up, in jail!" cried the voice of Dick. "Father got him out, and then he made a holy show of himself trying to ride Ginger. He was thrown, and he screamed like a woman! The whole Drayton tribe is laughing. The whole range will be laughing at us tomorrow. We're disgraced, Mother! We're shamed forever! He screeched and yelled for help!"

VII

That was the introduction of Paradise Al to the Pendletons—at least, to the head of the clan. But much followed the mere introduction. There were, in that household, besides big Thomas J. Pendleton, and his little, sharp-faced, gentle wife, a single daughter, Sally, tall and brown, as imposing in her directness of speech as she was imposing in thews and sinews. Above all there was a crown of growing manhood in the form of three huge sons. There were Dick, Jerry, and Ray, each one taller than the other, ranging from Dick, the eldest, to Ray, the youngest, tallest, handsomest, most promising young berserker in the entire clan Pendleton.

He was one of those men who bear about them all of the signs of eminence from childhood to the grave. He was not only inches taller than most men, but he possessed size without awkwardness, and without the rough finish and lack of perfect proportion that is the drawback of most large men. One thoroughbred in a million or more stands seventeen hands high and is compactly and powerfully built from the nose to the heels. And Ray Pendleton was one of these rare creatures among men.

He was only twenty-one or twenty-two, but already his opinion was as much listened to in the household as that of his own father. Yet, such was his natural modesty and proper sense of the fitness of things, that he rarely advanced his opinions except when asked.

It was he who delivered the final touch in the discussion of the new member of the family the very night of Paradise Al's arrival. Paradise had withdrawn very early, pleading fatigue. Then, sliding through the window of his room, he had faded down the side of the house with the adroitness of a climbing monkey and the silence of a stalking leopard, until he was back under the open window of the living room in which the rest of the family was informally gathered.

He was in time to hear Thomas Pendleton say:

"If he'd been trying to ride Sullivan, well, there might have been some excuse for it. But old Ginger, who does nothing but put up a bluff, to raise such yells because Ginger danced a little, I never was so disgusted in my life. A contemptible performance, that's my opinion."

"Dear, dear," said little Mrs. Pendleton over her sewing.

"We've gotta get rid of him, Dad," said Jerry Pendleton. "Maybe buy him a ticket somewhere, and turn him out with our regards."

"He'll ruin the family name all over the range," declared Dick Pendleton.

"I'll never dare to face Molly Drayton again, the spiteful thing," said tall Sally Pendleton.

Then the youngest son said: "You can't turn him out. You've got to make the best of him. And there may be something in him. There's something in every Pendleton, so the saying goes." Any other member of the tribe would have given that quotation in solemn seriousness, but Ray Pendleton laughed as he said it. Then he added: "You know how it is . . . maybe he has a dread of horses. People are that way, sometimes . . . they have a special fear of particular things, but they're regular lions with everything else."

"*Bah!*" exclaimed Sally. "You make me tired, Ray. Always trying to stand up for the underdog . . . and this time it's just plain dog."

"Sally! Sally!" exclaimed her mother.

55

"Well, she's right," said Dick. "There's a sneaking look about him. You've got to admit that."

Thomas laid his head on his hand and groaned. "In front of the whole town!" he exclaimed. "If it had been Sullivan that he was riding, but it wasn't Sullivan. It was just plain old Ginger. Thunder, he screamed like a frightened child."

Outside in the darkness, the tramp looked up at the stars and shook his head. What if he had made a little noise on the back of the pitching horse? And what sort of people were these, to refer to the gymnastics of the mustang as mere dancing?

"Let him alone for a while," said Ray Pendleton. "I'm going to make it my business to try to draw him out. There's something in him, mind you. He's got the right sort of an eye. It's just as steady as can be."

"He's got the eye of a hunting snake, is what he has!" cried Sally Pendleton.

Paradise Al went back to bed, climbing cautiously. They would have been interested, all of them, if they could have seen the rapid progress with which he mounted with bare toes and bare fingers to the upper story of the house, and faded through the window again. They would have been chiefly amused and amazed to see him finally hanging by one hand from the window sill, then drawing himself up with the single arm before he brought the other hand into action.

Back in bed, Paradise Al stared at the ceiling.

Sullivan was apparently some horse famous in the neighborhood for its meanness. Well, since it appeared that he was disgraced because he had put up such a bad performance on the back of Ginger, he would redeem himself, in their eyes, by his performance on the back of this Sullivan of evil name.

For difficulties never impressed Paradise Al greatly. He had a certain set of mottos that were deeply embedded in his mind and to which he was constantly referring. A few of them were:

"It's not the weight of the punch, but where you place it."

"A fast foot is better than a strong leg."

"What you can't meet, you had better dodge."

"The other fellow is as badly hurt as you are."

"Patience and a good pair of hands will open any lock."

"If the first lie doesn't work, lie, lie again."

"The bigger the man, the smaller the brain."

Such were the maxims with which the young man was equipped. He was young, indeed, but he had poured into his short years enough events to have filled a dozen ordinary lives.

As he consulted his preëstablished ideas, he vowed to himself that he would certainly not give up this easy home in a hurry, not until the real Rory Pendleton or his real son appeared on the scene. It was not any sense of disgrace that troubled Paradise Al. He was not in the slightest interested in the opinions of other people; he was merely perturbed because the disgust that the rest of the household felt might react in such a way that they would discard him, and set him on the out trail.

Lying in bed, he turned his head right and left, became aware of the big, airy spaces of the room, saw the dull glimmer of the top of the mahogany desk even in the starlight, and again nodded his head a little.

He knew nothing about riding, but he would win himself a place in the esteem of all by mastering the celebrated Sullivan, whatever that might be. He would learn, or else he would establish some system of hypnotism. According to his maxims, if there is not a way through the front door, there is a way through a window.

Having made up his mind, he fell promptly asleep, slumbering as peacefully as a child, until a hand fell heavily upon the door of his room, and a great voice summoned him for breakfast.

He was up, sponge-bathed, dressed, and down the stairs with a clean-shaven face within ten minutes, and this without hurrying, for he had learned, before almost any other thing in life, to make every move of his hands count for the best.

Downstairs, he found the family already eating, and a place reserved for him at the right of Mrs. Pendleton, who explained with her gentle, rather tired smile, that they had a punctual hour for breakfast, which was never postponed.

The others greeted him with nods and mutterings, all except the harsh, mechanical voice of the father of the family, inquiring how he had slept.

There was a better exception than that. It was Ray Pendleton, talking about hunting and wondering if he, Alfred or Albert, cared to make a day's trip to get a deer?

To get a deer? He would be delighted.

But before he had finished his porridge, he had recklessly turned the argument upon the subject of bucking horses and how they can be managed.

"Every horse can be ridden, and every rider can be thrown," said Thomas Pendleton.

"Sullivan has never been ridden!" exclaimed the girl.

"He will be, one day," said Thomas Pendleton.

"Who's Sullivan?" asked Paradise.

"Not the prizefighter. Sullivan is the stallion that belongs to the Draytons."

"Is he a fighter?"

"That's what he is. He's the finest piece of horseflesh that I ever saw," said Dick Pendleton, sighing and shaking his head. "And Tim Drayton will give him away to the first man that can stick on his back for ten minutes running."

"For only ten minutes?" asked the tramp carelessly.

"Only ten minutes? Only ten minutes of hell is enough!" exclaimed Dick.

"Well, ten minutes doesn't sound very long," said the tramp. "I'd like to try him."

"You?" shouted every voice, except the voice of Ray Pendleton.

"Well," said Paradise Al, "I don't know how to ride, and I might as well learn. The harder the teacher, the better the lesson will be."

"Sullivan will make a hard teacher," agreed Thomas with a sneer. "He'll eat you before the lesson's over, though. He's a man-killer."

"I've seen man-killers before," said the tramp softly, but with a certain meaning.

"Where, in the circus?" asked Sally Pendleton.

He looked straight at her, his brown eyes very soft and gentle. "Yes," he said, "it was a circus."

"You won't have a circus tent over you," exclaimed Sally, "if you try Sullivan! You won't try him, though."

"Hush, Sally," said the mother.

"You know, Mother," said the girl, "that Sullivan doesn't look like a horse, but more like a beautiful four-legged devil."

"I know, my dear," said the older woman, "but you mustn't try to tell Albert what's in his mind. Every Pendleton does his own thinking."

VIII

As a matter of fact, Paradise Al was doing his own thinking, and with a vengeance. He felt, on the whole, that he would have chucked the whole business had it not been for the way the face of Molly Drayton stuck in his mind. But she was there in the picture as a commanding figure. Therefore, after breakfast, he said to Ray Pendleton: "Mind if I borrow a horse for a while today? I've got to put off that deer hunt. There's that Sullivan horse, you know."

Ray Pendleton put a big, efficient hand on his shoulder and said: "Are you dead set on trying to ride Sullivan?"

"Yes, I'm set on it," said the tramp.

Ray Pendleton shook his head. He replied: "Let me tell you something, Cousin Al. I know that you're dead game. Most of the breed are. But there's no good in trying to prove it on Sullivan. You know his history?"

"No," said Paradise Al, yawning a little. For he looked upon the task that he had undertaken as one might look upon the blowing of the safe of a great bank, a difficult and a dangerous job, but one that had been done before and one that might be done again.

"I'll tell you about Sullivan," said Ray Pendleton.

61

"There was a pair of Irishmen by the name of Rourke and Sullivan. They were prospectors, and they'd worked together all over the Rockies, but one day, away up in the desert in Nevada, they looked down from the shaft they were sinking in the side of a mountain and saw a herd of wild horses going by. In the front of that herd was a big, long-legged, red son of a wide-stepping chunk of a hurricane. When they saw that horse go down the valley, leading the rest, his mane up in the air like a flag, and his tail pouring out behind him like it was floating on a fast river, they forgot all about the gold they were after in the rock of the mountainside, and they packed up their stuff and hit the grit after the stallion.

"Matter of fact, along comes a pie-faced Dutch bartender, after them, and finds their hole in the ground. He sinks a drill into it, lays in a shot, and blows off the face of a couple of million dollars. But that doesn't matter to Sullivan and Rourke. They're after the horse and they keep after him for six months."

"That's a long time," said the tramp, shaking his head.

"Yeah, but they were long men," answered Ray Pendleton. "There was nothing weak or short about 'em. They walked all through the winter. They walked that horse right out of his herd, and they kept on walking, and they kept on starving and driving themselves, until Sullivan lies down, one night, and wakes up dead the next morning, so to speak, if you know what I mean."

"Heart trouble, maybe?"

"Quick pneumonia on top of a bad heart, and no food in his hide," said Ray. "It fetched him off like a poison. Rourke woke up in the middle of the night and heard his partner raving. At daybreak Sullivan was dying, and Rourke says to him . . . 'It's all right, partner. I'll catch that son of a he-wind and a lightning flash, and I'll saddle your name on him.' That was what happened.

"Of course, the pair of 'em had worn themselves out, but they'd rubbed the stallion down to a stack of bones. When Rourke started out the next day, he cinched up his belt and cut a new hole in it to keep his trousers from sliding down over his hips. That same day he got his rope on the horse. Once on the back of the big brute, he was bucked off, but, ten miles farther on, he caught the end of the lariat again. And so Rourke worried the horse down in two days from the mountains to the Drayton Ranch, and Tim Drayton himself met him on the range. With his 'punchers he herded and dragged and beat the red devil into a corral, and in that corral Sullivan has been ever since.

"Twenty men have tried to ride him, and twenty men have been shied off his back the way that you'd flick watermelon seeds out between your thumb and forefinger. Understand? Dolly Simpson hit a corral post with the back of his head and was buried. And Mex Taylor hit the ground, and then Sullivan jumped on him and punched him full of holes. There was a Negro, too, and I disremember what his name might have been. He was savaged to death by Sullivan, too. He'd come all the way from Canada, that Negro. Those three he killed, and everyone of the rest had a mark put on 'em, one place or another. Some got a broken leg, and some a cut across the face, or smashed ribs, or something like that. Everybody that tackles Sullivan has to pay for it. And that's why I tell you that you'd better not try your hand with him. He's a devil, is what he is."

"Is he?" murmured Paradise Al. And to himself he was saying: *Patience and a good pair of hands will unlock any door.*

"I'm not joking," said Ray Pendleton. "It's been months, now, since anybody has tried to claim Sullivan by sitting on his back for ten minutes. Tim Drayton is ready and willing to give up all the good that that big devil may do for his string of saddle horses. He'd rather see Sullivan ridden than to keep on supporting Rourke, maybe, because the deal is that Rourke has an easy job until some man can ride Sullivan and take him away. And there you are. It sounds funny. It is funny. But it's a fact."

"It sounds like something else to me," said Paradise Al.

"What's that?" asked young Pendleton.

"Sounds as though I'm going to try that horse and get my foolish neck broken," said the tramp. "Will you show me the way to the Drayton place?"

Ray argued no more, and ten minutes later they were jogging down the trail and over the hills toward the Drayton Ranch.

It was a different matter, that house, from the tree-embowered place of the Pendletons. It was simply a wide-armed rambling shack of a house or, rather, a collection of many broken-down shacks, all adjoining. There was not a tree around it. There was not even a stroke of paint to hide the rotting nakedness of the wooden walls. There was not a green blade of grass nearby, but all was beaten to brown dust by the hoofs of many horses. There was a hitching rack long enough to accommodate fifty horses on one side, and the wooden top bar had been gnawed into waves by the teeth of horses, and the ground had been pawed full of deep holes.

"That's the Drayton layout," said Ray Pendleton. "Confound them, the place looks like them . . . pretty bleak and miserable. The Draytons are like that."

"What started the trouble between your two families?" asked the tramp.

"Uncle Rory never even told you that?"

"No, not even that. He was pretty silent about things out here in this neck of the woods," said the tramp.

"Everybody knows that yarn. And it was a pretty silly thing, I suppose," said Ray Pendleton, "except that it's been dignified by the number of times it's been told, and the number of years we've fought over it. The first Pendleton to come out this way was named Thomas J., too. He had a fool yellow dog that ran out one day on four legs, and came back on three.

"So Grandfather Pendleton took the back trail of that yellow dog, and it brought him to the camp of a prospector up in the hills named Drayton. When he asked Drayton if he'd shot a dog recently, Drayton said that he hadn't, but that he'd shot a sneaking yellow coyote that had been around his camp. So grandfather damned Drayton and, to cut a long story short, they up and shot one another. Grandfather thought that Drayton was dead, left him in a pool of blood, and crawled onto the back of his horse and rode home. The next day he died from the loss of blood, but Drayton hadn't died at all. He'd just been stunned.

"When he came to and found out what had happened, he said that one Pendleton was not enough for him. He wanted more of our blood. So he gave up prospecting and squatted on a piece of land. Then he built a shack, which is the first part of this house in front of you, and fetched out his wife and kids. Ever since then we've been fighting the Draytons and the Draytons have been fighting us. Just now it's an even break. There're six men dead on each side, but that doesn't count the women that have died of heartbreak and things like that."

"Maybe it's time for this feud to die out," suggested the tramp curiously.

"Die out?" repeated the other, looking up at the sky. "Well, I suppose it would be a good thing, but it won't happen, not at this late day."

"Why not?" asked Paradise Al.

"Because," said young Pendleton, "nobody knows who's in the wrong. We say that the Draytons are, and they say that we started it. Of course, neither side will give in. The Pendletons don't quit in the middle of a fight, and you can bet your bottom dollar that the Draytons don't, either. They're a hard lot, and they're fonder of fighting than of chewing tobacco." He laughed a little as he said this.

Paradise Al looked at him with a sort of cold, calm wonder. Twelve men had died, and still the foolish quarrel about one wounded dog had not ended.

"Look here," said Paradise Al suddenly, "aren't you running into danger, coming over here to their house this way?"

"Of course, I am," said the other, "but so are you. But I don't think that Tim Drayton would let us be hurt, so long as we've come to try Sullivan. He'd rather see that horse ridden, and get rid of Rourke, than kill all the Pendletons in the world,

I'm sure." He looked up, and then added: "There's Rourke now!"

A little red-headed man came out of the house, a red-headed man with a ragged white beard and a ragged red mustache.

When he saw Ray Pendleton, he raised a shout: "Pendletons!" And he pulled a revolver with either hand. Ray Pendleton pulled up his horse.

"Hold on, Rourke," he said. "Any reason why a Pendleton can't try his hand on Sullivan?"

Three or four other men had come to doors and windows in the ramshackle house by this time, and now the shrill voice of a woman cried out: "Don't none of you dare to shoot a bullet or I'll be after you! Lay down them guns!"

IX

A screen door was pushed open, closed with a jingling slam, and there stood little Molly Drayton. Paradise Al looked at her with both pleasure and pain—pain because he had hoped that on second sight she would prove a disappointment; pleasure because she fitted into his conception of what a woman should be as exactly as a bullet fits into a rifle gun barrel. The color of her hair and eyes, her size and her weight were all perfect. It was not that she was so very beautiful, but she combined all those variations from ideal beauty that were, to him, more than perfection.

"Hello, Ray," she said. "What's all the noise about?"

"We're not making any noise," said Ray calmly. "Your tribe is doing the shouting, old son."

It seemed a little odd to the tramp that the girl should be addressed as "old son". He registered the term, to be thought over later on.

"Yeah. They seem to be a little noisy. Pipe down, you!" called Molly Drayton. "I see you've got the young cousin along, Ray. What's he for? Trouble?"

The calm insolence of this did not disturb the tramp. He had been insulted before, and to a skin like his mere words were as water to oiled silk.

"Al has come over to ride Sullivan. That's all," said Ray Pendleton.

"He's come over to which?" she repeated.

"He played a little joke on you people, there in Jumping Creek," said Ray Pendleton, embroidering a trifle upon the facts. "And now he wants to show you what a real rider can do."

She turned her glance upon Paradise Al, and then she smiled. It was not a friendly smile, either. Never before had Paradise Al seen such an expression on such a face. He could realize, as he looked back at her, the full extent of the deadliness that underlay the feud.

"There's the corral . . . here's Rourke to show you the way . . . and there's still enough of us left to enjoy the play," she said.

Paradise Al understood perfectly. The play, to her, would be a tragedy, involving the death of a Pendleton. Therefore, it would be a very good play, indeed.

The tramp shrugged his shoulders; then he followed the example of his companion and slid from the saddle to the ground.

Other people came out of the big house now— women, men whose clothes bulged significantly, here and there, and sagged as with the concentrated weight of metal. An eye less keen even than that of Paradise Al would have suspected Colt revolvers instantly.

Rourke came up to him. He was at least two inches short of even the meager height of the tramp, and, when he was very close, he halted and grinned. "You're going to try Sullivan, are you?" he said.

"Yes, I'm going to try Sullivan," repeated Paradise Al.

"You're young," said the other, "and that's kind of too bad. "But this way, brother." He turned, laughing.

"Hold on," said Paradise Al. "I've come to get the horse. I'm riding him back here a week from today. Right now, I'll take him off on a lead, thank you." For, as he said to himself, patience and a good pair of hands will open any lock, if only there is time enough.

Rourke halted and spun about. "It's a game, is it?" he said.

A very old, very white-headed man came slowly forward. "What would you be doing to Sullivan for a week?" he asked.

"More than you people have been doing to him for a year," said Paradise Al.

The old man blinked. "I dunno," he said. "I dunno what Tim would say to this. Molly, what you think?"

"Dad would say that it's a bluff," said the girl.

"A bluff," said the old man, nodding his head. "Yeah, that's what it looks like to me."

"Look here," said Ray Pendleton to Paradise. "You're not letting us down, Al, are you?" He added, after a moment: "You wouldn't make fools of us . . . ?"

Again was the word implied, but not spoken. The inborn courtesy of Al prevented that.

"You see, Ray," said Paradise Al, "the fact is, the Draytons are the ones who've been throwing the bluff. They talk of their challenge to the whole world to ride the stallion. That's all right. But they'll give nobody a chance to work on the horse. They want the whole show here under their eyes, and maybe they put pins in the saddle blankets, for all we know. That would be a real Drayton trick."

Ray Pendleton blinked at him when he heard this remark.

A wide-shouldered youth stepped forth from the gathering cluster to say: "You don't look like much to me, Al Pendleton. And no Pendleton ever lived that could talk like you've done and get away with it."

"Hush up, Sammy," said Molly Drayton. "This is only pure bluff. Al Pendleton will no more try to ride Sullivan than . . . well, that hawk is nearer to being a dead buzzard than he is to doing what he boasts about."

Her glance went upward, and, following it, Paradise Al saw a hawk sweep out of the top of a tree and dart up into the blue road of the upper sky.

"Excuse me, Ray," said the tramp, and instantly conjured the long Colt from the scabbard that was strapped to the leg of his "cousin".

The saddle might be a strange world to Paradise Al, but guns were his element. In the land of electric lighted streets, gun plays were more common, in fact, than ever they had been in the wildest days of the West. In that same land, men stood for hours every day in the shooting galleries, trying to shoot the celluloid ball from the dancing top of the fountain, counting it very bad work, indeed, if they missed one in ten times.

This was not a shooting gallery. The range was long, and the target was in an awkward position far above his head. But he jerked up the gun confidently and fired. As he drew the steel, he was aware that half a dozen other weapons had instantly gleamed in the hands of the Draytons. But that pleased, rather than concerned him.

In answer to his first shot, the hawk swayed to the side, dodging like a runner on firm ground and leaving a thin tuft of feathers floating in the air. It seemed to the tramp that, having found the right range, he hardly needed to look, in firing the second time. The next shot, in fact, tumbled the wide-winged bird of prey out of the sky as if off a high perch. Down it came, whirling, and by chance it struck the ground not two steps from the place where Molly Drayton was standing.

As the heavy, solid noise of the impact came to the ears of Paradise Al, he said: "There's one half of what you wanted. It's not a buzzard, but it's dead."

Rourke ran and picked up the dead bird by one wing. High as he lifted it, the long feathers of the other wing almost touched the ground.

"By thunder," cried Rourke, "a man that can shoot like that can ride, too, no matter what you say!"

"But you people won't give me a hand with the stallion," said Paradise Al, with a ready discourtesy. "I know the cut of you . . . and you talk about wanting to see Sullivan ridden, but you won't give anyone a fair chance."

The same young man who had spoken before cried out now in a shrill voice: "You gonna try to bluff us out because you managed to make a lucky hit with that bird? I'll take you on, and I'll take you on right now. Ride a horse? You couldn't ride a hobbyhorse!"

Al looked at him. Then he said: "Somebody take that young fool away and shut him up. He's too young to die. A week from today, I'll ride Sullivan back here and, if anybody in the Drayton outfit wants trouble, that will be the time to get it. I'll take you one by one, as many as there are to come." As he spoke, he laughed just a little. It was not pleasant laughter. There was too much cruel confidence in it. Saddles were not the element for Paradise Al, but guns were a different matter. Death by being hurled to the ground from the back of a horse was one thing. Death by bullets was quite another. Already there were sundry scars upon the body of Paradise Al. He knew all about the pain that guns can inflict, and he was not afraid.

Suddenly Rourke said: "What kind of bunk is all this here? Here's a gent that'll take Sullivan and keep him for a week, and guarantee to ride him back to us. Well, let him have him. If there's anybody here that wants a party with this Pendleton, a week from today is the time to claim him for a dance. Ain't that right?" He did not wait for a vote or an answer. He simply called out: "This way, Pendleton! I'll get the hoss out of the corral for you."

He turned his back and strode away, and the whole crowd followed him, compelled by that ready mastery of the situation. So they turned a corner of the house. As they did so, Paradise Al saw Sullivan in the corral.

There was no other animal in the enclosure. Even had there not been, he told himself that he would have known the beast. There were sixteen hands and an inch of him, and he was by no means pretty to see. His hips stuck out too far. No amount of good oats would ever fatten those great outstanding ribs. His knees and his hocks were like the iron-hard joints in the boughs of an old oak tree. His head seemed like the work of some inspired but half-demented sculptor. Even from a distance, it seemed to Paradise Al that he could see the red flare of the eyes of the stallion.

All the courage oozed out of the heart of the tramp. He had come expecting to find a horse; he felt that he was face to face with a winged devil.

X

Ray Pendleton was staring at the beautiful animal. "There's a horse for any man," he said. "Any man would want to ride it . . . or a flying dragon, too, or a wishing carpet, say."

"How many men did you say that brute killed?" asked the tramp.

"Three or four," answered Ray. "They all needed killing, too. Some people say that Sullivan had a real job in the world . . . that he was sent down here to weed out a few of the thugs."

This suggestion did not seem to make the tramp feel any more at ease.

"There's Sullivan," said the red man, Rourke, pointing to the blood-red stallion. "I'll fetch a saddle onto him for you." He went into a shed, brought out a saddle, and climbed the fence into the corral. At sight of his coming, the stallion lifted its head and whinnied a soft welcome.

"He likes Rourke, anyway," said Paradise Al.

"Sure he does, the way the lions like the keeper at feeding time. You might as well get yourself ready and loosen up to tackle him. Or are you only going to lead him home?"

"You let me do things my own way," said Paradise Al. "I'm going to make that big red spot behave like milk and honey down the throat. You've got a rope on the pommel of your saddle. I'd like to have it."

He was given the rope, and Rourke himself, having saddled the horse, stood by and hitched the rope to the neck of the stallion. "Now you're all right," he said to Paradise Al. "Gonna hypnotize that hoss, are you?"

"I'm going to ride him back here at the end of a week and give you a show," said Al.

"Good," said the other, grinning. Rourke was a rather pale little man, and there was an evil in his eyes and in his whole face that peered out at one, particularly it peered out at Paradise Al at this moment.

"I throw in the saddle," said Rourke. "It's made to order to fit the back of that stallion without squeezing him none. There's three or four of the boys that've died out of that saddle, but you'll have better luck, I guess. That saddle has steel in it. When he falls over backward, if you was to be caught under, that saddle wouldn't crush in on you. There's enough steel in the arch of it to hold up five tons. Believe me, because I seen it made."

He nodded and laughed as he spoke, and the red of his hair was like the red in his eyes, and that was the red of the great horse, also.

Al accepted the horse and the saddle on him without a murmur of thanks. He led the big fellow back to his own borrowed mount and climbed up on the back of the mustang.

"One week from today, folks!" he called to them cheerfully. He took off his hat and waved it at Molly Drayton. "I hope that you'll be here laughing, Molly," he said.

Her head jerked up a little. "I'll be here to cry on your shoulder, Al Pendleton," she said, "if you're here to ride red Sullivan."

"Will you cry on my shoulder?" said Paradise Al, sneering.

"I will," she said.

"Will you wear my ring, too?" he said.

"Your key ring?" she asked.

"Stop this nonsense, Molly!" said an angry woman's voice.

"I'll mind my own affairs," retorted Molly. "I'll see the day when a Pendleton dares to try to bluff a . . ."

"One week from today," mocked Paradise Al, "little Molly Drayton will be my sweetheart." And he sang the words of an old happy tune with a sudden ring to them, and his laughter followed the singing. "Is that right, Molly?" he said.

"Why," said the girl, "if you can ride Sullivan . . . honestly, fairly, and squarely, with all the lot of us here to see it . . . I'll marry you. I'll squaw for you, darn your socks, pack your grip, and follow you over the hills, Al Pendleton. But if you don't ride him a week from today, I'm going to blow myself to a party and tell you what I think of you."

"That won't be all you'll hear," said Red Rourke. "When you come back here with that hoss, you're comin' back alone, Al Pendleton." He laughed, a sound like the cawing of a crow.

"I'll come back alone. Sullivan will be my company then," said Paradise Al.

"Here, come along!" exclaimed Ray Pendleton curtly.

And they were off on the return journey.

A grimness had come over Ray Pendleton, so that he rode most of the way back with his jaw thrust out, set in a rock-like, beetling formation of muscle and bone.

Just before they came to the Pendleton Ranch, he merely said: "Look here, Al. I'm for you. I want to be behind you and help. But if you're only staging a big bluff, then . . ." His voice had mounted high, but now it gradually died out.

But Paradise Al could fill in the interval that had followed well enough. It meant that once before the whole Pendleton clan had been shamed by the antics of Paradise Al, but they would not endure being shamed twice by any living man.

Well, that was a threat worth hearing; there was a certain weight and substance behind it, of course. Still Paradise Al smiled. He had smiled in just this way more than once before, with an unconcealed and real joy, on certain occasions when his last dollar or the safety of his neck hung upon the turn of a card.

Life was a flat and dull and unprofitable thing to him, except when it was a great game of chance. He gave no answer to Ray Pendleton, and the other seemed shamed into adding: "That was a mighty fine shot you made. A fine trick shot. It shut them up for a minute, too, all of those Draytons. If it were as easy for you to . . ." He paused once more.

And again Paradise Al knew perfectly what had remained unsaid: *If he could shoot a man as easily as he could shoot a bird, that would be a different matter.* And again Paradise Al smiled. Horses were not his province. Guns and men distinctly were another matter.

He put the stallion in a small pasture behind the barn and unsaddled him. It was a nervous moment, and he wondered if the beast would lose his temper and try to destroy him. Try to destroy him? Why, this sleek, shining thing under his hand, from which he dragged the saddle, was a machine made as much for battle as for speed, it seemed to him. When the ears were flattened, that was the bony head of a dragon, equipped with teeth that could crush the skull of a man like an egg. And those iron-dark hoofs were so provided with driving force that they might easily punch holes through a human frame.

Force—that was the thing. Sullivan oozed and shone with it. In the glint of his eye was electric power. Standing flat-footed, he looked capable of jumping over the roof of the barn, and there was something in the carriage of his head that made one feel that Sullivan himself realized all of his powers.

Paradise Al backed toward the corral gate, and Sullivan put down his royal, ugly head, and quietly began to feed on the good grass of that field.

"Now what?" asked Ray Pendleton.

"I'll leave him there to ripen for a while," said Paradise Al.

He was aware of the darkening of his companion's face. They went back to the house in silence.

He spent the rest of that day strictly by himself, brooding. He took a pencil and a piece of paper and made upon the paper little scrawlings, little jottings, for he had found of old that out of random words ideas will often spring. Still, when the night came, he had blundered on no good ideas for the taming of the great horse.

His mind had ranged from starving the monster to using some sort of drug to turn the edge of that destructive temper until someone could ride the stallion for a few turns, proving to the beast that there was nothing dangerous in having the weight of a man upon his back.

Of course, the talk at supper was all about the horse. The Pendletons were looking with a solemn eye of doubt upon Paradise Al, but in those eyes there was also a faint glimmering of hope. For there was one chance in a hundred, or perhaps in a thousand, that the wanderer might perform a miracle.

"He seems quiet enough when there's no rider on his back," said Paradise Al.

"He's as quiet as a house pet, when there's nobody trying to ride him," replied Thomas

Pendleton. "That's the way with a lot of mustangs. There was Bill Dekker's cream-colored mare that was the toughest and fastest thing that ever rattled a buggy over the mountain roads. She was a lamb in harness, but, when you tried a saddle on her back, she turned into a devil and tried to eat you."

That was all the information that Paradise Al received from the family, and it could hardly be called useful information at that.

They were simply waiting, with more or less bated breath, for the moment when he, the tramp, would come into action with the famous horse.

Paradise Al vowed to himself that, when he tried to ride the horse, he would make it a matter of mystery. So, early in the evening, after dinner, he went up to his room and waited there until the lights were out in the rest of the house and the place quiet. Then he departed by the window route, which he had tried before, and went out to the pasture field.

When he stood by the fence, before him loomed the bulk of the stallion against the stars, and the ugly head reached across the topmost bar and sniffed at him. He laid a hand gingerly between the eyes; Sullivan playfully nibbled at his sleeve, and all the fear that had been building up in the tramp like a thunderhead in the sky suddenly vanished and left his mind clear and assured. There was no evil in the horse; there was simply something wrong in the way in which it had been handled.

XI

But if Sullivan had been wrongly handled by experts, who was he to strive to find a better way? Grimly he acknowledged that truth. One thing at least he could do, and that was to become better acquainted with the stallion. So he slipped through the bars of the fence and walked up and down the field. Where he walked, the horse followed like a dog.

This animal a man-killer? He would not believe it. He had known killers before, men and dogs, and he knew that they all possessed one trait in common, which was a sullen malice that might work quietly, but which was always present. Yet, there was no malice in the stallion, so far as he could see. He tried walking and he tried running. When he ran, the big fellow broke into a canter and threw circles around Paradise Al, flipping his tail in the air and kicking up his heels.

It was not that he was very fond of Paradise Al. That much was clear. But it was simply that the stallion had grown accustomed to human society and, therefore, had to have it. Killer? No, there was some mysterious reason behind this thing.

Paradise Al brought out the big, heavy saddle from the shed, the saddle that had been specially fitted to this horse. He strapped it on Sullivan and found that the stallion made not the slightest resistance. He stood with perfect good nature while the tramp went back into the barn and carried out a ninety-pound sack of barley. Al reasoned if once he could get the horse into the habit of carrying any sort of a lifeless burden in the saddle, he would be quicker to endure the weight of a man in the same way. That sack he slid, therefore, onto the saddle, but no sooner did the horse feel the added poundage than he fairly exploded under the nose of Paradise. The sack went one way sailing into the air, and Sullivan went another. All over the face of that field he bucked and raged in a constant fury, snorting and groaning as a horse will do when it is being spurred beyond its strength.

It was a full hour before Paradise Al could get close enough to take the saddle from the big fellow's back. Then, for another full hour he remained with Sullivan, petting him, talking to him.

Killer? There seemed to be nothing of the killer in Sullivan. Yet, it was true that in the past he had killed three men, all of whom had needed killing, according to Ray Pendleton.

Very tired, very troubled, and confused, Paradise Al went back to the house and gained his room by the window again. And again he slept late.

"Working on Sullivan today, Al?" asked Sally.

"I'm going to go out and give him some treatment," said Paradise Al.

That was what he did. He simply got some old magazines and sat with them under the tree in the middle of the pasture field. In the heat of the day, the horse came and stood beside him in the shadow. Once he came over and nipped the hat off the head of the tramp and raced off with it, exactly like a playful child.

Killer, said the tramp to himself. And he laughed a little. He found himself reading very little in the pages of the magazines, but very much in the glorious body of Sullivan. When he walked, a ripple of shining strength passed over his polished skin, and even when he stood still, he always looked as though he had just lighted from the sky and was about to leap back into it again.

Suppose that, on a certain day, he were to sit in the saddle on the stallion and let him go, turn him loose at full speed, jockey him forward. What of that? Why, it would be like being hitched to a kite that was flung loose in a great storm. It would be like that, except that this storm he might be able to control, turning it this way and that with the touch of his hands.

The heart of Paradise Al leaped up into his throat. He had raced across the continent many a time, but always on the trains, and they were confined to their steel roadbeds. But to have at his command such an animal as the stallion would be to have freedom to go where he pleased, free from danger of pursuit, to soar among those ragged mountains, for instance, almost like a winged eagle. Why, a man who had such a horse as Sullivan was able to do as he pleased. He could live according to his own law.

A grim joy thrilled through the nerves of the tramp. There was a predatory soul in him that was savagely contented by such a prospect. But, at the end of the day, he had attempted no more with the stallion.

"What's the game? Hypnotism?" asked the older Pendleton sourly as they sat together at the supper table.

"That's the idea . . . hypnotism," said Al lightly.

But that night, under the stars, once more he tried the saddle on the back of the stallion, and once more he slid the barley sack into place. He was prepared for the explosion again, and he saw one worth ten of the first. The big horse went up into the air with a squeal of pain, hurling the sack far off. Then, whirling, Sullivan went for that fallen burden and beat it to pieces with his hoofs, seized it with his teeth, and carried the empty rag of a sack around and around the pasture, shaking it violently.

Paradise Al looked on with horror. Suppose it had been his body that had been cast from the saddle.

It was a full two hours later before he could get

close enough to Sullivan to strip away the saddle, and, as the flap of the saddle dragged across the back of the stallion, the horse winced and grunted. Paradise Al moved his hand gingerly down the back and found a spot that he pressed upon lightly. The horse winced suddenly and jerked about that ugly, snaky head, with mouth gaping.

The tramp went thoughtfully back to the barn with his burden. Something was decidedly wrong. In his room again, he lay awake for a time and stared into the darkness, puzzled, until sleep closed his eyes. The first glimmer of the dawn was enough to waken him, so uneasy was his mind, and straight out to the barn he went, and to that peg from which hung the made-to-order saddle of the stallion. He took it down, laid it upside down on top of the barley bin, and examined it.

What he had dreamed of was there, in the form of two small spots of blood on the inner face of the heavy, folded saddle blanket. He jerked up his head and stared straight before him. A very ugly expression distorted his handsome features now, and what he was seeing in his mind was the strange face of Rourke and the leering evil in the eyes of that man.

He tossed the blanket aside and carried on his examination of the padded under part of the saddle. There was nothing to be seen. No matter how old the saddle might be, it had been used so little that the strong, woolly cloth of the lining was almost as white as the day it left the shop of the maker. That was not very strange, for the saddle had probably never been used except on the back of Sullivan, and very few unfortunates had dared to try their luck with the famous stallion.

With both thumbs, he began to press on the thick padding just over those points where the bloodstains had dimly appeared on the saddle blanket. Suddenly he was stung to the thumb bone. His hands leaped away and he cursed, looking down at the drop of blood that was welling up on the surface of his finger. But there was no anger in his heart, only a bubbling happiness.

He could understand very well why Rourke had insisted on sending the saddle with the horse. This was the reason. This had caused the pain that had turned Sullivan into a raging devil. It was perfectly clear, all except the mind of Rourke, who had devised such a malicious scheme. Three men had died. Well, it was not the horse, but Rourke who had killed them.

With his pocket knife, he cut the stitching of the outer cover, removed the inner covering also, and then pulled out the padding. There, affixed to the strong frame of the saddle, were two points of steel. A man's weight in the saddle must have driven them deeply down into the back of the tormented horse, and there followed one of those fiendish explosions of temper, not temper at all, properly termed, but rather torment. He removed the stings, replaced the padding, and, securing needle and thread, sewed down the inner and the outer cover.

What should he do now? Let the world know about the villainy of Rourke, or continue with the working of his miracle? The latter was a temptation too great to be passed over.

They saw him in the field that day as before, and once again, in the night, he brought out the saddle. It was no easy matter, this time, to persuade the stallion to stand for it. Once it was cinched in place, however, Paradise Al, without fear, climbed into the stirrups.

It was as though he had sat down on the top of a volcano, for he was hurled suddenly toward the whirling stars, and landed on the flat of his back in the pasture grass with a *thud* that knocked all the breath and half the wits out of him.

Then he saw above him a darkness sweeping over the stars. It was Sullivan, rearing aloft, to descend with battering forehoofs on the body of his persecutor.

For that half second, the nerves of Paradise Al refused to react. He lay still, and his leaping mind was struggling with the clear truth. It was simply the pressure of the saddle on the sore back that had caused the horse to buck—that and the anticipation of the thrusting agony. Now would he, Paradise Al, pay the cost of his folly?

The forehoofs dropped down straight at his head and landed beside it, making the ground tremble, while Sullivan bounded away to the farther side of the field.

Gasping, trembling, the tramp rose to hands and knees. All his pain was as nothing to him. He had hurried the work a little too much, but that did not mean that he had definitely failed. Little by little and step by step he must go systematically about this work, but he was assured of his success in the end.

XII

It was a week of such satisfaction as the wanderer best understood and appreciated. For he was sitting in at a game where the rest of the players paid him very little heed, indeed, but in which he knew that he held the best cards up his sleeve.

As that week wore on, the nervousness of the entire Pendleton family increased. Hardly a word was spoken, except a bit of forced conversation, when Paradise Al was present.

The morning of the fatal day, when he was to ride the stallion back to the Drayton place, found a dozen other members of the clan present. They were all big men, these Pendletons. When they gathered in force, they made Paradise Al seem more of a stranger and an outcast than ever. He said aside, to Sally Pendleton, from whom he got most of his intimate information about what was passing in the mind of the family: "Why has the clan gathered and brought all of their guns along?"

She looked narrowly at him, for her frankness in speaking to him never sprang from any liking she had for him.

"The Pendletons have come together," she said, "because if you disgrace us today . . . well, something has to be done about it."

"Shooting, eh?" he said.

She shrugged her shoulders, turned, and left him.

Watching her height, her suppleness, the fine swing of her stride, he forgot her insulting demeanor in his admiration of her as a woman. In fact, he continually found himself at ease among these people, even when they most showed that they were suspecting or despising him. He felt that they were a superior race, better bred, molded in a purer air and under a stronger sun than any that he had known.

He had never been a rogue who excused his own roguery. He knew that he was a knave, and he looked at good people as one looks at actors upon a stage, with admiration, but not with a real envy. He felt that he was fallen too low ever to rise again.

That was the mood of Paradise Al, on this morning, when he went out toward the pasture in which the stallion was grazing; the entire clan followed him, men and women, children and farm hands as well. About thirty people stood at the fence with him.

"He ain't done a day's work to break that hoss," he distinctly heard someone say. "Claims to be hypnotizin' him, or something like that."

"Maybe he's hypnotized Sullivan, but, if he tries to ride him, Sullivan will hypnotize him right back," was the answer.

Paradise Al hastily turned toward the barn, concealing a smile, and came out carrying the saddle and the bridle. He climbed through the fence and whistled, but Sullivan was already coming up at a trot. What horse will not come to a whistle, when from the same hand it has been fed good barley or oats during every visit for seven days? There was another handful of oats to reward his coming on this occasion. While he munched it, gathering it from the palm of the tramp with a dexterous pair of velvety lips, an angry murmur ran down the line of spectators.

"Why do you waste time, Al?" demanded Thomas J. Pendleton.

Sullivan himself turned his big, bony head and stared at the speaker, while he munched the last of the oats. Then he lowered his head to sniff at the saddle, while Paradise Al answered: "It's just a way of saying hello to Sullivan. A handful of oats is nothing to a horse that's going to carry you six miles or so."

That was the distance to the Drayton place. Next, the tramp swung the saddle onto the back of the horse with a decisive flop, and reached fearlessly under to get at the cinches.

"That's all right," said Thomas J. Pendleton rather too loudly. "Even that red rascal, Rourke, can do that much with Sullivan. The riding is the thing."

Paradise Al was annoyingly slow and careful in the drawing up of the cinches and in the arrangement of the stirrups, which he affected to find not quite the right length. Finally, when he was satisfied, he said: "In case old Sullivan takes it into his head to run a bit, just open the gate, will you, somebody?"

The gate was opened. Paradise Al settled his hat more firmly on his head, thrust a foot in the stirrup, and swung himself awkwardly up into the saddle. In fact, his weight dropped into it— he fumbled for and found the other stirrup—and the terrible Sullivan merely pricked his ears and switched his tail.

"The thunder'll start pretty quick," said one of the cowpunchers. "And Satan help that tenderfoot then."

Paradise Al ran his eyes down the line of faces and was content. Never an actor thrilled with more pleasure in holding an audience spell-bound than did this thief as he saw the stern, set, resolved faces of those brown men and women of the West. His own knavery delighted him all the more. It had only been a trick, a mere quiet bit of experimenting, that had earned for him this triumph. To be sure, he had once measured his length hard on the ground, and he had seen the front hoofs of the stallion dropping at his head like a pair of ponderous sledgehammers. But that moment was forgotten in his moment of triumph. He gathered the reins. He slapped the stallion cheerfully on the flank. "Get up, old fellow," he said.

In response, Sullivan did not hurl himself at the sky. Neither did he fling himself backward upon the ground, nor indulge in one of his outbursts of snaky twisting and rope snapping that had unseated so many an expert rider. He merely switched his tail and walked slowly forward toward the gate.

A whisper, a murmur, a voice, a roar of excitement and applause came from the watchers. Al saw the face of Thomas J. Pendleton, crimson with joy; he saw the old gentleman shaking a burly fist in the air. He saw hats waved, and, through all of that commotion, Sullivan walked calmly on.

He could do better than that. Every night for five nights the tramp had ridden him in the pasture and began to know his gaits and paces very well. So he put him to a trot. And what a trot it was. The powerful fetlock joints gave whole inches, like hydraulic shock absorbers of infinite delicacy, self-adjusting. Even Paradise Al could sit that trot and hardly move in the saddle. Then he brought the stallion to a canter that swept him around the corral in a moment.

He headed Sullivan straight out over the field at full gallop, with the wind suddenly fierce in his face, and the ground shooting back beneath him as it shoots beneath a running train.

He turned the stallion in a wide loop and brought him back. When he stopped the sorrel again, the Pendletons swarmed about him with worship in their faces.

"Albert, I'm going to confess that I've been doubting you," said Thomas J. Pendleton. "I'm going to confess that I was afraid that you'd shame us. I'm taking this moment to make an apology. I want you to forgive me, and forgive the rest of us, because we haven't had faith."

"Why, that's quite all right," said Paradise Al. "I know how it is. You never can tell what a tool's worth until you try to make it cut."

He was glad that he had thought of saying that. He heard a murmur of approbation in answer to his speech. Only, looking among the faces, he saw Sally Pendleton watching him with a cold expression of doubt.

She has a mind of her own, that girl, he said to himself. Then, to Ray: "Will you ride over with me, Ray?"

"To the Draytons?" asked Ray Pendleton.

"Yes."

Ray looked to his father.

"Trouble may come of it," said Thomas. "There generally is trouble, when the Draytons lose out. They're not the kind to be put down and lie still and take it. But you'll have to take your chances. You went with him before. You can go with him again."

"Why, if it comes to that, I'll ride over by myself," said Paradise Al. "I'd rather, except for the company. I'll ride over and then swing back toward town. Anybody who's thirsty, meet me there for a drink. Is that a go?"

"Steady," said Thomas J. Pendleton. "D'you mean that you'll go to that nest of tigers alone?"

"No, not alone," answered Paradise Al, "if one of you will give me a gun."

Twenty guns gleamed in twenty hands, thrusting forward, butt first, toward the hand of Paradise.

"Take this," said a single voice.

He took the nearest one and knew that the owner of it felt honored by the choice. Odd people, these Pendletons. He looked them over with a strangely guilty sense, knowing that he had been taken suddenly into the heart of the clan and that every one of these men was willing to die for the new member.

"It may be better if he goes alone," said Thomas J. Pendleton. "The Draytons know that one man is one man. But whenever they see two Pendletons together, they're apt to think that it's a whole crowd and start a war. Albert, I'm going to meet you in town, but you can't pay for any drinks today. We'll all meet you in town, every man of us, and hear how the Draytons took the bitter pill. There's only one thing I have to say."

"Yes?" said Paradise respectfully.

"When you were there before, you made some foolish remarks to Molly Drayton. You won't remember them today, I hope?"

Paradise Al drew in his breath slowly. He had never quite rubbed the picture of the girl out of his mind. It grew burningly bright before his eyes now.

"You know," he said, "she damned me with her eyes, the last time that I was over. I don't think that Pendletons ought to take a damning quietly, even when it's only in the eyes, do you?"

He smiled at his "uncle", and his "uncle", with an answering smile, shrugged his shoulders and made a gesture that left the matter to the disposal of the rider's good sense.

So he turned the head of Sullivan toward the outer road and heard a cheer behind him. When he came to the gate leading to the road, he saw that the person who had run ahead to open it for him was none other than Sally, and she stood there with the heavy panel flung open behind her and looked steadily up to him, saying: "Al Jones, or Brown, or whoever you are, if you want to keep yourself and the rest of us out of a devilish lot of trouble, drop Molly Drayton. There's nothing but poison there for you."

XIII

There was nothing particularly soothing about the knowledge that Sally Pendleton saw through him and knew perfectly well that he was a mere pretender to the name of her family. There was nothing agreeable, likewise, in her prophecy that the best thing for him was to keep away from Molly Drayton.

He went on down the road, shaking his head from time to time, and vainly struggling with the problem. The stallion went along easily on a loose rein, as though there were nothing whatever on his back and as though he were picking his own way across country, meanwhile looking out for all manner of possible dangers on the way. Now and then he paused, with a forehoof raised like a fox, while he sniffed the wind or eyed a grove of trees. Once, he turned halfway around and looked back down the road at two riders who were slowly overtaking them. Always his head was high to study the wind, or lowered to sniff at trails on the ground. It was very plain that he had not forgotten the earlier days when he was the wild leader of a wild herd. He went across country with the caution of a beast of prey.

Paradise Al was beginning to feel that the horse was both a means of travel and a guide and guard while traveling, when the two riders came up, one on either side of him. Their faces were not welcome. They were the detectives who had worked so industriously for the railroad, Jay Winchell and that same Harry Tucker who had beaten his fist against the face of the tramp with such pleasure and energy.

"Hello, boys," said Paradise, undisturbed, to all appearances, by the arrival of this pair of enemies. He was taking note, at the same time, that one was on either side. They did not know, perhaps, some of the little gun tricks of which he was capable.

"Hello," said Winchell. "You rolled us, finally, did you, you worthless bum, you?"

"You don't think that you put anything over on us, do you?" added Tucker. "You don't think that we swaller this gag about you being a Pendleton, do you?"

"Why, Harry," said Paradise Al, "are you accusing me of playing a rôle?"

He shook his head in mild rebuke at Tucker, and the latter growled like a dog.

"We're gonna get our teeth into you," said

Tucker. "Went and got us rolled, did you? We'll get our teeth into you for that, brother."

"They fired you, finally, did they?" asked the boy. "I'm glad to hear that, and sorry to hear it, too."

"Why, damn you," began Tucker, his voice rising and his face reddening.

"Shut up, Harry," said Winchell. "Let's get at his idea. You're glad and sorry?" he repeated.

"Glad that they kicked you out before you made any more trouble for poor bums coming along the railroad in this direction," said Paradise. "But I'm sorry that you're fired, because that means that I may have to go a long distance to find you, when I'm tired of staying around here."

"You're not staying around here? You're not a Pendleton? You admit that?" barked Tucker.

"Certainly I admit it to you two."

"You got an idea we like you so good that we wouldn't spread the news anywhere. Is that it?"

"It doesn't make any difference what you say about me," said Paradise. "The more you talk, the more these people will laugh at you. They're a queer lot around here. They know the difference between a talking man and a barking dog, for instance."

"We're barking dogs, are we?" demanded Winchell. "But go on and tell us why you'll be sorry?"

"Because," said Paradise Al, "when I'm through

with my place here with the Pendletons, I'm going to look you both up. You, Winchell, I'll let off easily. But you're a dead man, Tucker. You are really a dead man. I'm going to kill you. And I want you to know what I intend to do. You may get more taste out of the thing, if you know it in advance."

"Thanks," said Tucker. Then his rage came roaring out of his throat: "I'm gonna bash your head in for you, and right now!"

"Will you?" asked Paradise Al. "You're going to beat me up, Tucker?"

"Yes, and right now."

"Shake hands on that, and then you can start," said Paradise, and he actually extended his slender brown hand with a smile toward the other.

Tucker hesitated, cursed, then grasped the hand. But it was like laying hold upon an electric wire, for the forefinger of Paradise Al touched and pressed down upon a nerve in the back of Tucker's hand, and that pressure sent an icy wave of numbness shooting up through the wrist and forearm of the ex-detective.

He had intended, as a matter of fact, to crush that slender hand in his own more massive grip. But now, with a grunt of pain and rage, he tore his hand away from the deadly pressure. It was still numb. He would have reached for a gun, but he knew beforehand that a gun would slide out of his nerveless fingers. Raging inwardly, he saw the faint, calm smile of the tramp regarding him, mastering him.

"What the devil's the matter with you, Harry?" asked Winchell of his companion.

"He tricked me," said Tucker furiously, massaging his still tingling hand.

"Mind you, Tucker," said the tramp, "I'm going to hunt you down, when I'm ready for the job. And when I find you, I'm going to put you under the ground."

With that, he touched the tender, sensitive flank of the stallion with his heel, and Sullivan galloped down the road with a long-reaching stride.

The two did not follow. Something had happened to them during that brief interview that was highly depressing to their spirits, and they merely stared after the slender rider, realizing that not once did he turn his head to mark whether or not they were unlimbering rifles to shoot after him.

Very well did Paradise understand what must be going on in their minds, and he laughed to himself as he galloped on his way.

He pulled the stallion down to a trot and at that gait he at last approached the house of Drayton.

Even in the distance he saw that an audience waited for him. There were men lingering about the house; there were others nearer the barn; two or three were in the pasture, overlooking the horses there. As he came nearer, there was a sudden stir that brought the entire body of people near the house itself. From that wide-spreading shack of a place, out came women and children. Still from afar, he thought that he could recognize Molly Drayton, almost lost among the others. He laughed to himself, but felt, as he laughed, the cold leap of fear, something that went to his heart like the bright glinting of a sword.

They were drawn up in a wide arc as he finally drew the rein of the stallion before them. A silent group they were, and every face hard and cold with anger and astonishment. Only Rourke, like a red pestilence, leered, open-mouthed, with a mixture of wonder and rage, fear and malice. There was a devil in that small man.

Molly Drayton? She seemed actually less moved than any of the others. But her father, Timothy Drayton, the sheriff, stood close to her, with his big, strong arm cast about her as though to protect her from any coming evil.

"I'm to stay on the back of Sullivan for ten minutes now. Is that correct?" said Paradise Al as he lifted his hat to the crowd.

"Ten minutes?" said Tim Drayton in a harsh, grating voice. "I reckon that you've been on him ten minutes, all right. I reckon that you've won him, Pendleton."

Paradise Al slipped to the ground. Very frail and unimportant, he looked as he stood before those massive men, those silent, staring women.

He bowed toward Molly Drayton. "I hope that you feel it's a lucky day, Molly?" he said.

Tim Drayton burst out: "Young fellow, a joke's a joke. We can all laugh at it. You got the horse, and that oughta be enough. If you begin to talk about the fool bet you made with Molly here . . ."

"Was it a fool bet, Molly?" asked the tramp.

She shook her head. "I've given my word," she answered, "and I intend to keep it."

A groan came from every throat about her.

"Keep it?" shouted her father. "Are you plumb crazy, Molly, darling? I'd rather see you . . ."

She stepped from the shelter of her father's arm suddenly and stood before Paradise Al. "Now, say what you want," she commanded fearlessly.

"A claim on you," he said intently. "I file a claim that can't be jumped, with this ring, Molly. Is that right?"

"You can do as you please," she said. She stepped still closer to him. With her voice lowered so that only the murmur of it, not the words, could reach the ears of the others standing so near, she said: "Paradise Al, or whatever your name is, you know what will happen if you take me at my word. There'll be murder in the air. If you have half an eye, you can see it and feel it now. The men won't let you take me. You knew that before. There'll be a killing before that happens."

He answered her, aloud: "If I take you, your

tribe will come for my scalp. That's all right, Molly. What I want from the Draytons is their scalps and you. If there is killing, I'll try to do my share. But here's my claim, and here's how I file it."

It was a man's ring, a broad band with a flat-faced emerald set in it. This he slipped upon her finger, and raised her hand to his lips. Then he stepped back.

"You understand, Molly," he said. "If I send for you, you come. I'll choose my time. The rest of you, good luck, and may you shoot straight when we meet again." He climbed into the saddle.

The high, whining voice of Rourke was crying out: "Stop him! If he gets away this time, you'll all have a chance to groan about it later on. Stop him! Stop him!"

There was a snarling answer from the throat of Timothy Drayton, the sheriff. Molly Drayton herself, her face as pale as stone, stood motionlessly, looking down at the ring on her hand, and that was the last that Paradise Al saw of them as he turned the head of Sullivan and rode back down the trail toward Jumping Creek.

It had been bad enough to leave the two ex-detectives behind his back. It was far worse, now, to have the assembled Draytons behind him.

He knew that the thunder and the lightning had gathered over his head. He knew that the least word, the smallest wrong gesture, would be enough to draw the thunderbolts down on him and blast him. Shudders chased up his spine. He was weak with fear, but, as he had done with the two on the road, so he did now, and went away toward Jumping Creek without looking back.

As he rode, he looked down at the short, pricking ears of the stallion, at the length of the muscular arching of his neck. It seemed to him that the great horse was an engine to carry him over something more than mere miles, or mere mountains, but on to face destiny itself, in a fated country.

It seemed to Paradise Al that all his world had changed greatly. He had been playing all his life a game of many tricks, of danger, and he was still playing a game, but the stakes seemed more important—more important than money, for instance—for greater, loftier, nobler things.

XIV

He did not go straight in to Jumping Creek. No, that would be a folly, he felt. In Jumping Creek all the electric currents had to gather and pile up, all to be set in motion by his arrival. Something was going to happen. He hardly knew what. When he arrived in the town, deviltry of all sorts would be precipitated.

He took Sullivan off the trail, pulled the bridle from his head, and let the stallion graze. He had spent enough hours alone with the horse to have built up a close relationship, particularly in the hours of the night. To all animals, one hour of human companionship by night is worth a month of work in the daylight. Sullivan, as he strayed and grazed, repeatedly kept coming back to his master, lifting his head and staring around the horizon like a sentinel.

What he meant to Paradise Al was more than the tramp could have put into words. In fact, new emotions were growing up in him with every moment of his existence. The width of this horizon stretched his very mind until it ached, and the clear, sun-washed blue of the sky opened above him, as it were, a new conception of life. He was worried, he was vaguely but greatly distressed. Somehow he felt that a new system of values was impinging upon his mind, and that he would have to admit it before long. It was like preparing to put on a new soul. He could not tell what was going to happen to him.

Then these people with whom he was mixed— they were all different from those he had known in the old days. Winchell and Tucker, they were the last links with the old types. He could understand them, close, savage, bitter, cunning men. But the Draytons, they were another kind of being, sinister in their strength and their resolute courage, no doubt, but nothing shifty or tricky about them. The Pendletons, also, those lions among men, were of a new breed. He, Paradise Al, had foisted himself upon that great family. He shuddered with a strange mixture of joy and dread when he thought of them.

Finally, there was Molly Drayton.

He had put his ring on her finger. That was true. Although he had announced it as a claim, he felt with a sickening fall of the heart, that such a claim was too absurd. She, incapable of deceit or lying, as it seemed, might be willing to fulfill the foolish contract she had made with him, out of the very excess of contempt that she felt for him. But that willingness of hers would not be enough. Fate, itself, he felt, would put down its hand to prevent such a match between a girl like Molly Drayton and an unclean thing like Paradise Al.

For so the tramp saw himself, for the first time. As he remembered the white, still face of the girl, as she had looked down at his ring on her hand, Paradise Al dropped his face into both his hands and groaned aloud. His past life came over him, flickering as rapidly as the shadows that sweep under the wheel of a windmill.

He saw the city streets, the dark, twisting lanes among high buildings that fenced irregular ways through the smoky sky above. He saw the companions of his youth, the pale faces and the eyes filled with evil knowledge too great for their years. He saw back to his life in the foundling's home, the mechanical charity, the dreadful monotony of the days, the sense of hopelessness. He saw his youthful days, his training by older wits in the ways of crime, and those first glorious years, as they had seemed to him, when figures celebrated in the underworld accepted him with respect, as a rising master. There had been an intoxicating sense of power in all of this. His wits were better than those of other men. His eye was calmer and clearer. His hand was more swift and subtle. He was not large, but his natural gifts were such that he was as an Achilles compared with his fellows.

Yet now, within the brief compass of a single week, he had stepped across the border into a strange new world wherein all of the old values were dissolving. Somehow it seemed to him that perhaps the greatest thing in the world was not strength of craft and cunning, or strength to slay, but strength to be brave and honest, strength to keep one's soul so clean that all the world might look in upon it.

At last he started up, choking, dizzy, his heart racing. And he thought to himself bitterly, fiercely, slowly: *I've trained myself for only one thing. I can raise hell. That's all I can do. That's the only way I can make people look up to me. So I'm going to raise hell again today. I'll show them what I am, when I turn loose my guns.*

He got the bridle back upon the head of the stallion, as this thought went through his mind, and then he climbed into the saddle again and let the horse wander gradually back along the trail to Jumping Creek.

Even before he came to the town, he saw that the situation was being built up for his arrival there. On the verge of the place three cow-punchers galloped past him, coming in, and, as they went by at full speed, he heard one of them exclaim: "There's Sullivan! That's Paradise Al Pendleton!"

All three turned their heads and stared back at him. They drew down their horses to a trot. Through the dust they raised, the three still looked back until a turn of the street cut them off.

Paradise Al, in his dark heart, smiled with gratification. It reminded him of the old days when he went down the street in New York, and the young chaps whispered together and looked after him with their eyes as big as moons, or when he had entered Dill Morgan's place after Shorty Welch, the gunman, had hunted him down, only to die at his hands, and everyone in Dill Morgan's stood up and drank in his honor.

Well, it was something like those good times to ride into Jumping Creek, to be pointed out and whispered about, except that there was a difference. For, coming past a corner house, he saw a tall old man standing in the vegetable garden, resting on a long-handled hoe, and the old man looked at him with eyes of calm knowledge and watched him down the street.

To save his soul, Paradise Al could not meet that glance. The cold, clear knowledge of that look pierced him to the soul. And how had the old man been able to look so easily through him? Why had there been such penetrating knowledge and disdain in that glance? Was it that here on the frontier a man's fighting ability was respected as a blessing or despised as a curse, according to the way he used it?

He passed on into the heart of the town, aware of a growing murmur before him. When he came to the center of that murmur, which turned out to be the pounding feet of galloping horses, combined with human voices and the *rattling* of carriage wheels, he found himself in front of the biggest saloon in Jumping Creek, Chuck Lewis's place.

He dismounted, found a place to tie the stallion at one end of the long hitching rack, and went in through the swinging doors. In front of the saloon there were a full score of idlers. The instant that Paradise Al entered the doors, he seemed to set up a draft that blew the others quickly in behind him.

He easily recognized them. They were the spectators. Even the West, it appeared, could furnish men who appeared in the sky like

111

buzzards, prepared to fatten on the crimes, the follies, as well as the tragedies of other men.

But he had no opportunity to give his mind to these affairs. Once inside of the saloon, he saw that he was surrounded by danger in its most electric form—high-spirited men, armed all of them to the teeth, and only waiting for the fall of a pin, as it were, before they engaged in battle.

He saw the faces of Winchell and Tucker. Well, they hardly mattered, except that they were sure to join the opposition. He saw instantly, what mattered more—half a dozen of the Drayton clan, all looking at him askance and then fastening their eyes on a man among them who he had never seen before.

To balance the Draytons, there were several Pendletons. Big Ray Pendleton stood out among the others. Instantly he was at the side of Paradise Al, saying: "Mind yourself, Al. They've brought their ace of spades with 'em. And he's going to try his hand on you . . . that's Joe Drayton over there. The one with the beard. He's their black sheep, but they can use him in a pinch like this. He's going to start in on you. And then the whole gang will jump up. We're ready for them. But mind that murderer, Joe Drayton. They've brought him here to get you. Hell is going to break loose. Tim Drayton has resigned his office as sheriff. He'll die fighting to get you out of the way. It's all about Molly. Watch yourself, Al, and bank on me."

XV

Murderer Joe Drayton, the man of the black beard, had been called, and Paradise Al, with an eye to professional skill, probed the fellow to the soul and saw that he was worthy of his name.

But Murderer Joe was only one element in the crowding dangers of that moment. It was veritably like standing inside a powder barrel, with sparks flying, to stand in that barroom. It was a big place, where fifty cowpunchers at a time could change their pay for whiskey, and now men were crowded everywhere. Scores of them filled the place, and the air was filled with blue wreaths and clouds of cigarette smoke.

Death was certainly in the air, but, more than that, there was a strange gaiety. Men laughed loudly. Whiskey glasses were being filled rapidly up and down the bar. Men were not gathering Dutch courage, Paradise Al could guess, but simply celebrating a wild and famous occasion.

Well, when once the shooting began, that floor would run deep with blood. As for him, he saw his maneuver beforehand. He would fling himself slithering on the floor behind that table and shoot up through the legs of it. Then, as he made this decision, he remembered that tall old man with the clear, cold eye, who had looked through and through him.

If he were young and standing in the boots of Paradise Al, what would he do? What would Thomas J. Pendleton do? What would Timothy Drayton do? Allow the massacre to begin?

It seemed to Paradise Al that something cracked open in his soul and let in sudden light. He was a little dizzy with the new idea that burst upon him and for a moment he gripped the arm of Ray Pendleton and looked down to the floor.

"Don't weaken, Al," begged Ray Pendleton. "We're all counting on you to fight like a man."

Paradise Al smiled a little, and, looking up, he saw the fierce eyes of Blackbeard fixed upon him.

Straight through the crowd stepped Paradise Al and faced Murderer Joe Drayton. The latter squared slowly around at him. His eyes narrowed to gleaming points.

"You're Joe Drayton?" said the tramp.

"Yeah, that's my moniker," admitted the big fellow.

"There seems to be some trouble in the air," said Paradise Al, "between the Pendletons and your gang. Now, Joe, you and I both know that guns are going to start working before long. A lot of people will be hurt and that's a pity. What I suggest is that you and I take on the fight for the rest of the boys. Let it lie between the pair of us. Does that sound good to you?"

A wild joy leaped into the eyes of Joe Drayton.

"Do you mean that, kid?" he said. "Where'd you like to start the ruction? D'you mean what you say?" He seemed to be clutching at the idea as at a joy too great to be possible.

"Here is as good a place as any," said Paradise Al. "Stand back there at that end of the bar. I'll stand here. That makes about ten yards. If you want it closer, we'll grab ends of a handkerchief and have it out that way."

Joe Drayton licked his lips with a red, pointed tongue. "Ten yards is all right for me, brother," he said. "I see you're a good, game kid, and I kind of hate to . . . Here, you, clear out and give us room. It's between the kid and me. He's asking for it."

Many voices rose in a clamoring protest. Paradise Al raised his left hand, and that clamor was stilled. "Joe and I are having this little trouble out," he said, "but we've got to learn something first. If we finish this fight, and a finish fight is what we'll make it, there's not to be any quarreling afterward. Not a single damn' gun is to come out of leather, no matter how the fight turns out."

Joe Drayton exclaimed: "The kid's game, and he's right! This little party ends the deal. You boys agree?"

No one spoke, but there was a nodding of heads, here and there. At the same time the men moved suddenly back against the wall. There was not much extra space, but two experts like Joe

Drayton and Paradise Al would not fill the air with flying, random bullets.

They were facing one another, the left hand of Paradise Al resting on the bar, Joe Drayton opposite, leaning a little forward to get the weight on his toes, as though he were prepared to rush at his enemy. A smile of joyous anticipation kept the black beard of the killer writhing.

"You start, kid," said Drayton.

"Somebody count to ten. We'll shoot when he drops his hand," suggested Paradise Al.

"Listen at him," said Joe Drayton. "He's been there before. Rudge, will you do the counting? Stand over there where we can both see you."

Rudge Drayton obediently took his place at the side, midway between the pair, and, raising his right hand, he began to count: "One, two, three . . ."

He had reached seven. As that count proceeded, a quiet and calm pleasure filled the heart of Paradise Al. He saw the twisting, tense faces of the others in the room. But it seemed to him that it hardly mattered how the battle turned out, for he, Paradise Al, had won a victory in the beginning, a victory over himself.

Then, at the count of seven, the swinging doors of the saloon opened. His own back was turned to them, and he only heard the *squeak* of their hinges, but he saw a frown come over the forehead of Joe Drayton, while a catch in breath echoed around the room.

"Molly," said Joe Drayton. "This here ain't any place for you."

It was Molly Drayton herself who stepped suddenly before Paradise Al, her face set and her blue eyes shining with resolution.

"There'll be no murder because of me," she said. "There'll be no reopening of the feud, either. Al, will you come away from here with me?"

He stood like a statue before her. But all the will went out of him and all the resolution. He felt her hand on his nerveless one. As she drew him, he turned with her and like a blind man allowed himself to be led out of the room.

The sun was in his eyes and he could hardly see what was before him in the street. Behind him, in the saloon, a dead silence held them all.

"You're riding out of town with me," said the cold, grim voice of the girl. "Get on Sullivan and come along."

He obeyed as a small child will when it hears the voice of authority.

Now he was on the back of Sullivan, and vaguely he was aware of the girl riding a cream-colored mustang beside him and seeming very small and weak. Then the town was behind them and the sweeping brown hills were before, with the great mountains beyond going up incredibly high into the heavens. Only gradually his brain cleared and recovered from the shock that it had received.

"What's the idea?" he asked. "And where are we going, Molly?"

"Anywhere. I don't care where," she said, "so long as it's away from Jumping Creek and all those crazy men who are so ready to butcher one another."

"What made you do it?" he asked. "Joe Drayton and I . . . we would have settled it. There wouldn't have been any more trouble. That was agreed on."

"Was it?" she said. "And how long do agreements last between honest Draytons and murdering Pendletons? Can you tell me that?"

He could feel the fierceness of the feud in her, and, looking down into her face, he said: "Molly, was one bit of your coming due to me? Do you care a rap about me?"

"About you?" she said, lifting her voice and her brows at the same time. "Why should I care about any Pendleton? I'd rather . . ." She checked herself in the full flow of anger, adding bitterly: "But here I am. I've pledged myself, and the Draytons keep their word. Much good may you have of me. Much good."

They had come into the entrance of a long ravine that reached deep into the hills, with precipitous slopes that went up on either side. There Paradise Al drew rein.

"You go back home, Molly," he said. "You don't have to come along with me. I give you back any

118

promise you made. It was only a fool bet. That's all."

"I go back home . . . and you go back home," she said. "And in twenty-four hours some Pendleton will shoot some Drayton, or the other way about, and the whole feud breaks out again. Oh, to think that trouble should come on us all on account of such a thing as you are."

"You hate me, Molly," he said.

"I hate you. There's never a Pendleton that I haven't hated," she said.

He nodded his head. "I'll do another thing for you, then," said Paradise Al, and he wondered at his own voice speaking the words. "I'll cut straight out of this part of the world. I'll go East. You'll see no more of me, Molly. With me out of the picture, there'll be an end of the feud. Isn't that the best thing?"

She frowned as she looked at him. "What sort of a bluff are you making now?" she asked. "What d'you mean by it, Al Pendleton?"

He smiled just a little, because she had used the name in speaking to him. "I mean what I say," he replied.

"You mean that you'll go away and stay away?"

"I mean just that."

"I don't believe it!" she said. "It's not in you. You've made yourself a great man around here by riding Sullivan."

Again his voice amazed him as he said: "That

119

was only a trick. That devil, Rourke, had planted two needles in the saddle. I got them out, and Sullivan became as gentle as a house cat at once."

"Are you telling me this?" she said. She held out her hand. "Al, are you a square-shooter, after all?"

"Not very. But I'm trying to be," he said. Could he tell her, also, that he was not a Pendleton? He wanted to say that, but he could not, for he felt that this new name he wore was giving him the right to a new existence, with a new soul, and this he could not surrender. If he left these mountains and never returned, it would be sweet to feel that he was remembered here as a man among men, a clean man, and a strong one. So he sighed and said no more as he grasped her hand.

"There's one Pendleton in the world that I'll remember, and that I'll pray for, Al. Good bye," she said. "But here's the ring."

"Will it hurt you to keep that?" he asked. "I'd like you to have it. You don't need to wear it, but keep it, will you?"

"Why, Al, I'll keep it forever and on my hand, too," she said.

Then she was gone, galloping her horse hard out of the mouth of the ravine.

Paradise Al did not look after her, but blindly he rode Sullivan up the valley. He was sad as he never had been sad before, but there was a sort of exultation behind his sorrow, a lifting of heart and soul. For the first time in his life, he felt the old life of streets and gutters and crime fading far away, as though he never had been a part of it. Paradise Al was dead and gone, it seemed, and Al Pendleton had taken his place. He smiled a little, as he thought of that. As for Molly Drayton, well, she would never have had anything to do with him. It was far better to let her go free without the weight of her promise yoking her to trouble.

As for the ache in his heart, perhaps the pure air of the mountain uplands would cleanse him of that, also. But all of life lay dim and vague before him. There was only one reality, and that was the bony, ugly head of Sullivan, nodding before him as he slowly climbed the trail.

Then a hot needle plunged through his thigh. The weight of the blow jerked him sidewise. Not until then did he hear the *clang* of the rifle shot down the ravine and, turning, saw three riders charging toward him.

XVI

His whole left leg was numb, from hip to foot, and the crimson was beginning to run rapidly down. He never could sit the saddle with such a wound, he knew. So he slumped out and lay flat on the ground, with Sullivan sniffing the hair of his head in inquiry.

There was no use in letting Sullivan be killed or

ruined by a stray bullet aimed at his master. It was quite clear that he, Paradise Al, had come to his last day, and there was no reason why he should bring the stallion to his end, also. So he waved and shouted, and the stallion, taking alarm, fled at full speed down the ravine.

Past the three riders he ran, and they came on, fanning out as they galloped. They came closer, so that the tramp could recognize Winchell on the left, Tucker on the right, and in the center the black beard of Joe Drayton, divided by the wind of the gallop.

To be killed by such people as these? A sudden rage came over the tramp. He dragged himself up. There was a rock of convenient height, and against this he propped the knee of his wounded leg, and so he stood, revolver in hand, ready for any emergency.

They opened fire, flattening themselves along the backs of their horses as they charged in, but the bullets missed the target. He heard them, almost felt them, wasp-like in the air about him. But, with revolver poised, he waited until he could be reasonably sure.

He had a strange feeling that, if he were about to die, the Paradise after which he was nicknamed would be sure to permit him to lay his enemies low before the end.

Then, with his first shot, he smashed the left shoulder of Winchell and hurled him screaming with agony to the ground, where the shock of the fall blotted out the voice of pain.

Tucker, as he heard his companion shriek, involuntarily pulled on the reins of his horse and swung it a little sidewise. It was as though he had deliberately swung broadside to offer a better target. At the center of the body the marksman aimed, but knew, even as he fired, that he was shooting rather low. As his finger pressed the trigger, Tucker flung his head far back and clapped both hands to his hips.

Farther and farther back he leaned, as the horse galloped onward. Now his hat, caught by the breeze, whipped from his head, he was lying back almost on the hips of the mustang, and suddenly he rolled from the saddle. One foot caught in a stirrup, but, he was hardly dragged two jumps before he was disentangled and lay still.

At the same moment, a bullet ran a burning furrow down the cheek of Paradise Al. He had time to think, as he watched the black-bearded man rushing in on him, that now he was marked for life, and many of the easy old disguises would never be useful to him again. Scarface, they would call him, instead of Paradise.

Big Drayton, in the meantime, was covering himself almost perfectly with the body, head, and neck of the horse, as he charged on, firing now pointblank. But the outline of head and breast appeared through the flurry of the blowing mane, and at that dim target Paradise Al fired his third shot and his fourth.

The mustang rushed furiously past him; Joe Drayton lay in a senseless, broken heap at his feet.

"Are you dead, Joe?" he found himself saying as he sat beside the fallen man.

Joe Drayton groaned, twisted, sat up, putting a hand to his head. Other muffled groans were coming out of the distance from Winchell and Tucker.

"You nicked me. It was mighty pretty shooting, kid," said the gunman. "Where'd you get it? There in the face. I see. Oh, and the left leg, too, eh? That's nothing. Listen to those tramps groan and holler. They're feelin' sick. So'm I, a little. I felt a couple of ribs crack like kindling wood under your heel, when I hit the ground. That was a tolerable hard whack. Lemme give you a hand with your leg, kid. You'll need to have a twist put on it to stop the bleedin', and then we'll take a look at the Winchell and Tucker gang. They were the skunks that persuaded me out on the trail after you, partner."

Now, swiftly racing up the ravine, Paradise Al saw Sullivan returning, the girl in the saddle upon his back. Joe Drayton saw this, too, and groaned again, with a worse pain than his wounds.

"I'd rather be in hell than where Molly can talk to me about this job," he said. "I'm going,

and believe me, I'm going fast. Excuse me, kid."
Lurching to his feet, he made for the nearest of
the unburdened mustangs, caught it, and,
mounting, was soon gone up the ravine.

An odd, singing sound was buzzing in the ears
of Paradise Al. His eyes were growing a little
dim, as when an invalid too suddenly comes from
a sick room and faces the blazing sunlight. He
saw the girl only vaguely as she slid from the
saddle and rushed to him. It was rather a blind
sense of happiness that came over him.

And he heard her saying: "They've murdered
you, Al. Oh, the cowards!"

"Look, Molly," he said. "I'm going to live forever, if nothing worse than this ever happens to
me. Tell me, did good old Sullivan bring you
back?"

"I managed to catch him. I thought at first . . .
and then I heard the guns and guessed the truth.
Al, you don't think it's a trap I led you into?"

He shook his head. His dizziness was increasing.
"Where are you, Molly?" he asked her.

"Are you fainting?" cried an anxious voice
through the darkness that was suddenly welling
up before his eyes.

"Of course not," he said. "I wanted to ask you
about Sullivan. He's a grand stepper, isn't he?"

"He's a grand horse," he heard her saying. "He's
almost worthy of the master that rides him. Al,
I thought you were a gunman . . . but you could

have killed them all, and you let them go, you let them go, and I . . ."

She talked softly to him while her swift hands bandaged his wounds. It was music to him, and, listening, the mists lifted from his befuddled brain.

PARADISE AL'S CONFESSION

The follow-up story to "Paradise Al", "Paradise Al's Confession", appeared in the July 16th issue of Street & Smith's *Western Story Magazine*. In it, Paradise Al continues his charade as Al Pendleton, the son of artist, Rory Pendleton. He is planning on marrying Molly Drayton and is busy at work, starting up a ranch, when an unexpected visitor arrives who could put an end to all of his plans for the future.

I

The road turned into a trail, the trail turned into a cow path, the cow path turned into a plain, open slope of pasture land, whose grasses *swished* around the wheels of the buckboard. Now those wheels began to bump and bounce over the many irregularities of surface that the grass masked. As rocks were struck, right and left, the pole of the wagon jumped to one side or the other, bumping against the shoulders of the mustangs.

However, they were accustomed to bad treatment, and they continued to moil and toil in their collars, to jolt the wagon forward until it arrived at its goal, which was at the bottom of a little, round-topped hill. Halfway up its side a spring leaped from the ground and hurried down with silver twistings to tumble into a brawling creek in the middle of the valley. That valley was a spacious one, largely covered with big pine forests that here and there gave back, revealing good, rich fields of grass, where a few cows grazed.

The particular goal of the driver in the buckboard stood beside the spring, a solidly built, one-story log cabin, not quite completed. At least half of the roofing had to be laid on. The furnishings, furthermore, were not all installed, and it was plain that a certain proportion of them were being made at home. Near the cabin there was a yellow-haired girl on her knees, planing smoother the well-laid surface of a big table.

The tall old man who was driving the buckboard stepped out of his rig, smoothed his long, white beard, and, having tethered the team with a long rope to a sapling, he went up the slope of the hill with a step surprisingly long and athletic. It was clear at once that his white beard was not in tune with his actual years, which could not possibly have been more than forty-five or fifty, at the most. But the silver beard, swung aside by the thrust of the wind, gave a touch of dignity and strangeness to his appearance that was already set off by his great height and the width of his shoulders.

Furthermore, as though consciously building up the picture still more, he wore a very wide-brimmed black felt hat whose curving outline made one think of old Spain. His coat, also, was so long that it almost gave the formal effect of tails.

When he came nearer, the girl jumped to her feet and gave the stranger the brightest of smiles. For in the lonelier parts of the West a stranger is always sure of his welcome by the very fact that he comes from another part of the world. He will bring news of far places and of other people, it is hoped. If he brings nothing else, he will at least introduce into the home circle a novel personality, and so enrich the time if he can be persuaded to stay a few days.

As she jumped up, smiling, the stranger took off his hat and bowed to her with an air of foreign grace; his brown eyes rested upon her with much kindness.

"You are Molly Drayton . . . I think?" he said.

"I'm Molly Drayton," she answered, and came forward a little, holding out her hand and waiting to hear his name.

He took the hand and shook it with a gentle pressure, saying: "I want to keep my name for a surprise, if you don't mind. The man of the house must have told you about me, I think."

"Al?" she said. "No, he hasn't told me. Not that I remember."

"*Tut-tut,*" said the stranger, still with his fatherly smile. "Can Al have let such a friend drift out of his talk completely?"

"He almost never talks about the old days," she said. "He's become all Westerner, you see."

"Has he? Good for him," said the big man. "You don't mind if I sit down here and wait for him, do you? The afternoon is still young, and I suppose that he'll be back before long. Or is he letting you do all this house building?"

She shook her head; the sun glanced brilliantly on her hair.

"Al works like a tiger," she said. "I'm only here

part of the time. You see, it's a ten-mile drive from my father's place."

"You drive over every day?" asked the big man.

"Yes, I come over every day from my father's place." After a pause she said: "Come inside. I'll stir up a fire and cook something for you. I suppose you've driven out all the way from Jumping Creek?"

She led the way into the cabin. Like most log huts, it was surprisingly spacious inside, and it was built with a thorough soundness that promised to make it outlive centuries. The beams and great uprights were huge affairs.

"You must have had a crowd at the raising," suggested the man of the white beard, looking around the room with apparent pleasure.

"Well, there were all the Draytons and all the Pendletons," she said. "And that made quite a crowd. And there were some others, too, who came to help."

"Yes, it's a good thing for the whole range, I suppose," he said as she began to lay the fire, ". . . to have the Pendletons and the Draytons bury the hatchet."

She lighted the fire in the stove, turned the draft, and stepped back for an instant, watching with pleasure as the flames began to roar up the chimney, while she answered: "You seem to know a great deal about what happens in this part of the mountains."

"Why," he said, "when I got to Jumping Creek and asked where I could find Paradise Al . . ."

She started so violently that he hastened to add: "I see . . . he's told you about some of his wild days when he was a youngster, has he?"

She looked steadily at the stranger, and for an answer merely sighed a little.

"That's all right," said the man of the beard. "I knew about some of his tricks, but I didn't help him in them, if that's what you're worrying about."

"I'm glad of that," replied the girl. "Very glad indeed." She began rapidly to slice bacon and cold boiled potatoes into a frying pan, having first put the coffee pot over the fire.

"As I was saying," went on the stranger, "I asked about Paradise Al in Jumping Creek, and the minute that I mentioned his name the whole town turned out to give me all the information it could. When it found out that I was a friend of his, nothing was too good for me. I was offered at least a hundred drinks. And talk ran like water out of a tap."

"Of course, they'd talk about Al," she said, her eyes shining. "Everybody loves him."

"Yes, it appears that you're going to marry a famous man," said the stranger. "I had no idea what he had been doing out here on the range, but I found plenty of people to tell me in Jumping Creek how he arrived, and how he was jailed, how it was discovered that he was a Pendleton, and how he rode the great red stallion, how he fought and downed three men, single-handed, when they tackled him in the ravine, and how, most of all, he became engaged to Molly Drayton. You're a very important part of the hero's story, you know."

She rested her hands on the back of a deep-seated, strongly framed, homemade chair and smiled on the big man.

"But lately he's been a little gloomy, it appears," said the old man.

"Did you find that out, too?" asked the girl, surprised.

"I found that out, also," said the big man. "And that's what I'm here about."

"Good," she said. "If you can help him to get out of his despondency, you'll prove a friend, indeed."

"It can't be done at a stroke," said the other. "But little by little we'll try to lift him out of the trouble, all working together."

She smiled again. "He'll be back here in a moment," she informed him. "He's gone down to see that the cows don't drift too far north with this south wind blowing. You know how even an easy wind will make them drift a little."

"I've heard that," said the big man. "I dare say that he's become a good cowpuncher by this time?"

She shook her head. "Not yet," she admitted. "He can't use a rope, and he doesn't know cattle at all. But he'll learn. And, oh, what a tigerish worker!"

"I suppose so," said the man, and nodded his head sympathetically. "But tell me why you people are starting in such a small way? The Pendletons and the Draytons are both rich enough and generous enough to give you a much bigger lift than this, I should think."

"Al won't have help," said the girl with a lift of her head. "We could have almost anything that he'd take, but he won't take a thing. He wants to start at the bottom and work up. I like that idea, too."

"It may be hard on you," said the stranger gently. He shook his head at her.

"You mean," she interpreted, "that it will be callous places on the hands and a red nose from hanging over a stove. But I don't care. The work's the thing, and we're going to make our place grow. See what a place it is, too. There's no better grass land in the mountains than in this valley, but people never paid any attention to it because it's tucked away among the trees. Al had the wits to see what could be made of it, and we're getting this for a song." She laughed happily, the brightness of an assured future in her eyes.

"Good for you!" exclaimed the stranger. "Is that Al coming along the road now?"

He stepped out from the door of the cabin. Along the slope of the hill a great, reddish chestnut stallion was galloping with a small, slender rider in the saddle.

"Yes, that's Al," replied the girl, following him outside.

The stranger started forward with long strides, waving his hand in greeting.

He was a little distance from the house when the rider drew rein before him, exclaiming: "Hello! Don't happen to place your face, stranger."

"You wouldn't, Paradise," said the stranger, "but I happen to be the man who's supposed to be your father. I'm Rory Pendleton."

II

A fighting dog obeys a first instinct by preparing to bite when in doubt, and so did slender Paradise Al show a glimmer of evil in his handsome face and in his brown eyes as he stared at the big man. To give point to his expression, there was the merest flicker of his right hand toward the inside of his coat, a gesture so rapid and fleeting that even the girl at the door of the cabin, watching with her heart in her eyes the man she loved, was unaware of it.

But the man of the beard, standing in the shadow of danger, was aware of the movement. He merely said: "You don't want a murder on your hands, Al. Not a dead man, Al. It would

136

spoil everything, and marry the girl to an outlaw."

Paradise Al slid gracefully from the red stallion to the ground, and that famous horse, Sullivan, began to lower his head and crop at the grasses, occasionally jerking his head up and staring about him, as all horses that have run wild are likely to do.

The young man was saying: "You're Rory Pendleton, you say?"

"I'm not bluffing." The other smiled. "I'm Rory Pendleton, and you're supposed to be my dear son. Isn't that the idea?"

Paradise Al drew in a quick breath, and, looking hard under the wide brim of the black felt hat, he examined the eyes and the soul of the other man. He could make nothing of the whimsical glitter in his eyes. "What's the game, Pendleton?" he asked.

"A friendly game, if I can work it that way," said the other. "And we have to talk fast. You haven't shaken hands yet. And Molly Drayton is watching."

Paradise Al gritted his teeth, then suddenly he thrust forward his slender, brown hand and gripped the stranger's. An odd grip it was, the forefinger finding a nerve in the back of the hand of Pendleton and temporarily paralyzing it.

But Pendleton merely smiled. "Full of tricks, Al, aren't you?" he said. "But you don't have to be afraid of me, I think."

"You don't think so?" said the young fellow grimly.

"No, I don't think so. We can play a game together out here."

"What sort of a game. Your own son, your real son, is alive somewhere."

"No, poor Al is dead. He got tired of poverty and went to sea. A Malay dagger was the end of him, I understand. No, no, Al . . . the real Al, the real Al Pendleton is dead, I believe, and I lead a lonely life in this world. That's why I'm so ready to talk business with you."

"Business?" said the boy. "What sort of business can you do with me?"

"You know, Al, that even in ordinary trade and business, a name has a value," said the big man. "When you buy out another firm's name, you want his goodwill and all taken together. You've simply grabbed off my name. You've called yourself the son of Rory Pendleton, but you wouldn't want to take that name for nothing, would you?"

"Are you asking for hard cash?" asked Paradise Al.

"Look here, Al," replied the big man, "you knew when you swiped the name and stayed on this range that sooner or later your bluff would be called. You knew that, didn't you?"

The young man shrugged his shoulders. "I knew it," he affirmed. "I've been expecting you, or the real Al Pendleton, to turn up here at any minute."

"And therefore?" suggested Pendleton.

"Therefore I've waited and played my cards high, wide, and handsome. I had something on the table."

"You mean the girl?"

"Well, perhaps we'll call it that."

"You mean other things," said Pendleton a little grimly. "You've been a gutter rat all your life until you graduated and became a gunman extraordinary and a safe-cracker. There are places in New York, Chicago, and Philadelphia, as well as some of the other big cities, where a few of the fellows in the know are pretty familiar with that face of yours. Isn't that true?"

Slowly Paradise Al nodded. A thoughtful and very cold look was in his eyes.

"And," went on the other, "the fact is you switched everything when you came out here. You've built up for yourself a new kind of reputation. You're the hero of the range. You're the leader of all the youngsters who punch cows, roll dice, and drink whiskey at the end of the month. You've been able to stop the worst feud on the range. You've engaged yourself to the prettiest girl in this part of the mountains. You're on top."

Paradise made a little gesture. "Everything you say is more or less true," he said.

The big man smiled, and there was a sort of kindness in his eyes, as kindness may appear even in the eyes of an old lion. "Now, then," he continued, "you're in a position to do something worthwhile, and I want to share in the profits. That's all. I want a cut. You get the lion's share. I get the leavings. Just enough to live on, is all I want."

"Only enough to live on the rest of your life, eh?" inquired the young fellow.

"That's all," said Rory Pendleton. "I hate to shock you," he explained as he saw a change in the expression of the young man. "But as you know, I'm the black sheep of the Pendletons. I never did very well out here, and I haven't made much money putting paint on canvas, either. Now I'm getting old enough to realize that I'm never going to make a great success. What do I want to do? Why, I want to get away from this neck of the woods and go off to another place where I'll be more at home.

"I'd take a couple of rooms some place on the Italian Riviera, say, or a little peasant's hut, and live there with one servant to cook and do everything else for me. I'm a fellow of simple tastes. I don't need the best Burgundies on my table. A little red Italian ink is good enough for me. After that I'll get on with pasta and fruit. Oh, I'm the simplest man in the world to take care of . . . very few luxuries, just the price of paper and oil paints, and such trifles. Then I'll amuse myself. You could do it easily on a hundred dollars a month, say. What about it, Paradise Al?"

Steadily the young fellow looked at the crafty old man. "Unless I come across with the money," he said, "what happens?"

"If you don't pay me, if you don't buy me off," said Rory Pendleton gravely, "then I'm forced to appear at the place of the revered Thomas J. Pendleton, the head of our clan, and show him that you're an impostor. And I'd really hate to do that, you know. You're reforming out here on the range, and you're actually reforming the range, as well. Paradise Al has become a reformer." He laughed a little.

"You know a good deal about me, do you?" asked the young fellow.

"A very great deal indeed," said Pendleton. "I didn't take the trip clear out here until I'd made sure of you. When I finally managed to get hold of your picture in a Western newspaper, you and the stallion at a rodeo, with the name and picture to go on, I soon was able to strike a few veins of information. Oh, they will talk and say a great deal about you in certain sections of the East, Al. Paradise Al was a great figure back there in certain sections and among certain sets of people. I know police detectives and private detectives that would give ten years of their lives to get their hands on you. Ten years!"

"There's nothing outstanding against me," said the young man.

"If they could find you, they'd make something stand out against you," replied the other. "They'd frame you, and you know it, and the chief reason you left the East and came West was because the ground was getting too hot under your feet."

Paradise Al nodded. "You're a clever fellow," he said. "Nearly every blackmailer is clever."

"Right you are," said the big man. "I don't mind being called names. I repeat, I demand very little of life indeed. I'm glad to furnish my own amusement by daubing my paints on canvas. All that I ask of you is that you put the bread in my mouth. You won't find me a waster."

"Man, man, I'm just starting life out here!" exclaimed Al impatiently. "How could I afford to spend a hundred dollars a month on you? Will you tell me that?"

"Out of your ranch work?"

"Yes."

"But ranch work is your poorest resource. You can do other things," declared Pendleton.

"Such as what, please?"

"You don't want me to turn over the pages and tell you what you used to do, do you?" asked Pendleton.

Paradise frowned.

"You don't want me to remind you, I'm sure," said the older man, "that once you were able to lose twenty-five thousand dollars in a day on the race track at Belmont Park?"

"And?" said Al.

"Why, the income of twenty thousand dollars would be quite enough for me," said the other airily, waving his hand. "I'm not a pig, Al."

"And how am I to get twenty thousand dollars?"

"How? My dear fellow, I appeal to your sense of humor. Here you are on a cattle range, established as the most honest man in the mountains, the first citizen. All about you there are little towns that have big, fat, rich banks in 'em, banks that have to be prepared to take care of the needs of the great ranchers in call. Why, you can tap any of those banks and crack open the safe, take out the lining, and there you are! Even suppose that the hick detectives and sheriffs and their posses finally should come on your trail, they'd never believe their eyes. And I, in the meantime, quietly slide back East, out of the picture and out of your life, never to bother you again."

III

There was no answer from Paradise Al, and the other went on: "In the meantime, if you give me your word that you'll go through with the scheme, we can walk back together and I'll tell your girl that I'm your father."

"You'll tell her?" said the young fellow. "Why, she's seen us meet like strangers almost."

"We've been estranged, that's all," replied Rory Pendleton. "We've been estranged, but now we're hand in glove again. Isn't that clear?"

"I'm to promise to rob a bank and give you twenty thousand dollars. Is that it?"

"I don't care where you get the money, Al. I'm not urging you toward robbery, my dear fellow," said the other, stroking his white beard and smiling very gently. "Perhaps you'll be able to crack open one of these golden mountains and take out its yellow kernel. I hope you can do that. Honest money has a better taste."

"You talk of honest money, do you?" asked Paradise Al. "And in the meantime you collect a blackmailer's capital. How am I to be sure that you won't come again and again to get the coin out of me?"

"How are you to be sure?" asked Rory Pendleton. "Why, very simply. This is a business deal between us. The first time I give you a base of rock to stand on . . . I tell the whole range that you are my son. I assure to you the Pendleton name forever. And that's what you want. That's the only way in which you can bury your past forever. Isn't that clear? After I've endorsed you, there is nothing I can do to harm you. If I go back to the cabin this moment and tell Molly that I'm your father, I can't unsay the thing afterward, because everybody would simply call me a lying fool. I'll give you that endorsement, now, that makes you a Pendleton forever in the eyes of the world. And then I'll have to trust to your word of honor to put through the deal that I want. Isn't that fair on both sides?"

"It's to be honor among thieves. Is that it?" asked Al.

"And where else is honor so binding?" said Rory Pendleton. "Shall we go back to her now?"

A groan came from the throat of Paradise Al. "I've always thought that I'd tell her the truth one day," he said.

"You never would," answered Pendleton. "You'd put the thing off and put it off, until after your marriage. And after that you never would dare, so long as you lived. Would you have the courage to tell her before the marriage?"

Paradise Al groaned again.

"Face facts and shame the devil," said the other.

"We'll go back to the cabin, then," said Paradise Al. "And I'm to introduce you as my father, eh?"

"Yes."

"Well," said the young fellow, "I hope that I don't murder you one day for this trick of yours."

"Steady, Al, steady. We go back affectionately," said the other. "It's a great and happy surprise for her, you know. Don't forget that."

They went on together. The stallion followed behind willingly, unled. As they walked, the big hand of Pendleton rested affectionately on the shoulder of the young man.

"Molly," cried Paradise Al, "I want you to meet . . . to meet . . . !" The word stuck in his throat. He could not speak the lie to her, and a flood of color came up in his face.

But Rory Pendleton said in a deep, rich, ringing voice: "His father, Molly! I'm Rory Pendleton!"

She was still amazed when he took her and held her in his arms and kissed her with unction. Joy and doubt, hope and fear were in her face.

Rory Pendleton put it quickly at rest, saying: "After years, my dear girl . . . after years, I'm reunited with my son. After years of estrangement. Ah, well, there were times when I thought that he would never speak to me again. Because I was very remiss as a father, Molly . . . very casual, very careless about my sacred obligations. However, I think that I have been forgiven. Tell me again, my son . . . you really forgive me?"

And he looked with an expectant smile toward Paradise Al.

The latter managed to smile, also. Then, looking at Molly Drayton, a strange mixture of fear for her and fear of her overcame him, with scorn for himself and the fear of staining her life by his very presence. It was that look that filled his eyes as the girl turned to him, but she, naturally enough, thought that it was for the old man, not for herself. If there were any doubt lingering in her mind after seeing the cold distance of their first meeting, the doubt now left her. After all,

Paradise Al was not an effusive fellow, and that one look that she found in his eyes was enough proof for her. She glanced up at the face of Rory Pendleton and accepted him instantly and forever as the father of the man she loved.

But the day was wearing out, and it was time for her to go. There was the meal, such as it was, waiting for Rory Pendleton inside the cabin, and he was seated in front of it, while she bustled happily about to add what more she could to the food already on the table. There was some talk about the great rocks that stood before the house.

"I've got to get some dynamite and blast 'em out," said Paradise Al. "They're too big. Maybe we could have some sort of a garden if the rocks were blasted out."

Rory Pendleton smiled very faintly. It was not for the rocks that dynamite was intended, he knew. But somewhere in a town on the range there was a bank whose safe would have to stand the force of the nitroglycerin that would be cooked out of the sticks of powder.

She was gone, at last, down the hillside to her mustang. Mounting, she waved and was gone, cantering down the road, turning to wave again and again, while Paradise Al, from the front of the cabin, waved in turn.

"Lucky fellow, Paradise," said Rory Pendleton. "She's a charming girl . . . you couldn't have picked a better one."

147

"I wonder," murmured the young fellow, "if I'll ever see her again?"

"Ever see her again?" exclaimed Rory Pendleton. "Why, man, this coming of mine, that seems a disaster to you, is really the foundation stone of your happiness. The news goes over the range at once that Rory Pendleton's back and is staying out here with his son. If ever any of the 'punchers have doubted that you're a Pendleton, because you lack some necessary inches, you know, to measure up to the Pendleton standard, the doubts will be gone."

The other simply sighed.

Rory finished his eating, and, slapping the broad flat of his hand upon the table, he went on: "There's one thing that you must do first of all."

"Well, tell me what that's to be?" said the young man.

"As simple as the nose on your face. You've got to pick out a bank that you'll enjoy robbing."

"Enjoy?" said Paradise Al gloomily. He sat bowed over in a chair, his chin resting on a brown fist, his frown directed toward the floor.

"That's what I said," replied the other. "There are banks and banks. Some of 'em are good . . . they help the poor devil who needs help. They fill in the gaps and take the hungry ranchers through the starving times. On the other hand, there are always banks and bankers who suck blood, by heaven. Lend money to a man only to corner him, if they can, and cut his throat when he's in their power. Don't you know any banks and bankers like that?"

Young Paradise Al looked sadly before him, striving to think, but finding no images whatever in his mind.

"There used to be a perfect picture of what I mean over in Jumping Creek itself," Pendleton went on. "When I was younger, there was a mean, lean, hard-tempered, cross-grained devil of a money-lender who was just commencing to make a fortune by cutting out the hearts of the fellows who took his money. He never loaned money to people who were sure to pay it back. He preferred to pick out some young rancher who'd make a fine start and built a solid house, worked up a good herd of cows, and ran some strong fence lines, built tanks, and got everything about the ranch in readiness. Then, if the young fellow struck a bad season, that man-eater in Jumping Creek foreclosed and gobbled the place up."

What was his name?" asked Al. "Seems to me that I've heard of somebody like that in the town now. He runs a private bank, and his name is Wallace Taggert."

"Why, Taggert's the very fellow," said Pendleton. "Made of iron, he used to be, and I daresay he still is. Now, between you and me, Paradise, would it break your heart to rob his safe for him?"

"Taggert?" murmured Al. "Taggert's not a man.

He's a wild beast. What he does is murder, not banking."

"Exactly . . . worse than murder. Why, my dear fellow, you'd be conferring a benefaction on the whole town if you wiped out Taggert. You see?"

Paradise Al sat up straight and looked before him with a set face and an intent eye. He said nothing, but Rory Pendleton smiled with a quiet content, because he knew that his idea was taking hold, strong and fast.

IV

The bank of Wallace Taggert was a very small affair indeed. He was the president and everything else official. The rest of the staff consisted of two clerks who did long lists of figures all day long, two day porters armed with rifles, and four night watchmen armed with double-barreled shotguns.

Eight men, therefore, were working daily for Wallace Taggert, and it seemed miraculous to observers from the street that this should be the case, for very few, very few indeed, were the customers who entered the door of the bank. And these, furthermore, generally seemed to enter not with the gladness of men going to get spending money, but with the desperation of men about to venture life and soul.

Sometimes days would go by while Wallace

Taggert, lean, brown, and dangerously cold of eye, sat brooding on the dismal affairs of his heart, and not a single visitor to entice him to business. Finally someone would enter, and those who entered the bank of Wallace Taggert entered, indeed, as deep as the roots of life and happiness.

Often a year went by in which he concluded hardly more than a dozen business deals, merely one a month. For who would go to Wallace Taggert so long as there remained another possible court of appeal?

For desperate men, desperate measures; on the range it was commonplace to say to a fellow who was down on his luck: "Cheer up, brother. You don't have to go to Wallace Taggert yet."

The name of Taggert began to take on a sort of legendary character. Likewise a mythical horror gathered about it. He himself was aware of this reputation he had acquired, and he was proud of it. Furthermore, it paid him, for he was advertised far and wide by the detestation with which men looked upon him. Men who were states and states away from him would come, out of despair, to talk about money.

It was true that once he had made a $10,000 loan to an unknown man on the strength of a few photographs. And that deal, when he foreclosed, made him $100,000 of clear profit. The very years during which he consulted no more than a dozen clients were often his best years.

He had piled up millions of dollars, and he kept a considerable sum in the safe in his offices.

On this morning, into the office of Taggert, came Paradise Al Pendleton. The banker looked him up and down, nodded to him, half rose from his chair, gave him a hand as dry as paper and as cold as earth, and sat down again. He spent a moment looking over his client, bending outward the sharp, high points of his collar. At the base of the collar, at the bottom of his long, skinny neck, there was tied a black bowtie, so narrow and so loosely put on that the glistening white head of the collar button always showed.

"What can I do for you this morning, Mister Pendleton?" said the banker. "And this, I suppose, is a very happy time for you. I understand that your father has returned to the West and is staying with you?"

His speech was full of pauses, during which he cleared his throat with a sound very like that of dead leaves being crushed under foot. As he spoke, he smiled a little, and the lines of his face, which seemed to be filled with dried soap or dust, wrinkled without in the slightest increasing his appearance of cheer.

"My father is back," said the young man, "but he's spending most of his time at his old home. I've only got an uncompleted cabin out in the hills, you see."

"Well," said the banker, clasping his lanky hands

together, "that is the way that fortunes are founded. Young men start at the bottom and work up. And what can I do for you, Mister Pendleton?"

"I want money," said Paradise Al. His glance flickered to the farther end of the room, where stood an old-fashioned safe with the name of the maker painted in gilded letters at the top: *Wesselmann and Hyde, Troy, N.Y.*

It was like the face of an old friend, for Paradise Al had encountered Wesselmann and Hyde safes before. He knew all about them. In imagination his nervous fingers were already running the mold of soft, yellow laundry soap around the rim of the door; in imagination already he was pouring the soup into the mold. The door of that safe would lift off as simply as the cover of a box of candy.

Robbery? No, it would be no robbery to take money from this walking skeleton of a man, who employed his wealth only to accumulate more, and to spread misery through the world. His business was simply a trap with which he caught living creatures for the sake of draining out their blood.

"You want money," said the banker. "I've never met a man who didn't. So many men, Mister Pendleton, that my own resources are now severely overtaxed. I am overextended, and the times are hard. However, for the sake of accommodating a rising young man, if the security is

153

good . . . But just why do you want money, Mister Pendleton? What is your particular need, if I may ask?"

"My particular need," said the young fellow, "is that I have to expand in order to get on."

"Expand? I thought you were only beginning, and yet already you are talking of expanding." He shook his head and put on, like a mask, his exceedingly mirthless smile.

"The way of it is this. I have the land out there," replied Al. "All I need is the cattle to fill up the grazing acres. Plenty of woods to give the cows shelter from the heat in the summer and from the cold in the winter, you understand. Plenty of good big trees that will make fine lumber one of these days. There must be a quarter or half a million dollars in timber out there, if only I can get the stuff to a market."

"That's it! How often that is true," said the banker. "If only we could get the goods to the market. If such things as rivers and railroads were not really necessary, why, then life in this world would be like life in a paradise, I'm sure." He gripped his hands together harder than ever, and wagged his head at the young man.

"Maybe you're right. Maybe it's an old problem," said Paradise Al, "but I want to go into the thing in a big way. Not the timber . . . let that wait. It would simply make your security better and better as time goes on."

"Time goes on slowly," said the other, "when a man has lent money. And death is always coming nearer. But how far would you go, Mister Pendleton? How much credit would you like to have?"

"Hard cash to go into the market and buy cattle," said Paradise Al. "I know where they can be got cheap."

"*Ah,* do you? And where?"

"Mexico!"

"That would mean a long drive."

"I can make the drive, all right," said Al.

"And what happens to your place while you're away?"

"I can get one of my cousins to take charge. That's easily managed."

"No managers like a man's own self," said the banker.

"I want to go in deep," said Paradise Al, putting into his voice an energy and a hope that he by no means felt.

"How deep, then?"

"Fifty thousand dollars."

The banker whistled. "Fifty thousand dollars? *Whew!* That's a great sum of money."

"Nothing less would do me," replied the young fellow. "With that amount I'll fill the whole valley with cheap Mexican beef. This next spring the price is going to be high. I know it. And I can winter cows in great style up where I am."

"What makes you think that the prices will be high?" asked Taggert.

"Why, look at the number of states that have suffered from summer droughts," said Paradise.

"It's a great, wide country, you must remember," remarked Taggert. "Inside of its ribs are three million square miles filled with intelligent, strong, hard-working people, always using their wits, just as you and I are. And millions of those people have cattle. Perhaps no more than a family cow, say, but, if the beef prices go up high enough, there'll be the family cow thrown into the breach. It's always that way. You may think that this country has its back to the wall, but beware, because the wall may turn into thin air. I've seen it happen too many times. You can't beat the United States of America, my dear young man, with a little scattering drought here and there."

Paradise Al leaned forward in his chair. "Mister Taggert," he said, "I've got a lot more to say about my idea. I think that I could turn cows into money mighty fast up there in my valley. I want fifty thousand dollars. What do you say . . . yes or no?"

Taggert shook his head, closed his eyes, and smiled until the dust in the wrinkles of his face quite disappeared. Then, his eyes still closed, the smile still there, he said: "Five thousand, perhaps, but not fifty. Young men always look too high." He opened his eyes, and, so doing, he was just in time to notice a burning glance that Paradise Al cast at the safe.

The younger man rose to his feet as he said: "That's short and sweet. It's better to get the answer without the waste of time. Good bye, Mister Taggert." And he turned and left the office.

V

That night Wallace Taggert wakened from a nightmare in which he had seen again the sudden, burning glance of Paradise Al as he glanced toward his safe. The banker sat up in bed, choking and trembling—not that there was enough money in the safe vitally to affect his holdings. In fact, he could have weathered the loss of ten times as much out of his millions. But thought of any loss whatever made him sick at heart.

He remembered that he had hired four men with shotguns to guard the premises every night, and at this memory he sighed and leaned back against his pillow. After a moment he recalled the fact that Paradise Al had the reputation of being to other men as a wildcat is to tame house pets. He had stood up to three expert gunmen all in one group, had he not, and faced their charge and brought down every one of the lot?

As for those four—well, there were strange whispers circulating about Paradise Al's past. He might be a fine upstanding Pendleton just now, but there were plenty of rumors about him in those other days before he came to the West.

This thought got the banker out of his bed. He stood at the window and looked out. His house stood on a hill, and the outlines of the other houses in the town seemed to him like darkly crouching figures, full of danger. How much malicious envy there was in the world. The night wind struck him and made him tremble. And there was that fellow, Paradise Al, likely to be prowling around through the town, bent on mischief.

$50,000! A great sum of money for a young man even to conceive. Wallace Taggert shuddered. Then he turned back quickly, looked at his bed, clenched a fist, and then cursed audibly in the darkness. Oh, the wicked youth of the world, ever hunting the wealth that wisdom and long labor have piled up, envious, devilish youth, trying to steal what it is too lazy to work for.

He lighted a lamp and got back into bed with a book of accounts that was to him a Bible. But tonight it was no comfort to him. His mind could not find a starting point. Names were merely names, and figures were simply so many numbers, grouped together.

At last he put the book gently aside and sat up once more, leaning upon one hand, gathering his thoughts, frowning. Nothing would do. He could not shut from his wits the memory of that burning glance that he had surprised upon the face of Paradise Al.

Whatever might come of it or fail to come of it, there was no doubt at that particular moment that the young man had reached with the hands of desire toward the treasures locked up within the safe. There was, in fact, cash amounting to more than $200,000 dollars waiting there.

As Taggert thought of this, his heart turned to stone, sinking through the shadowy regions of his spirit as into a cold abyss. He gritted his teeth and shook his head. He tried to tell himself that he was suffering from a foolish fancy, but presently he remembered many another occasion when sheer instinct had guided him.

Straightway he got up and began to dress. As he did so, he remembered the four night guards, one by one. They were all handsomely paid— $100 a week altogether for night safety, to say nothing of almost half as much more for safety during the day.

A cold sweat ran out on his face, and his upper lip curled with disdain and disgust. However, he could not solace himself just now with the memory of the little business affair with Widow Perkins that he was just concluding. If, when he foreclosed, no one bid in, he would have her three hundred acres for a song, and then, unless he were quite distraught, he would prove that what was regarded as simply good pasture was really excellent soil well worthy of being put under the plow.

When he had got as far along in his thoughts as this, he was already putting his black hat on his head. Now he pulled from beneath his pillow on the bed an old-fashioned single-action Colt .44. He examined it with a glance, then he blew out the lamp, left the room with his long stride, and went down the dark hall and the stairs outside to the street.

It occurred to him that perhaps he was a little foolish in living so alone. Nobody loved him. And someday a man hunting for vengeance, or a woman, might penetrate to his room and try murder to even some old account.

But he was a man of courage. He did not fear death any more than losing his money, and sometimes he told himself that his love of it was so great that surely he would be able to take the bright, golden ghost of it into the hereafter with him.

Now he stood in the street, still shivering a little in the wind, and, after a glance up and down, he turned toward the center of Jumping Creek.

Sometimes his footfall resounded hollowly upon a board walk—sometimes his heels *crunched* through sand or gravel—but finally he came into the vicinity of the bank. The familiar front of it was to his eye as welcome as the face of a dear friend—far dearer, in fact.

But the guards? Well, there was one of them now, walking up and down the street, and in an upper window another form moved steadily backward and forward, coming into the lamplight, its shadow sweeping across the window, then disappearing. There would be two more men toward the rear of the building, and all the beats were changed every forty minutes.

When he had assured himself that the posts were occupied, his hatred of these expensive guards lessened somewhat. Other men in the town pointed a mocking finger at him because he supported this army of protectors. But he could retort with pride and with joy that he never had lost a single penny of money in his life, neither his own nor that entrusted to him by another man. That was a record worth having. Somehow it was far better to spend $5,000 a year for defense than it was to lose even so much as $500 to thieves!

He went around to the rear of the bank, going down the adjacent alley. There he paused. He heard voices, heard his own name.

"He eats people like some eat bones," said one voice.

"Yeah, I know that," said another. "Who's he eating now?"

"*Aw,* the Perkins woman, the widow of old Perkins."

"Is he gonna take her over the jumps?"

"He's foreclosing, I hear."

"The dirty dog!"

"Yeah, he's a dog. He's got starvation under his ribs, is what he's got, and all the money in the world would never fatten him, curse him."

"I'll curse him with you. You know what's a wonder to me?"

"What?"

"That the four of us don't get together some night and, instead of protecting his joint, rob it."

"I've had the same idea."

The heart of Taggert stood still, then bounded wildly with rage.

The first speaker went on: "I dunno that I'd have the nerve. If Taggert ever lost five cents to a thief, he'd spend millions getting it back."

"Yeah. You know something?"

"What?"

"That devil, he's never given a penny in his life to anything or anybody."

"Sure?"

"Yep."

"Seems like he'd have to give something sometime to a feller that's down on his luck or a crippled beggar."

The other agreed, saying: "Yeah, I forgot about the cripples. Even a skunk like Taggert, he'd have to give away money to a cripple, I guess."

In the darkness Taggert smiled to himself. That was the beauty of his character, he felt. It was so astoundingly simple and true to itself. He never deviated from his principles. This thing that rumor said was the actual truth. He never in his life had given a penny to any charity. And he never would. He did not believe in giving. He never had asked so much as a cigarette. Then why should he offer anything to others out of the folly of his heart?

He moved on now, well pleased. As for the curses he had heard directed against him, they were as nothing compared with a reputation that made men fear to steal from him as from a pursuing devil!

VI

So, guarded as this building was, could any human being possibly enter? He, perhaps, could do so, because he carried with him a passkey that would turn the lock of the door at the side of the building. He went back down the alley, fitted the key into the lock, opened the door, and slipped inside just as the figure of one of the guards turned the corner and started down the alley.

Had he been seen? For once in his life the fear that comes upon breakers of the law came upon the banker, also. He leaned a hand against the wall and listened. But the step of the guard came down the alley, seemed to slow and pause by the door, then went on again.

Anger swept over the mind of Wallace Taggert. He wished that he had been able to recognize that guard so that the fellow might be discharged the next day. He wanted no one so slow of eye to guard the contents of that building.

His anger deepened, and then gave place to a sense of pleasure. He had gained entrance into the place unseen. That pleasure vanished suddenly. If he could do it, others might be able to manage it, and once inside—well, it was not a very new and not a burglar-proof safe that he had in his own office with the money inside.

He went to that office.

There should be a new safe, he had felt for some time, but the expense was large, and the news of its installation was something that he wished to avoid—large, new safes mean money, and attract the attention of burglars.

From his key ring he took the key to his office door, opened it, and walked in. What he first saw was a blur of darkness, of course. Then, through the darkness, a ray of light plunged straight into his eyes, and through that ray darted a clenched fist that landed on the bony point of his chin.

Taggert slumped toward the floor, tried to shout for help, failed owing to a numbness of all his nerves, and found himself caught in sinewy arms that carried him to a chair.

Said a quiet voice in his ear: "If you whisper, I'll give you the heel of the gun between the eyes."

"Paradise Al Pendleton," breathed the banker.

"Certainly," replied the other. "Make the world believe it tomorrow, if you can." Then he added: "I'll have to make you uncomfortable for a moment or two."

As the robber spoke, already he was binding the arms of Taggert behind him, working with incredible speed and surety in the darkness. Then a wadded cloth was jammed into the mouth of Taggert. Having got this done, Paradise Al went back to his work.

There was only the most meager ray of light from his dark lantern, but it was sufficient to show the agile hands of the thief running the mold of soap around the crack of the safe's door.

As he worked, the safe-cracker said: "You see, Mister Taggert, that a large policy and a big heart are sometimes the best thing. Fifty thousand dollars is not a lot of money. As a matter of fact, I was prepared to come down a long distance. Down to twenty thousand in a pinch. But I wanted something over that. Besides, you would have got your money back. Yes, if I had had to work my hands to the bone. You'll still get it back, but it may take more time. You or your heirs would have had it, however. And you still will have it. This is only what might be called a forced loan. And I hope that you'll see the point of that joke one of these days." As he talked, he was still working like lightning. "This is the soup, Mister Taggert. I hope it runs in and fills the mold well. Otherwise the explosion may be disastrous . . . and you and I are in a very small room with it."

Suddenly he came back to Taggert. A single ray of light played across the face of the banker, but that ray was sufficiently strong to show, in its reflection, the revolver poised and ready in the hand of the burglar.

Paradise Al removed the gag from the mouth of his victim. "If you want to open that safe for me, Taggert," said the young man, "we'll both avoid all risk from the explosion. When you answer, make it a whisper only."

"Damn you!" gasped Taggert.

"Of course I'm damned," said Al. "Every evil-doer is damned. But the evil-doing is a lot of fun when the victim is a bloodsucker like you. What will you have? The nitroglycerin or a turn of the combination by the hand that knows it?"

"I'll get you," said Taggert through his teeth.

"Very well," said Paradise Al. "Then we have to go ahead on the old basis."

And the gag was roughly thrust back into the mouth of Taggert.

A moment later Paradise Al moved across the room, vaguely seen through the darkness. Taggert almost stifled with rage when he saw a spark of light applied to a length of fuse. Up the fuse ran the fire, dancing and sparkling.

Something more than rage invaded the heart of

Taggert, unwilling as the heart was to give the feeling harborage. It was a sense of admiration at the deft sureness of this youthful rascal. Suppose that he, Taggert, were gifted with such a surety, would he spend so many dismal hours working in that office, squeezing dollars laboriously out of the hearts of his clients?

The young man glided to him, touched his shoulder. "Over in the corner, and lie down on your face, quickly. Better stuff your fingers in your ears," was the rapid advice.

Taggert obeyed it, grinding his teeth. Just beside him, Paradise Al slipped to the floor. At that very moment the red eye of the fire disappeared against the face of the safe.

It's out, thought Taggert. On the heels of that thought he heard a dull, soft, muffled explosion. He felt a pressure over his entire body. The floor seemed to sag and give upward again, like a great spring that has been stepped on. Then he saw Paradise Al leap up and race across the room.

The unsheathed ray from the dark lantern played on the scene and gave it a dull light, by which was revealed Paradise Al, receiving in his arms the door of the safe as it slowly sagged outward.

Oh, fool that Taggert had been not to replace that clumsy old contraption with a new marvel to baffle the wits of the burglars. But what device would have baffled the wits of Paradise Al?

The door of the safe was on the floor. Now the

drawers inside were being pried open, with the use of a short crowbar that was far more effective than a mere key. There was a light *jingling* sound, afterward the grating of steel on steel. Every minute or so a drawer was pulled out and its contents dropped upon the floor.

But where were the four valiant guards? Yes, where were they? Must the city fall about their heads before they stirred?

In the meantime, the contents of the safe were made into an astonishing large heap, and through that heap the enchanted hands of the young man were going like magic. A thin, short parcel wrapped in brown paper passed through those fingers, was deposited inside the coat pocket of Paradise Al.

Dizziness seized the brain of the banker. He knew that the sum of $30,000 was in that little bundle. He sat upon the floor, bewildered, unhappy, sick at heart.

Then, sweeter than any music to the soul of Taggert, he heard the footfalls of men entering the bank from the rear. He heard voices. He recognized Murphy, the head night watchman. Those footfalls went straight on to the door of the office. There they paused.

Was the thief deaf? Had the explosion had that effect on him, or was he too intent on his spoils? But on went his hands, rummaging through that pile of treasure, hands that moved rapidly, but not rapidly enough, considering the peril that waited for him only a few steps away.

Just outside the door, Murphy was saying: "Have you got the key? I'm dog-gone' certain that the noise came from the inside."

"You're crazy. I'll tell you what it was," said his companion. "It was a bed broke down in the lodging house next door. That's what made the noise. Kind of muffled and deep, like when the slats slip and the box springs come down with a whang on the floor."

"Maybe you're right," said Murphy, "but I took it to be something else."

"What else could it be?"

"Well, maybe I am crazy, but I thought it was an explosion."

"Explosion!"

"Yeah. And I'm gonna take a look inside this here room."

"I've got no key. You're wild, Murphy. Say, you don't think there could be a crook at work in there, do you?"

"Oh, I dunno. Maybe not. I just had an idea."

"You make me laugh, Murphy."

"Maybe I'm a fool," said Murphy. "Only . . ."

"Say, you just kidding yourself?"

"I thought the building kind of shook," said Murphy.

"Stuff and nonsense," replied the other, laughing.

Taggert could have eaten his heart raw, without any seasoning other than his rage.

"Well, maybe I'm wrong," said Murphy. "I wouldn't go and break the door down for nothing."

"You better not," said the second watchman. "That old shark would fire you in a second if you spoiled a fifty-cent lock in this joint."

"You're right," said Murphy. "Come along, then."

The footsteps actually began to retreat. It was too much for nature to endure. A mighty groan burst from the stifling throat of Taggert.

VII

It was a sufficient warning. It was also a sufficient cause, as Taggert suddenly feared, to bring a leaden bullet through his own skull, for Paradise Al swerved toward him at the sound, with the flickering gleam of a revolver naked in his hand.

But the gun was not fired, and, to the incredulous amazement of Taggert, Paradise Al leaned above his work again, sifting through the articles that composed the heap of loot.

Many a time before this, in his long life, Taggert had seen men show consummate coolness under fire, but never had he seen such work as this. At the same moment that he felt the thunder stroke of greedy rage, he felt also a chilly tingle of admiration that went up through his spine and lodged in his brain.

The heavy footfalls of Murphy and his companion watchman had thundered back to the door of the office, Murphy shouting: "Who's in there? What's happened? Open the door or . . ."

As the handle of the door was seized and shaken, still Paradise Al Pendleton continued to pick over the heaped-up loot, extracting here and there what he seemed to feel was of the greatest value. Every one of those familiar parcels Taggert well knew, and he thoroughly agreed with the cunning of the young fellow that led him with so sure an instinct to the selection of his prizes.

"Open the door or I'll smash it in! You're caught, whoever you are. Go around into the alley and watch the window! Here come the rest of 'em, the deaf men! I thought they'd never have sense enough to know that something's happening here!" Thus spoke Murphy.

Now was the time for Paradise Al to flee, surely. He could still, perhaps, shatter the glass of the window that gave on the alley, and, slipping through, he might be able to escape from the roused town. He might be able, although there were many doubts of that. For the town of Jumping Creek never slept with more than one eye shut, and it was as readily roused, night or day, as any wild mountain lion.

171

What a rush of men and horses there would be once it was known that the bank had been raided. Not that they loved the banker, but because Jumping Creek had a peculiar pride of its own about being a town that would tolerate no evil-doers.

All of these things poured through the mind of the banker. He was in the strangest emotional crisis of his life. While one part of his being clamored for the capture and the destruction of this bold thief, there was also a perverse devil of instinct working in his brain that desired the escape of the robber, and that wanted the gag from his mouth only in order to shout out advice, instructions as to how he should flee.

There was not to be much time left to this rascal, however. One man had run around to the alley, and, as though to announce his presence there, had fired a bullet straight through the window. The fool, thought Taggert, breaking an entire pane of glass over a job of capture that was almost as good as completed! Or, perhaps, the man in the alley was wishing, on the one hand, to frighten this thief, and on the other hand to rouse the town. In that case he was a wise and clever fellow, and Taggert must reward him. He must reward all of these fellows. $1,000 apiece?

A pain took hold upon the vitals of Taggert— not $1,000 apiece, considering that it was only a moment in the work of the night. Would not $500 apiece be enough, with a speech in praise of the four heroes?

He was pondering these thoughts at the same time that he marked, far away beyond the bank, the rousing of the uneasy town of Jumping Creek. It was living up to its active name, its very active past.

He heard shootings far away, and the slamming of doors near at hand.

"We'll break down the door," said Murphy, just outside. "Come on, together, now."

And the weight of a strong shoulder beat against the door, sending a sound of brittle thunder through the room. The end was coming.

At last Paradise Al moved. Partly with a savage hate, partly with a vast, instinctive relief, the banker saw the young man stand up and move, with guiltily bulging pockets, toward the door at which Murphy and the other two were thrusting with their shoulders. Murphy was counting now, so that their movements would be synchronized.

Standing inside the staggering, bending door, the lock was turned between two movements of the guards by the hand of Paradise Al. That done, the young fellow stepped to the side.

Taggert, watching with desperate eyes that probed at the gloom, saw the idea and tried to shout, but gave out only a stifled roar. Then, hitting the door with a united effort, Murphy and his first helper dashed it open at the next movement, of course, and floundered headlong into the office.

As they fell in, Paradise Al was out at their heels and flickering off into the darkness.

"Stop, thief!" howled one of the watchmen.

Then guns barked with a sudden, terrible, deep-coughing sound that went to the heart of the banker.

Men would die for money. He had known that well enough. For his own part, he had always thought that it was the only thing worth dying for, but now he changed his mind just a trifle. The life of that cunning vagabond, that desperately calm and cool robber, that Paradise Al—well, it was a pity, in a sense, that it should be flung away in this manner.

Perhaps the young fellow would be sent to prison—fifteen years, at least, for a job like this. Faster than light, the mind of the banker darted into the future.

In the meantime a lantern was unhooded and flared upon him. Murphy howled with surprise. The gag and the bonds were removed.

"Murder! Robbery!" thundered Wallace Taggert. "You four worthless devils have let a robber in here that's cleaned out my safe. You see what's happened there! Now every damn' one of you oughta be hung, unless he was snagged in that fracas out there. Somebody fell. Find out who it was!"

They were already pouring, shouting, into the

long outer room of the bank, and there they stumbled over a figure that was writhing on the floor.

It was not the robber. No, it was only Jemmy Weeks, the newest and the youngest among the force of night watchmen who had charge of the bank's precious treasures. He was also the worst blackguard of the lot, a tried and proved gunman, and a cheating rascal to boot, who had been employed by the banker only because he felt that one rascal with teeth might be a good thing in his body of four resolutes. But now Jemmy Weeks was lying on the floor, grasping his left thigh with both hands, and writhing back and forth, cursing through his teeth.

When they leaned over him, Murphy asked excitedly: "Are you hurt bad, Jemmy?"

Jemmy Weeks did not answer. He merely glanced up at the face of the boss watchman with a concentrated fury of hatred in his eyes. He would not speak. He would rather tear out the throat of this man who asked the foolish question. Words were not what Jemmy Weeks wanted, but a good opportunity to murder the whole of Jumping Creek. And all of this pleasant emotion showed very clearly in his eyes.

The banker even shivered a little, almost forgetting that instant that the thief had probably managed to get away—not clear away, but beyond the bank. They would not need to do any trailing, the heavens be praised. They merely had to ride at full speed for the place of Paradise Al.

Now he found his voice. So, shouting out his tidings, Wallace Taggert ran out through the back of the bank. In an instant, or so it seemed, whole throngs of armed riders were there about him, he was mounting a horse, and Sheriff Timothy Drayton was there to lead the posse.

How glad the banker was of the enmity that had flowed for so long and so bitterly between the Draytons and the Pendletons, for now the sheriff would follow this trail with passion, and to the death. There was not the slightest doubt of that.

First, however, Timothy Drayton laid both of his powerful hands upon the shoulders of Taggert and exclaimed: "Once before I was made a fool of by this same Paradise Al! What he done then seemed clear enough. But him going now to rob a bank, him letting his face be seen, throwing away everything just when he was on the point of marrying . . . that ain't likely."

"I tell you," cried Taggert, "that I didn't see his face! He was masked, all right, but I know."

"How do you know?"

"Because he'd been in the bank, asking for a ig loan . . . fifty thousand dollars. That's what he was asking for. And I had the sound of his voice in my ears. He acted funny, too, when he was in the bank. It was remembering him that got me out of bed and started me down to the bank here in the middle of the night . . . and a damn' lucky thing that I came, because I found the young scoundrel at his work."

"Did he know you recognized him?" asked the sheriff.

"He knew it! He talked to me. He said that no matter what I said, he'd outface me tomorrow when the posse came."

"He knew that you'd recognized him, did he?" said the sheriff. "And still he didn't take and bash in your head with a gun butt? Maybe he's too decent to be a robber. But now we'll ride hard. He's sure to have Sullivan under him tonight. And that means that we'll have to fly to catch up with him."

VIII

Now, when young Paradise Al had flickered through the midst of the night watch and come to the rear of the building, he went right on sprinting through the backyard, jumped the seven-foot fence by catching the top of it and swinging himself up like a pole vaulter. He landed on the other side on top of a woodpile, rolled off of this with a crashing of wood, in the midst of which he landed on hands and feet, cat-like, and then raced on.

Out of the starlight a voice called to him. He

made no answer, but increased his pace. Three revolver shots in rapid succession, so rapid that they indicated the practiced skill of a man able to fan a gun, whistled about his ears, but with the third one he entered a small clump of young poplars, and on the other side of this he found his mustang waiting.

Ordinarily it would have been easy going from this point. There was plenty of broken country, plenty of draws, groves of trees, thickets of high brush, through which he could have laid a trail problem that all of the frontier wits of Jumping Creek even could not have unraveled easily. But now his problem was different.

He regretted, almost, that he had not smashed in the skull of Wallace Taggert with the butt of his revolver. It would have been no loss to the world. Rather, it would have been a wiping out of a poisonous influence. Instead, he had allowed the man to live, and Wallace Taggert would tell the crowd the name of the robber and send them head-long in pursuit.

There was nothing for it now except to outride the men of Jumping Creek to his cabin in the hills and to appear to be sound asleep in his bed when they arrived. After that he must outface them. That was all.

Outface that bloodthirsty posse with the cunning of the despoiled banker to lead them? Well, there was nothing else for it, unless he chose to take his stolen money and ride out of the community, to disappear, to leave behind him Molly Drayton and his hopes of honest happiness.

However, for one thing, he had prepared a quick return to his cabin. He swung the mustang out of the brush and gave her the whip and spur. She was a long-legged mare with a valuable dash of hot blood in her. She had no wind to speak of, and she was not overly intelligent in working cattle, but she could speed up as long as her strength and her wind kept those legs of hers working. He raced at full, breathless speed for two miles of straight sprinting.

He had put a long stretch behind him before he heard the roar of the pursuit break out at Jumping Creek. Looking back over his shoulder, he saw that the town that he had left buried in night was now blooming with lights as though this were no more than supper time.

He was not a fine rider by any means, but he had had constant practice since he came to Jumping Creek, and he had sense enough to listen to good advice and to follow it. There were no better riders in the world than the Pendletons, and they had given him the benefit of their advice. He used it now. His instinct was to ride with a loose rein and to let the racing mare have her head, but he had been told that it was far better to steady a racer in its stride, to swing the body of the rider in the rhythm of the horse. So he swung himself now, and carefully jockeyed the mare straight down the road.

Was there any means of cutting him off on the way by telephone? He hoped not, if he could get past the McGuire place, which was the last station out from the creek. So he burned up the road past the McGuire house just as the lights began to flash on in that darkly outlined building on the hill.

Yes, they had been warned, and they would be out, riding hard in the pursuit, but he, half a mile farther up the road, flung himself from the back of the half-exhausted mare.

He had loosened the saddle while she was still at full speed; now he stripped the bridle from her lean head and pulled the saddle off before she had fairly halted. A slap on the flank sent her cantering ahead. She knew the way home, and she would keep to it, wandering across the open fields, perhaps pausing to graze here and there, until she reached the place.

Here, in a tangle of brush, there was a staunch roan gelding on whose back he was flinging the saddle, tightening the cinch straps with a single haul against them, and speeding on at full gallop. There was no need of whip and spur now. The roan would hit his own upper limit and would keep at it without any urging.

At that pace the mustang would last, as Paradise Al knew from experience, a full five brisk miles. After that there was another relay.

He had three return horses in his string, and they were all pressed into service on this night of nights.

The five miles slid away behind him. The sound of the pursuit died out behind him.

Now he was peeling the saddle from the roan and sending it on ahead, relieved of its burden, while that same dripping, hot saddle was clapped over the wincing loins of a strong brown mare. She was the best of the lot, mountain bred, and therefore at her top in the ups and downs of the last stretch toward home. She knew the dying of the road into the trail, and where the trail itself faded out, every hole and every rock that might endanger her running. Her gait was smooth.

As Al leaned above her, close along the neck to offer less resistance to the wind, patting her neck now and then, speaking to her gently, never touching her with whip or heel, he watched the tremor and the pricking of her ears and told himself that he was a fortunate man indeed. She was no trickster. It was all honest service.

When they came, finally, to the long upward slope, he pulled her back to a trot, although she was willing enough to break her heart in making that lift, and, although he was fidgeting to get on, for he had much to do before he could rest with any security, waiting for the coming of the posse.

At last the slope was mounted, and on the rolling level of the upper plateau he gave her free rein again. Valiantly she ran, until the obscure outline of the cabin appeared and grew plain before him.

He sent his shout ringing before him: "Pendleton! Hey, Rory!"

A half-dressed man ran out to meet him as he arrived.

Paradise Al sprang from the horse. "Take the horse. Off with the saddle. Turn her in the pasture."

"You should have rode Sullivan," gasped Pendleton. "He would have whisked you away from danger."

"And been found dripping with sweat, eh, when the posse arrived?"

"Is a posse coming?"

"Yes. There's no way out from this except to bluff them. We have two or three minutes. Run like the devil. I'll pile out of my clothes and get into bed. Understand? Get to the haystack, mark the place. Here's the loot. Jam it into the hay as far as your arm will stretch."

"A haystack! You mean to say that there's twenty thousand dollars in this wad?"

"More than that. Are you going to stand talking here like a fool when they're burning up the ground to get at us? Hurry!" He was turning into the door of the shack as he spoke, loosening buttons from their holes, and rapidly he shed his clothes. He stuck his head out the door again to shout: "Stick that wet saddle blanket into the haystack, too! And rub down the saddle flaps a couple of licks."

His own riding trousers were sweat-stained about the knees, and up from the ankles along the calf of the leg. He felt them anxiously. Far away he heard the clamor of armed hoofs upon rocks. It beat against his ears, and then failed again.

They were coming, and they were coming hard. Would Pendleton have sufficient time to do all that was required of him? Would he bungle things in a moment of confusion? One wrong step, one thing left undone, and that keen-witted fox, the banker, would be sure to find the missing clues.

He could thank heaven that he had not ridden Sullivan, tempted as he had been to do that. For Sullivan found in the pasture, still panting, would have been in himself sufficient evidence against him.

The moist riding trousers he hung on a peg against the wall under a slicker. He took another pair and draped them over the chair beside his bed. In another moment he was deep in the blankets. There he lay in the bed, with his arms flung out sideways, his eyes closed, his breath coming deeply. Gradually his heart stopped racing, his nerves quit jumping. But it cost him a great effort of the will.

A man's eyes, when he wakens from sleep, are always filmed with moisture. Perhaps they are swollen and reddened a little. Now he compressed his eyelids with all his might, until he felt the moisture of tears oozing out on the lashes.

In the meantime there came the pounding of hoofs; they were coming across the rolling ground; they had mounted the slope.

Pendleton came hurrying in.

"Into bed!" snapped Al. "It's Wallace Taggert himself. He blundered on me in the middle of the job. He knew my voice. But we'll bluff him out. Did you do everything?"

"Everything you asked," said the other. "Twenty thousand, you say?"

"And more," said Paradise Al.

IX

The storm of the posse poured up about the cabin, and what a storm. It seemed as if half the riders in Jumping Creek must have made up this mob.

"Yell out!" he called to Pendleton.

Rory Pendleton rose magnificently to the part.

"Who's there? Hold on! Keep out of this house! Who's there?" thundered Rory Pendleton.

"We'll show you damn' soon!" called several in answer.

"Keep back or I'll shoot!" said Pendleton.

"Who are you?" said voices from among the crowding figures at the doorway.

"Rory Pendleton."

"You are, are you? Has your son come back?" demanded the panting voice of Wallace Taggert.

"Come back from where?"

"From Jumping Creek. Is he there?"

"He's where he's been all night. He's in his bed. No, he's up now. Al, don't let them in. There's bad blood in the air."

"Here . . . I'll take charge," said Timothy Drayton, getting to the front at last, for his weight had made his horse backward. He stood at the door of the cabin, breathing hard.

"Al Pendleton, are you in there?" he called.

"Hello!" said Paradise Al. "That you?"

"Yeah. It's me," said Drayton.

"Come in," said the young man. "It's all right, Father. It's the sheriff."

"Sheriff or not, it's a Drayton," said Pendleton. "I don't like this business."

"Stuff," said Al. "It's Molly's father."

"Don't count on that," broke in the sheriff. "I'm here in the name of the law. I want you for burglary . . . the worst kind. I want you for robbing the Taggert Bank!"

Paradise Al whistled. "Robbing the Taggert Bank?" he said. "That's all right, too. Light that lantern, Father, will you, beside your bunk?"

The lantern was lighted. It revealed Paradise Al in the act of stepping into his trousers. He paused to wave one hand in greeting toward the excited, dusty, curious faces.

It had not been expected that things would go this way. Paradise Al was a fighting man.

But there they were, with guns in their hands, and there was he, disarmed and helpless before them, actually rising from his bed and dressing.

Wallace Taggert, with a burning eye, stared at Paradise Al. How would this rascal attempt to escape from him, an eyewitness, backed by the power of twenty armed men?

Al was completing his dressing without haste as the sheriff laid a strong brown hand on his shoulder, saying: "Al, I hate to do it, but I arrest you in the name of the law. Anything you say may be used against you. I gotta warn you of that. I'm sorry about this."

"Yes," murmured Al, looking calmly into the eyes of Tim Drayton, "I know how sorry you'd be to see me in the soup. I know how happy you've been about Molly's plan to marry a Pendleton. I know all about it." And he laughed a little, but without great malice. He went on: "When was this bank robbed? I never heard of Taggert losing a penny in his life."

"The bank was robbed tonight, son," said Taggert, thrusting out his long, lean jaw as he spoke. "And you're puttin' up a wonderful bluff, but the bluff ain't good enough. I heard your voice. You know what we said to one another."

The young man paused in the buttoning of his shirt. "I see how it is. Oh, I see." He turned suddenly on the sheriff. He pointed an accusing finger at the banker, saying: "D'you understand, Mister Drayton? I went in this very day to try to raise some money. I wasn't satisfied. I wanted to take a big chance, so that Molly wouldn't have to start like a beggar when she married me. And just because I tried to borrow a lot of money from that skinflint, now he says that I've robbed his bank."

He walked up to Wallace Taggert. That long, lank man towered above him. Dropping his hands on his hips, Paradise Al looked up to him with gleaming brown eyes and said: "I wish that I had robbed the bank. It would have been a good thing if I could have carted away every penny that you own. It would have taken a curse off the range, and every man here knows it."

Two or three men grinned and involuntarily nodded.

The sheriff, frowning, muttered: "A couple of you go out and look for Sullivan. I guess you all know what he looks like. He's in the pasture field behind the house, yonder. Look him over with a lantern. He'll come up to the light, I guess. And if there's a drop of sweat on him, it means a long rest in stripes for you, my son." He said the last grimly, staring at the young man.

"Thanks, Sheriff." Paradise Al nodded. "As a father-in-law, you're a shining crown, all right. But I didn't expect anything else. Go out and look Sullivan over, fellows. Or, wait a minute. I'll call him in, and you can look at him here."

He pressed to the door through the crowd. Two or three of the posse looked questioningly at the sheriff, but the latter, his face as hard as a rock, merely said: "That's all right. I guess he won't try any of his shifty tricks this deal."

It was apparent that was the very thing the sheriff hoped for—a break on the part of Paradise Al that would be the equivalent of a confession of his guilt.

From the doorway the young fellow whistled, waited, whistled again. Presently a beat of hoofs was heard. It swept up to the house. A neigh rang louder than a trumpet in front of the house, and there was the stallion, thrusting in his long neck and nosing at the hand of his master, then stepping back, snorting, and stamping defiance at the rest of the crowd.

"Why, he's as dry as a stubble field," said someone. "There ain't a speck of sweat on him. Taggert, have you gone and sold us . . . damn you!"

"You people are half-witted," said Taggert, "if you think that Paradise Al would ride the horse on a job like this. He knows that we'd hunt for Sullivan as soon as for him. He knew that, so he took some other nag. Look over the rest of the horses, and see if you find some wet saddle marks."

"Where are the rest of the horses?" asked the sheriff, scowling at Paradise.

"You know I let 'em run on the range," said Al. "I'm not working anything but Sullivan this season of the year. But you fellows go out and comb the range. You may find some of 'em here and there. You know my brand. Sometimes they get tangled a little with the Wilson horses, but you can weed 'em out with a little time and care."

There was a general exchange of gloomy glances. It was no one's pleasure to hunt for stray horses on a big range by night.

"Let the horses go for a minute," said the sheriff. "I thought that we'd find Sullivan dripping, by thunder. Al," he added, turning sharply on the young man, "are you really square in this?"

It was a peculiarity of Paradise Al that, although he often had had to dodge telling the truth in the eventful course of his life, he disliked telling a direct lie if he could avoid it. Now he simply said to Drayton: "I want no more talk out of you, Drayton. I see your hand, and I don't like the look of it. Did you and Taggert work up this crooked deal for the sake of breaking me and running me out of the country? Is that the way you're trying to keep Molly away from me?"

He worked himself into a cold passion as he spoke. We do not have to have the right on our side in order to scale high peaks of wrath. Now, leaning a little forward, with his lips pinched hard together and his eyes gleaming, a very dangerous man appeared Paradise Al, and other men, watching him, knowing what he could do with weapons, drew back a trifle from him.

Drayton, however, took the affront in a large way, saying: "It sounds hard, I know. But I ain't got a strong grudge against you, Al. It may be that I don't like everything that you plan to do in this here world. But . . . that's not my business. I'm here for the law, and not for myself. You've got to believe that."

Al shrugged his shoulders and turned away. "If I robbed the bank, the loot is somewhere around here. You'd better search. Search that bed first, because I'm turning in again as soon as you're through with it." He sat down on a chair and crossed his legs.

Stiffly and helplessly the cowpunchers and the citizens of Jumping Creek stood about the room. It was not the sort of scene they had prefigured. The capture of a bank robber, when a fighting man is involved, is supposed to call forth exciting gun plays. Instead, it seemed that there was to be nothing but a dreary bit of house searching. No one was ready for such business as that.

Even the sheriff was dumbfounded, and he said to Taggert: "Now let's have the best part of your evidence. The quicker that we get through this deal, the better for all hands. What have you got to say that'll put this man behind the bars?"

Said Taggert: "I talked to him in my own office. I heard his voice. I named him, and he answered back. I told him that he was a goner, and he told me back that he'd get out here before the sheriff could, and that he'd bluff us all out of our faces. And that's what he's doing."

"What you say, you sneaking bloodsucker," exclaimed Paradise Al in what was apparently another hearty outburst of wrath, "doesn't weigh against the word of any decent man!" He whirled back toward the sheriff. "You mean to say," he cried out, "that you've dragged this crowd out here because of what that thing said? Where's the proof that the bank was robbed, after all?"

"A safe was blown open, Al," said the sheriff sternly. "Is that proof enough to suit you?"

"Well," replied the young fellow, "get your dirty work over, will you? I'm tired. There's a working day ahead of me, unless I'm railroaded into jail. And I want my sleep."

He sat down again, and yawned profoundly in front of them all.

X

They searched the place for eight hours. The morning was well along, and still men were dredging here and there, prying into odd nooks and corners, with the lank form of Wallace Taggert in the lead, making suggestions. He offered a $5,000 reward to the man who found the loot, or any important part of it. That was in the dawning of the day.

At least half of the men returned to Jumping Creek, heartily cursing the sheriff, and, above all, furious with Wallace Taggert. They declared that he deserved worse than the robbery that had befallen him for leading them on a wild-goose chase.

When that party went off, every man of them came and shook hands with Paradise Al, apologizing for joining in a hunt against him.

He was at his best in making his answer to them, saying merely: "You don't have to apologize. I know how it is. If there's a hunt on hand, every fellow wants to get in on it. As long as there's a wolf afoot, nobody much cares what the name of the wolf is, or whose calf it killed. It's all right, fellows." He gripped them all by the hand and watched them ride away.

Those who remained were still probing in the shed, lifting rocks, prying into the hollows of trees and holes in the ground, while Paradise Al worked busily on the top of the house, completing the roofing. There was need for haste, because this day clouds were blowing over the sky and piling up in the darkened north. It might rain.

In the meantime, from his post of vantage he could sweep a wide section of the country with his eye and follow the workings of the searchers. But he was not at all excited until he saw the tall, crane-like form of Wallace Taggert approach the haystack.

Well and widely and loftily had that stack been built, but Taggert took a ladder that leaned against the pile and went around it bit by bit, probing, with the handle of a pitchfork, sometimes boldly, sometimes gingerly, holding his head askance, as when a man has to trust to a delicate sense of touch and hearing rather than to sight.

The heart of Paradise Al turned to stone. However, a full hour of this work continued, and then Taggert stood back and stared at the stack with a grim face, leaning on a pitchfork. Finally he turned away, shaking his head, and the heart of the young man began to beat normally again.

He called down through a gap in the roofing: "Hello, there!"

"Hello?" said Rory Pendleton, looking up from the preparation of the lunch for that day.

"Slice some more bacon into the pan. Slice in all we've got. Clean out the big kettle and start some coffee, a couple of gallons of it, because we're going to give these hounds a bit to eat before they go home."

The face of Rory Pendleton darkened. "Feed 'em?" he said. "I'd see 'em damned first!"

"Because they have the nerve to suspect me of breaking the law. Is that why you'd damn 'em, Father?" said Al, smiling as he looked down.

Pendleton at last grinned in turn. He set to work

enlarging the scope of his preparations at once.

So they cooked and offered a meal to the last half of that sleepless, weary, grumbling posse. At the sight of the meal, and above all when they sniffed at the fragrance of the strong black coffee, such a change came over the spirits of the men of Jumping Creek that they looked upon the sheriff and Wallace Taggert as though the latter had been a pair of snakes.

The oldest man in the party was Jim Wade, and he gripped the hand of the young fellow in parting, as he said: "Paradise, we were a lot of fools ever to come, and we were a lot of hounds to stay."

"Why, Jim," said the young man with an air of surprise, "any fellow will stand around a while if there's a chance to make five thousand dollars in half a day's work."

"That's it, son," said Jim Wade. "That's it. But the next time that anybody tries to ring me into helping in a hunt for you, I turn my back and start the other way."

The sheriff, also, had something to say. "Al," he began, "I suppose that Molly will be over here before long. She's a pretty high-spirited girl, and, when she hears about what I've done, she's going to be cross with me. I'm sorry that I came at all, because it looks as though Taggert must have been wrong."

It was some distance toward an apology, but Paradise Al, guttersnipe and foundling, who never had possessed a family name, stared at the sheriff with eyes of the true Pendleton brown, saying: "I've heard what you've got to offer, and it doesn't sound good to me. No good ever came to a Pendleton out of a Drayton up to now, and I don't expect that any good ever will come. So long."

He would have said more. There was a passion in him. Then he realized, with a shock of surprise, that he had no right to indulge in that passion. He, Paradise Al, was no Pendleton at all. He shrugged his shoulders and turned away as the sheriff started off.

That left Wallace Taggert alone in the cabin with Rory Pendleton and the supposed son of that rascal.

It was in character with the makeup of Taggert that he should have come into the house with the rest of the posse, and that he should have tasted the food and drink offered to him by the man he was trying to hunt down. He seemed perfectly at home now as the other two glowered at him. Seated slumped far down in a chair, his legs crossed, and the top foot wagging back and forth, he regarded his hosts with a comfortable air.

When he was assured that the rest of the posse was gone, he remarked: "You two are working this in cahoots, are you?"

"Working what?" demanded Rory Pendleton with dignity.

Taggert eyed him with care, smiling sourly. "You're working the game together," he decided aloud at last, "and you're doing a pretty good job of it. But tell me one thing. Do you expect to go on winning out against me all the time?"

"This thug," said Rory Pendleton to Paradise Al, "seems to think that you really are guilty of something."

"And you," said Taggert, "seem to think that your son was safely home all evening. You didn't know that he rode all the way into Jumping Creek. Oh, no, you didn't understand that, I guess."

"Father," said Paradise Al, "suppose you step out and leave me alone with this thug for a while, will you?"

"I'm glad to have the open air," said the grave Rory Pendleton. "This atmosphere of accusation and suspicion is stifling to any honorable man."

It was spoken magnificently and with an air, but there was just a shade too much magnificence and air, and, as Rory Pendleton walked out of the cabin, the banker followed him with a sarcastic smile.

He turned to the young man with that smile and lifted his brow.

But Paradise Al merely shrugged his shoulders. "Now what's on your mind, Taggert?" he asked.

"Congratulations, first," replied Taggert, and held out his hand.

Paradise Al shook his head. "Not that," he said.

Taggert nodded, insisting. "You shake hands,

brother," he said, "and call it a day. You did a good job, and you trimmed me. I'll tell you something else. It's the first time in my life that I've ever been trimmed that close."

His hand was still extended. Paradise Al crossed the room, and after a light touch abandoned his grasp again.

"You seem game, Taggert," he said. "I'm sorry that I had to touch you so far."

"Tell me this. Would you really have come down to twenty thousand when you first walked into the bank to talk to me?" said Taggert.

"Yes."

"I was a fool, then," said the banker. "What did you want twenty thousand dollars for?"

"Cows."

Taggert shook his head. "Not cows," he declared. "I know the look of men that are going to buy cows, and I know the look of men that are going in for other things. You had the look of somebody . . . well, somebody with a wife and kids at home, with the winter long and cold, the larder empty, and no money in the wallet. What was the pinch?"

Al shrugged his shoulders. "You can talk your head off," he said. "It doesn't bother me."

"Was that the main call? Is that the fellow who put on the pressure?" asked Taggert, jerking a thumb toward the door to indicate Rory Pendleton in the great outdoors.

"What would he have to do with it?" asked the young man.

"Let him go, then," said the banker. "I'll tell you what I'll do. I'll let you have the twenty thousand and a chance to pay it back honestly and squarely, and never have a blot against your fair name, young man."

"Thanks," answered Al. "You mean what by that?"

"You can sign a note for twenty thousand dollars with interest. I'll charge you a low rate of interest, Paradise. Four percent, say. That's practically making you a gift of the money. And I'll let the note run for three years. What can you ask fairer than that?"

"And anything above twenty thousand?" asked Paradise, smiling. "Anything above I may have?"

Said the other surprisingly: "Every penny you've stolen above the twenty thousand you give back to me as fast as you can."

XI

Al smiled a little. "I like to hear you talk, Taggert," he said. "You're so plausible and easy about it. Go on, now, and tell me why I'm to give you back the coin. You know how much coin there is above the twenty thousand?"

"No, I don't know. Not exactly. I saw the

198

packages that you took. There's between a hundred and fifteen and a hundred and eighteen thousand dollars altogether, isn't there?"

"Great Scott, man," said the young man, "how can I tell? You fellows didn't give me a chance to stop and count the loot, did you?"

"You don't even know yet how much you grabbed?" The banker sighed.

"Not yet, but I judged that it was a handful."

"It was," said Taggert with an odd admiration in his eyes. "The way you went through the insides of that safe, I thought that you had X-ray eyes in your fingers."

"It rounds up," suggested Paradise Al, "that I take twenty thousand and give you a note at four percent for three years . . . and you take the hundred thousand or so that's left to put back in your bank. I don't see how you get on in business, Taggert. You don't expect people to be as simple as that, do you?"

"You call it simplicity," said the other, "but I call it necessary common sense."

"Necessary for you . . . I can understand that. But why is it necessary for me?" asked Paradise Al.

"Well, what would you do with the money in the first place?" asked the banker. And he laid his long, lean, dry hand under his long, lean bony jaw and stared at the young man.

"I wouldn't eat the coin, I can tell you,"

said Paradise, "if that's what you're afraid of."

The other grinned at him. "You think it over, Paradise," he said. "They say that you've stepped around the corner of the law before this, but now you're trying to lead a different life. You're trying to go straight. When you were leading the free and easy, that was very different, my son. You could pick up the money wherever you pleased, and spend it as you liked. It's easy to throw money away, but if you begin to sink it into the ground or in the making of a house, you start talk. Understand?"

"You mean that people will ask where I got the money?" asked Al.

"That's it, and you couldn't stand the questioning."

"Couldn't I?" said Paradise Al with a ghost of a smile.

"Not now," insisted Taggert. "Not with a wife in your house who might hear the question asked of you. You can't take chances any longer. You'll be having children. You can't let them so much as hear the question asked. Am I wrong?"

The young fellow grinned. "I'll rush right out and get all the money for you, Taggert," he said. "I'll rush right out and bring it in, you're so persuasive."

The dusty wrinkles suddenly chopped up the face of Taggert. He, too, was smiling. "Perhaps we'll get to understand one another," said Taggert.

"Someday we may," agreed Al. "But I don't know what you're driving at just now."

"You want to be an honest man. I'm opening the corral gate to let you into the honest pasture," suggested Taggert.

"Go on and explain some more."

"You don't want dirty hands for the life you're to lead out here."

"Who talks about dirty hands?" asked Paradise Al sternly, and leaning forward in his chair.

The brows of Taggert clouded, but he answered with a certain dignity: "Saints are not the only good teachers, Paradise."

Al nodded. "That's true," he said. Lifting his head, he looked at Taggert as though the latter suddenly had receded to a great distance. But it was not the face of the banker but his own new thoughts that Paradise Al was seeing. Then he said: "Suppose you give me some advice then, Taggert? What d'you want me to do?"

"Go straight," said Taggert. His eyes were suddenly burning. "Go straight," he repeated, "and then you'll beat the game. Money will never make you happy. But a good reputation will. I don't care about reputation. Money is all that matters to me, but you're different. You're entirely different. If you can't be honest and turn back everything that you've stolen, turn back a part of it."

There was a feverish pleading in the eyes of

the banker, and the young fellow sneered openly at him.

"Like a woman pleading for her baby," said Paradise Al.

"Turn it back and I'll give it to charity," said Taggert, glaring.

"What's the matter with you, man?" demanded Al. "What's in your head, eh?"

"Listen to me," said the banker. "The money's gone. I know that. I've lost it, and you have it. Well, if you use it, you're a goner, my son. Crime doesn't succeed this far west. It may give you a start in life, but it will give you a finish, too. Will you believe that?"

"I can believe that," muttered Paradise Al. "But what difference does it make to you, Taggert, what becomes of me, unless you can get me into a jail?"

"I'm asking myself the same question," said Taggert, "and I don't find any quick answer. I've lost the money. I know that well enough, but I don't want it to poison you. You think I'm lying. I'm not. I'm telling you the truth. Why should I care what happens to you? I don't know. Perhaps it's because you're the one man who's managed to beat me at any game, Paradise. Perhaps it's because, if you'd been a lower cut of a fellow, you would have given me the heel of your gun between the eyes, or a bullet through the same spot. But you let me go, even after I'd made a noise that put you in a corner. You robbed the bank, my son, but you didn't do a murder that almost any other thug in the world would have done."

The same far-off look that had been in his face before was in the eyes of the young man again as he said: "I'm going to believe it. You're coming clean with me, and I'll come clean with you. I'm a crook, and I was cornered, so I went back to an old trade. Taggert, I was cornered for twenty thousand dollars. Let me have that and I'll give you back every penny of the rest. I'll even give you a note for the twenty thousand. I'll pay it off when I get a chance. I'll work myself to the bone . . . it'll take years, but I'll manage to pay it off. I don't believe my ears when I hear myself saying this . . . but I'll do it."

"We're getting kind of sentimental, we're both so good," said the banker, sneering. "But d'you mean what you say?"

"Yes."

"What cornered you for twenty thousand?" asked Taggert.

"I can't talk about that."

"Was it . . . ?" said Taggert, and, breaking off, he made another gesture with his thumb toward the outdoors to indicate Pendleton.

Al waved the suggestion away.

"How could you be cornered except by . . . well, a pinch out of the old life, son?" asked Taggert.

"I'm not talking," said Paradise Al, and he set his jaw like a rock. He stood up.

"Stay here, will you? And I'll go out and bring you the money."

"Not now," answered Taggert. He was pale, and his face was drawn as he stared at the youth. He added: "Think it over. You're impulsive now, and excited. But think it over. Wait till tonight, say, and if you're still ready to pay the coin back, you come into Jumping Creek and I'll be waiting for you. Not at the bank, but at my house on the edge of town. You know where it is?"

"Yes, up on the hill. I know."

"Think this over, Paradise. I'll be sitting up for a while tonight. I won't be expecting you. But if you come . . . well, I'll be glad to see you."

With that he started up from his chair and hurried out of the cabin like a man who fears to be detained by one spoken word that would be irresistible.

He mounted, and, leaning over the pommel of his saddle, he spurred his horse furiously away.

It seemed to Paradise Al that he could understand. Taggert was fleeing from a new and strange soul that had entered his body. And he, Paradise Al, felt very much the same sensation as he realized that he had agreed to take back almost $100,000 in hard cash.

He watched the banker out of sight, then he went to the haystack and found Pendleton sitting on a stump beside it, nursing his knee between both hands.

"All right," said the young fellow. "Let's have the money, Pendleton."

"How much of it is there?" asked Rory Pendleton, rising and approaching the place at which he had thrust the loot into the hay.

"I didn't have a chance to count," said Al. "There's more than sixty or seventy thousand, I suppose."

"That leaves you a good big margin," said Pendleton. "Plenty for your night's work . . . and I'm glad you have it, Paradise. Because you've been a life-saver to me." He reached into the proper place and brought out the saddlebag that contained the stolen money.

"I'll meet you inside in a moment," said Al. "You count out the money, will you, and we'll go over it again when I come in."

He went to the shed, whistled Sullivan in from the pasture, and gave him a feed of oats. As he watched the greedy horse grinding teeth against the feed box, he smiled faintly. He might have need for the strength of the red stallion this day, for never had murder been so close to the surface of his mind.

XII

He might need Sullivan and he might need a gun. He watched the horse eat for a moment, and then he walked slowly back toward the cabin.

Molly Drayton should have arrived by this time. What was holding her back? Was she waiting to hear from her father, the sheriff, that nothing had been proved against the man she was engaged to marry? He was savage with jealous suspicion at once. The greater his love for her, the more easily he could be wounded, of course, by the least of her actions.

Still, from the front of the house he scanned the hills in vain to see the bobbing of a rider coming out of the horizon.

He went inside and found Pendleton busily counting money.

"More than you think, brother!" cried Rory Pendleton. "A whole lot more! Ninety-one . . . no, wait, ninety-two thousand dollars!"

"Much as that?" asked the young fellow.

"Yeah. Ninety-two thousand dollars! That leaves you more than seventy thousand up after you've given me my little spot." He leaned back in his chair and entangled the fingers of his right hand in his white beard, smiling upon Paradise Al, his eyes benevolently soft and gentle.

"You're a winner, Paradise," he said. "You're the sort of a fellow who can't be put down. Now tell me, my son, aren't you glad that I came to you in my time of need? How else would you ever have had the inspiration? Seventy-two thousand dollars to sweeten life just when life needs sweetening. That's what I call the proper start. You can make your wife happy now, my son. You can use this cabin for your servants or cowpunchers and build yourself a proper place, eh?" He beamed upon the young fellow as he sketched this coming happiness.

"Rory," said Paradise Al, "you're a wonderful man."

"Am I?" said the other.

"You are," replied Al, "but there's one trouble ahead of you. I can see it coming."

"What, Paradise?"

"A gun accident."

"Gun accident?" echoed the man of the beard, the softness passing instantly out of his eyes.

"Yes, gun accident."

"Where, Paradise? What are you talking about?"

"Gun accident. Right here in this room. Gun going off and the bullet will split your wise head open right between the eyes."

"Paradise," said the other, "what's the matter?" He leaned forward and spread out a hand confidingly flat on the top of the table.

"Can't you guess, Rory?" asked the young fellow.

"I haven't any idea."

"Reach in your pockets and you may find some ideas," said Paradise Al.

The other paused. Then he shook his head. "Can't imagine what you mean," he said.

"All right. This house needs a christening, and just now I feel like christening it with red," said Paradise Al. "Say your prayers, Rory."

"You mean . . . ? *Ah-ha!*" cried Pendleton, not in the least embarrassed. "You young fox, you had counted the money, eh? Oh, I thought you weren't as simple as that. But, ah, Paradise, to put temptation in the path of an old man like me. Very sad. I wouldn't have believed it of you." His hearty laughter rang and re-rang through the cabin. And from inner pockets he took out several sheaves of bills and added them to the pile on the table. "Making, altogether," he said, "a hundred and seventeen thousand dollars one hundred and something . . . I forget what." Again he beamed on the other. "There you are, Paradise," he said. "And there are no hard feelings, eh?"

Al put the Colt away. Then he stepped to the table, thumbed two of the piles of bills, and gave them, with a few additional hundreds, to the blackmailer. "There's your money," he said. He passed it across.

"Thanks a lot, son," said Pendleton. He stood up, sliding the money carelessly into a deep coat pocket. "And now," he said, making a wide gesture almost of embrace, "you see what you've done for me, Paradise. You've remade the world for me. You've given me a chance to die happily after some more years of quiet, steady work. The simplicity of my life, Paradise, will be a thing that would amaze you if you were to see it. And see it you will, because, with all of that remaining money, you'll want to take a trip abroad."

"All this remaining money goes to the bank tonight," said the young man.

"What?"

"To the bank," insisted Paradise Al. "To Taggert, to put it otherwise."

The mouth of Pendleton fell open. "Great Scott!" he cried.

Paradise Al smiled at him. "Queer idea, eh?" he said.

"Queer? It's crazy, I tell you. Ah, but I see, I see, Paradise. You don't want your own hands soiled, after all. And I don't blame you. Not a young fellow of your age, with life before him. You want to be clean. But give that money back to Murderer Taggert, who's ruined so many harmless lives? Give it back to him? He ought to be bled, and you've done the bleeding. No, no, son, if you want to give that money away, give it to someone who will know how to distribute it where there is crying poverty. When I think what good could be accomplished with such a sum in a place like the Riviera, for instance, and you could safely entrust it to me, Paradise, because I already have all that I need for my modest needs."

Paradise Al pointed toward the door. "Get!" he ordered.

"Ah, my son, I'm sorry to see you in this humor," said the old blackmailer. "Suspicion breeds black thoughts, Paradise, and hard feelings. I'm sorry to see you in this mood."

"If you ever see me again in any mood," said Al, "I promise you the bullet that you ought to have today, Pendleton. You're a hound, and a sneaking hound. You've stuck a knife in me . . . and now get out of my sight."

"Savage words, Paradise." The other sighed. "But I see that it's not a time to argue. I won't attempt to stand up against the storm. Well, my son, heaven bless you. I'll go hitch up the mustangs to the buckboard and drive along. But I'm a sad man."

"Rory," said Al, "I've stood about all that I can manage. Now move."

And Rory Pendleton moved.

Paradise Al watched him finally jogging away in the buckboard, controlling the horses with singular skill in spite of the looseness of the rein that he held on them.

Bouncing and bumping over the rough ground, the buckboard climbed the slope, and now, over the skyline, came Molly Drayton, galloping her horse. She halted beside the buckboard. They talked a few minutes. Paradise Al saw them shake hands, saw the rascal drive on, then turn to throw a kiss after Molly, and he saw the girl herself come riding on, happily smiling.

She threw herself down from the saddle and ran to Paradise Al.

"Al Pendleton," she said, "I met Father on the way. I heard about the whole silly business, and . . ."

"Stand away, Molly," he said.

She had her arms stretched out to him already. Now she paused and frowned at him, shaking her head.

"What in the world is wrong, Al?" she said.

"I'm coming clean," he said. "That's all that's wrong."

"Clean?" said the girl. "What do you mean?" She grew pale. She stood, almost on tiptoe, with her arms stiffly extended at her sides and her fists clenched.

And Paradise Al, staring at her, thought that all the glory and the happiness in the world was centered in her slender body and gathered into the blue of her eyes.

His breast began to heave, for he was short of wind, as though he had been working hard uphill. It was desperately hard to do, but he had known the moment she came over the skyline that he would have to do it.

"What have you been thinking about me, Molly?" he asked. "My past, I mean."

"Your past?" she said, growing paler still. "I don't know, Al. I haven't been thinking much about the past. I've been too busy with our happiness right here in the present."

"You haven't asked any questions," he said. "No, you've dodged 'em. That's what you've done." He shuddered, and then got hold of himself again. "But you've heard rumors, though," he went on. "Everybody out here has heard 'em . . . about a past in which I was a tramp, a safe-cracker, and a gambler. You've heard those things, Molly. And you've believed 'em."

"Never!" she contradicted.

"You have," he answered grimly. "Otherwise you would have asked me questions about what happened, about the truth. No, you were afraid of the truth."

She made a blind, sweeping gesture. "I don't care about the past. There isn't any past for people who come out to the range. The past is forgotten. There's room out here in the mountains to let a man live a new life and accept him for it. Besides . . ."

He lifted his hand and she was silent.

"Molly," he said, "it's all true. Every word. I've been all kinds of a thug. I've cracked safes. I cracked the Taggert safe last night."

XIII

She started to answer, and then paused. "I'll tell you what, Al," she said finally in a low voice. "You're trying to make a joke of me, or to test me, or something similar to that. Isn't that the fact?"

He shook his head. "I mean it, Molly," he said. "I've been playing a kind of a part, and a pretty bad part, at that, and I'm sick of it. I thought that I could work the thing, but I can't. I've been shamed by sort of a human devil. I mean . . . well, I can't name him, even. Only, I tell you, Molly, that I've got to show you the truth. I'm not what I've seemed to be."

Still staring at him with the look of a sleep-walker, at last she exclaimed: "Oh, Al, I know that men are tempted . . . men who can do things with their hands and who have courage! They're tempted when they're young, and you're still young, Al. No matter what you've been through, you're young. You can change. You have changed."

He looked gloomily at her. As the sense of his own wrongdoing overwhelmed him, he stated suddenly: "Molly, even the name that I've carried out here isn't the right one. I'm not a Pendleton!"

The last vestige of color left her face then. And he, sick at heart, waited for an answer and received none.

"I'm going back into the cabin," he said. "You can think it over out here in the sunshine, and, when you've made up your mind what you're going to say, come and tell me."

So he turned from her slowly, because he hoped each second that there would be an outbreak of emotion and love from her that would bring her running to him. But there was no spoken word, there was not a sound to give him a pretense for pausing as he went into the house and sat down wretchedly, with his head between his hands.

He did not regret even then the impulse that had made him confess. Now he took his hands away from his face and lifted his head, for he felt that it was a shameful thing to be bowed like that, like a dog cringing in a corner when the crisis came. He had better be up and doing. No, he had better sit there calmly and face the future.

But there was no future when Molly Drayton was taken away from him. She would not be taken, though. There was too much red blood in her for that. After all, it was not with a name that she had fallen in love. That was not the thing. She had loved him for himself, in spite of the fact that she thought that he belonged to the rival clan.

A sound of hoof beats began very slowly, a mere scuffling through the short grass, but it brought him with a leap to the doorway.

It was Molly Drayton, riding away from him!

She was bowed a little in the saddle, her hands

were folded upon the pommel, and, although he could not see her face, he felt that she was suffering. Then why did she leave him like this without speaking?

"Molly!" he cried, that word involuntarily breaking from him.

At that she started, but she did not turn. And second by second the distance between them lengthened.

He ran out a few steps from the door, but still she did not turn, and now pride welled up in him and stopped his voice altogether. It was not right. Neither in man nor in woman was it right simply to turn the back upon a problem as she was turning hers now.

He could not believe it. He looked wildly back through all that he knew of her, and the only fault that he could find in her was a sort of fierce and almost masculine impulsiveness. There was no weakness of heart or affection in her. She was almost too guilty of those very emotions. But there was the fact, shattering to all preconceptions —she was going straight off from the house. She was leaving him, and all of the future life that they had planned with such joy together now dwindled into ghosts, mere phantoms.

She reached the brow of the farthest slope and sank beyond it, the horse first, then the rider to the shoulders, and finally the hat disappeared, and he was left alone.

He thought that he had known pain before, but it was not at all like this. There was no comparison. This was a sickness of the very soul.

At last he turned away toward the house. But it struck him with a sense of revolt when he faced it. All of the work that he had poured out on it was to him a poisoned thing because he had not a single thought connected with the house that was not connected with the girl, also. She was gone, and everything that had to do with her was grief to him.

Sullivan whinnied from the pasture, and now he saw the great red stallion standing in the field, hanging his head over the topmost bar.

Like the yielding of a dam, his will gave way, and his pride. Stinging tears rushed into his eyes, and he went forward half blindly to the pasture fence. He put his arms around the smooth, hard neck of the horse; he buried his face against the mane of Sullivan and remained there for a long moment, shuddering violently, not daring to move lest the very sky over him might see the convulsion of his sorrow.

And Sullivan stirred not a muscle. All his foolish little tricks of hunting through pockets for sugar or apples, his ways of nudging at hand or shoulder, his inquisitive sniffing at the face of his master, were forgotten now. Still as the fence he stood.

Marveling at this understanding of his mood,

the young man mastered himself finally. He began to speak to Sullivan and caress his silky neck. His voice was shaking, and he wondered a little at that.

When they gave him the third degree for ninety-six hours, he had not weakened. Not when his nerves were screaming out for lack of sleep, not when his brain was battered out of all poise. Not for a single instant had he weakened. But the girl, at a single stroke . . .

Well, he knew what it meant, he felt, to be shot through the heart, to have come to the end of things. After this, to die would be no more than a silly, unimportant little gesture.

He whistled Sullivan to the shed and put a saddle on him, and then rode off on the range. He did not speak. He touched the stallion neither with hand nor heel.

Presently, looking out of his dream for a moment, he drew out his watch and saw with amazement that it was late afternoon. He could not believe it, unless time had taken wings. He held the watch to his ear, but it was ticking steadfastly. He glanced toward the sun and saw that it was sinking. Yes, some hours had dropped out of his life and left behind them only the poignancy of sorrow. So he turned back toward the cabin, and was amazed to see the miles he had come on Sullivan at a walk.

He fed the stallion again, entered the cabin, and

swept up the stolen money from the table. He stuffed it carelessly into the saddlebag and set about preparing a meal. He was not hungry, but he told himself that he would go through the mechanical motions of life until, perhaps, some savor of existence returned to him.

Wise men said that time healed even wounds as deep as this. And perhaps time would. But it was hard to believe. He felt that he was dying. He had the impulse of a dreadful homesickness to go somewhere—somewhere that was not on this earth.

So he cooked the meal of bacon and fried potatoes and found, as he sat down, that he had forgotten the coffee. That hardly mattered. Nothing mattered.

Presently he found that it was so dark that he could not see, except with difficulty, his plate and the food upon it. The potatoes were half eaten, and those that remained were icy-cold. The strips of bacon were glued to the plate by their own congealed oozings of white fat. Time once more had slipped away from his enchanted life. Hours had gone, and the evening was there before him.

He thanked God that he had something definite to do to take him away from the cabin. To have remained there would have driven him, he felt, to madness—with the lamplight pouring over him and the outer darkness, great and cold, extending over the mountains.

He fumbled along the wall through the dusk to find his sombrero, and his fingers touched a bit of soft, fluffy cloth. His hand closed on it like a vise. He wanted to leave it, but he could not. It held him like an electric current, for he knew that it was the red woolen scarf that Molly had left behind her the day before.

"How pretty she looked," said a voice. He started, but then he realized that it was his own voice.

And something like a resistless hand now bowed his head lower and lower, until his face was close to the scarf, and suddenly he caught it up with both hands in a brief frenzy. There was a faint, sweet odor of perfume about it, a mere hint of fragrance that came into his mind's eye the picture of her and brought her walking straight into his heart.

He could not wait after that. The saddlebag was already slung over his left shoulder, and, without waiting further to find his sombrero, he staggered out of the cabin into the open air. There he stood, uncertain, gasping in his breath, for he felt that he would choke.

People spoke sometimes of a swelling heart. And now he knew well what they meant. There was Sullivan, however. There was faithful old Sullivan. Well, if men and women could be created with natures like the stallion's, this world would be a paradise to live in.

He got to the shed, saddled the horse, and then, instead of mounting, he walked on over the hills, with the stallion following him behind. It was better that way.

XIV

Now, in the meantime, and well before this, of course, Rory Pendleton had driven in his buckboard to Jumping Creek. He was fairly well satisfied with the outcome of his endeavors. He had got his $20,000, for one thing. Furthermore, there was the possibility that he might tap this deep well of prosperity again and again in the future. Not immediately, of course, for he realized that Paradise Al was a fellow who could be led only a few steps at a time.

He was, as has been said above, fairly well satisfied, this Rory Pendleton, artist by profession, and callous adventurer by choice, but he was not thoroughly content. He had $20,000, a good fat haul. But what was it compared with the $100,000 that Al had kept? It was very little indeed. $20,000 was a year or two of real comfort. $100,000 was a dignified fortune.

He told himself that he would not have cared so much had the money really been used by the thief who stole it, but that strange young man had declared his intention of returning it to the hands of Wallace Taggert! He would as soon have seen this handsome fortune cast over a ship's rail into the unappreciative sea. And just as he would have made, at least, a gesture to save the world from such a loss, so his wits were making a gesture now, in the hopes of redeeming this money from wastage, for such he honestly felt it to be.

Now, there is a saying that when a man is seriously bent on a project, Providence will place the tools in his hands sooner or later. With Mr. Pendleton it was rather sooner than later. As he halted his rig in front of the biggest hotel in Jumping Creek and got out to tether it, he saw two men who were seated on the verandah scowl at him, and then commence to talk to each other.

It sent a singular chill up the spine of Rory Pendleton when he observed this. There were various little counts in various parts of the world that might cause police agents to be extremely interested in his whereabouts. That pair on the verandah had something about them that suggested either heelers of the law or followers of crime. And the law was nearer to the thoughts of Pendleton, with $20,000 in his coat. Distinctly he meant something to them, and distinctly they meant nothing to him, so far as he could remember. He did not recall ever having seen their faces before this moment.

It was characteristic of him that he did not wince from the tight moment. Like any confidence man, he imposed a vast trust in the control of his facial expression, and now he climbed straight up the steps of the verandah and confronted the pair.

They were both burly. Except for their complexions, they might have passed as brothers. Each man sunk his head a little and looked up with the expression of a surly bulldog that wants to bite.

"My friends," said Rory in his deep, genial voice, "you seem to know me. Is that correct?"

There was no answer, only the steady staring.

"My name is Pendleton," he said, "and I don't think that I know yours."

"Say," said the darker of the pair, "why start throwing that kind of a bluff?"

"Bluff?" echoed Pendleton gently, but feeling relieved, for it seemed certain they were not really trailing him. If they had even a suspicion of a clue against him, they would strive to refresh it by following his own invitation and opening up a conversation. They could not be so subtle as to lead him on by pretending indifference.

"But why should I know you, gentlemen?" he added.

"Pendleton," said one of them, "you're Al Pendleton's father, ain't you?"

"Why, yes, of course," he said a little surprised. "But what has that to do with my knowing you? Are you friends of my son?" He said it with the most amiable of smiles, and at this one of them laughed in a sneering, low-pitched voice like a growl.

"Friends of his? We're Jay Winchell and Harry Tucker, if you wanna know."

"Jay Winchell and Harry Tucker?" repeated Pendleton. "Well, let me see . . . let me see. I've heard those names before. Winchell and Tucker . . . why, those are the names of the two railroad detectives with whom Al had a little run-in when he arrived here in Jumping Creek."

"I punched his face for him, and then we chucked him into jail," said Tucker briefly. "And what's more, I ain't sorry for it. Not even if the railroad junked us. What I mean . . . I think that it'd be safer for the world if he was behind bars, and now you know what I think."

"So?" said Pendleton with no hint of anger. He even smiled forgiveness down upon them, and then he shook his head.

"I never carry tales," he said. "There's something in my nature that keeps me from carrying tales. I won't repeat what you said."

"You don't hurt no feelings here if you do," declared Tucker, but without quite the assurance of his companion. "He's one up on us, that's all. The next time we may be one up on him. What I mean to say is, we ain't hiding our heads to keep away from trouble."

It was then that inspiration came over Pendleton

as he looked down at the two brutal, not overly intelligent faces. "My friends . . . ," he began.

"We're no friends of yours," said Winchell savagely.

"Shut up, Jay," broke in Tucker. "Leave the old bird talk, will you? Words ain't bullets, I guess."

"If they were, I'd turn them the other way," said Pendleton, "because I want to ask you fellows how you're employed just now."

"We're employed just now being unemployed, and what the hell is that to you?" asked Winchell aggressively.

"If you'll think things over," said Pendleton, "you'll see that you gain nothing by being abusive. And the fact that I'm continuing to talk with you might mean to you that perhaps the three of us might combine to a very good purpose."

"We might combine, might we?" said Tucker.

"Not with me," said Winchell, shaking his head until his cheeks quivered.

"Hold on," interrupted Tucker. "Are you talking money or air?"

"I'm talking fortunes, my lad," said Pendleton calmly.

They stared at him, and Tucker muttered: "He means it. There's wool on this bird. Pendleton, what's on your mind?"

"I'm approaching you two gentlemen," said Pendleton, "on a very delicate matter . . . a matter of confidence that would be ruin to me if my connection with it were discovered. Do you realize what that means to me?"

Said Winchell: "I never yet heard a guy talk about what his reputation meant to him when his reputation was worth a damn. And that's straight from the shoulder, if you know what I mean."

"I understand, my dear fellow," said the other. "Perhaps if we had a chance to chat this thing over, you might see that I can speak just as straight from the shoulder as you can."

"This here matter, as you call it, what's the size of it?" asked Tucker curiously.

"Enough to interest all three of us," said Pendleton. "That is, if you two men can hold your tongues, take a chance, and don't mind danger that may be very great. On the other hand, there may not be any danger."

"It sounds to me like a frame," declared Winchell.

Suddenly Pendleton smiled and said: "Brother, there you have it. I'm proposing to let you in on the prettiest and the simplest plant that you ever heard of."

Tucker literally licked his lips. "I got an idea that we could talk to Pendleton," he said to Winchell.

"I'm getting the same idea, if we ain't the goats in the plant," said Winchell. "I been the fall guy before, and I ain't gonna be again. I sit down on the inside and see the whole show before I'm interested in anything whatever."

"I propose exactly that," said Pendleton. "But obviously we don't want to talk about a loose, straying hundred thousand dollars in the open street of Jumping Creek, do we?"

"A hundred thousand bones?" said Winchell.

"A hundred grand? Is that the story?" asked Tucker, jerking up his head.

"That's the story," said Pendleton.

"Brother," said Tucker, "I could stay awake all night and listen to that kind of a fairy tale."

XV

Taggert had waited in his house on the hill at the edge of Jumping Creek for a considerable time since the coming of darkness in a keener state of nervousness than he could ever remember. For the first time in a long life he was distinctly unsure of himself, and the sole center of all his thoughts was Paradise Al Pendleton.

He could not rid his mind of the young man. At last, he felt, he had encountered a force greater than himself. He was partly shamed and partly pleased—shamed to think that at last he had to admit a superior, pleased because now, in his coming age, he found something powerful and young carrying forward in the world. It is not in their own children only that older men feel a profound interest, but for everything in which are invested both youth and power.

It was a totally new sensation for Wallace Taggert. It made him feel suddenly close to the grave. He pitied himself, and at the same time there was a touch of pleasure in his melancholy.

So he went eagerly to the door when he heard hoof beats through the grove of second-growth trees that stood between his house on the hill and the street at the foot of that rising ground.

But there were two visitors instead of one. And he was dismayed when he saw before him the formidable front of Thomas Pendleton, the chief of all that wealthy clan. Behind him loomed the equally imposing shoulders and young fighting face of Ray Pendleton, the youngest of Thomas Pendleton's sons. One glance at them was sufficient to indicate that they had not come here merely for a pleasant call.

Pendleton came in with a nod, not noticing the hand that Taggert held out toward him. That made small difference to Wallace Taggert. He was used to encountering every species of discourtesy. Only not from the Pendletons.

He stood back from them, therefore, in the room that opened off his hall. It was a dingy, damp, shadowy room, only partially lighted by a lamp with a single burner and a rather smoky chimney. There were a few rickety chairs standing about, a sagging center table, and a moth-eaten carpet on the floor. But for Taggert this furnishing was enough. It did not matter what a chair looked like, so long as it was a place to sit; rugs and carpets were all right so long as they kept the floor from being noisy underfoot.

In the dull light of that room he watched his visitors, wearing the small, obscure smile that was his quizzical mask against the world.

Thomas Pendleton broke straight into his subject. "Taggert," he said, "for years you've been a poisonous spot in the life here in Jumping Creek. You've never done a stroke of good. You're a leech that sucks out the public blood. We could endure it as long as you didn't lay your claws on a member of our family. But now we've stood enough. I come here in the name of all the Pendletons to tell you that we won't stand for what you've done today."

It was a sore temptation to Taggert to say that, if the pair would wait a little while, they might see young Paradise Al come in carrying $100,000 of stolen money. But, in fact, Taggert did not really expect Paradise Al to do anything so romantic.

Now he merely muttered: "A man has to follow his real beliefs. I thought it was the voice of Paradise Al Pendleton. I thought that I recognized the voice when he spoke to me in my office."

"You thought so, did you?" exclaimed Thomas Pendleton. "And then, because of your precious thoughts, you went out straightway and cast a lasting slur, to the best of your ability, against the name of the entire family."

The banker shrugged his shoulders.

"Taggert," said the older Pendleton, "you're going to make some sort of public apology for this outrage. You're going to publish it in the newspaper, or else we'll find ways of making life hell for you in this town. Mind you, you won't have the Draytons to back you up . . . not against Al Pendleton. You won't have a voice raised on your side."

"I'm going to apologize for accusing Al," said Taggert slowly. "But not because I give a damn about all the Pendletons and the Draytons in the world . . . only because of the young fellow himself. He's worth the whole lot of the rest of you. It's because of him that I'm going to set him right before the town, if he needs any setting. That's all, Mister Pendleton. As for you and your son, I'm happier to have you out of my house than in it. Good bye."

It was rather a facer for the head of the entire Pendleton clan, but he took the blow fairly.

"Ugly language is no advantage to you, man," he said. "The important thing is that you should do the fellow justice. I have no more to say, except to thank you for making the withdrawal. Come, Ray. We'll go now."

They were about to leave when there was a

hurried beating on the door, and Taggert himself hurried out rather guiltily to open the door. If it were the young fellow, he would have to whisper two words of warning. When he opened the door, however, he was looking down into the face of Molly Drayton, very dimly seen in the light of the newly risen moon.

"Is Thomas Pendleton here?" she cried.

"Here, Molly, here," said the rancher, coming to her. "What's the matter, my dear?"

"I've been hunting for you everywhere, all afternoon and evening," said the girl. "Something's happened to poor Al. I don't know what. I'm frightened to death. It's this horrible fellow . . . this Taggert. He's driven Al out of his wits!"

"Hush, Molly," said Thomas Pendleton. "Steady, my dear. You're a little hysterical. What has Al done?"

"Lost his mind, or almost lost it," said the girl. "When I got to the house today, there was a terrible look in his eyes. He told me that he had robbed the bank, that he wasn't fit to marry me, and that he was not a Pendleton at all."

"What?" said Thomas Pendleton.

"And with his own father in Jumping Creek to verify him, too? It's his brain . . . it's this scoundrel of a Taggert who's badgered him out of his wits."

"By the eternal!" exclaimed Wallace Taggert. "I guessed it before. He's a cut above any of you.

He's a cut above the whole lot of the Draytons and the Pendletons. He don't belong to the worn-out blood. I might have guessed it. Mad? He was mad ever to talk down and call himself one of you. He hoodwinked you like a lot of fools. And I'm glad of it."

There was a sort of angry glory in the voice of the banker. And before any of the group could reply, guns suddenly began to crash among the moonlit trees before the house.

XVI

Here, in the dark of the underbrush, Rory Pendleton kneeled with Jay Winchell on one side of him and Harry Tucker on the other.

Down the thin lane that penetrated the trees they saw the rider coming. The newly risen moon struck between the trunks of the trees and over the tops of the brush, leaving all of the horse in darkness except his high head. It was Sullivan, the stallion, with Paradise Al on his back.

"Now," said Rory Pendleton, "there's two ways about it. You can stick him up and get the money off him, or you can drill him first and pick his pockets afterward."

"Sticking him up is a fool's way," said Tucker instantly. "He ain't the kind that can be held up without a fight. And once he begins fighting, there's the devil to pay. I know that . . . I've seen him fight before."

"We'll drill him," said Winchell. "I can see to shoot by this light. You take him high and I'll take him low, Harry."

"Too bad," said Rory Pendleton, shrugging his wide shoulders. "But then nobody should be such a fool as to try to throw a hundred thousand dollars back into the hands of a human maw like Taggert. Human nature revolts against such a thing."

"Stop your talk," muttered Tucker. "There's no time for that now. Jay, draw your bead. What's the matter with the damn' horse? He must smell a snake or something in the brush."

For the stallion had halted a little distance away and stood with forelegs braced and head raised high, the moonlight showing how the ears were flattened in angry suspicion against the sides of his head.

The rider did not make the slightest effort to urge the horse forward, but suddenly slipped from the saddle to the ground. As Tucker saw that maneuver, he exclaimed suddenly—"Now, Jay, now!"—and fired his own bullet. Winchell's rifle reported only a split part of a second later.

"Did you get him?" gasped Rory Pendleton.

"I saw him drop to the ground," said Winchell.

"I saw him jump into the brush, I thought," said Tucker. "Damn him if he got away."

"Wait a minute," said Pendleton. "If he went down, you'll hear a groan, or the horse will turn and sniff him . . . that horse loves the fellow."

He had barely finished that speech when a shadow came flickering out of the brush at the trio, and, as it came, fire and lead spat from the gun it carried.

Winchell fell face forward to the ground. Tucker, turning with a screech of fear, fled away, bounding high, like a rabbit making a spy hop. Rory Pendleton would have fled, also, but a wildcat in human form leaped on him from behind.

He turned about, gasping, staggering. "Al, my dear fellow . . . Al, wait a minute. I want to explain."

"Who's there?" called the voice of Taggert from the door of the house.

"A murder plot, Taggert," answered the voice of Paradise Al. "But it stubbed its toe and fell on its face. That's all. Rory, walk before me. We're going into the house."

"Al," said the criminal, "if you'll let me stop here for ten seconds and try to explain."

"March ahead," said Paradise Al. "I've a mind to let you have it through the small of the back, you dog!"

So it was that Rory Pendleton strode up the steps of the Taggert house and straight in upon an assemblage that could not have been more calamitously gathered, from his point of view. For there, above all, he encountered his brother, face to face.

Thomas Pendleton, amazed, looked from the stalwart figure of his brother to the gun in the hand of the supposed son of that man.

"Rory . . . Al!" exclaimed the head of the clan, "what under heaven is the meaning of this?"

Paradise Al did not look at the big rancher. Instead, his glance had found Molly Drayton standing behind the others, pale and staring, her hands clasped against her breast.

"Molly," he said, "why are *you* here?"

"Because I couldn't believe the things you said to me today," answered the girl. "Because I've been half crazy ever since. Al, what did you mean?"

"I meant every word of it," said Paradise Al. "Now I see everybody here that ought to know about what I've done and what I am. I'm going to tell you."

"Not now, not now!" exclaimed Wallace Taggert. He took the young fellow by the shoulder with a firm grip and glared feverishly at him. "I know what you're going to say," he went on, "but don't do it. There's no need. It would ruin you, Al."

The young man turned a desperate face toward the banker. "You're the cleanest and the best of the lot," he said bitterly. "But I'm going to tell the whole of it. I don't care if I rot in jail afterward." He turned toward the frozen faces of the Pendletons. "I was a tramp on the loose. When I hit Jumping Creek, somebody thought that I looked like a Pendleton," he said. "You came to see me. It was white of you, Pendleton. And I played my hand to get myself taken out of jail. That was all. I didn't intend to stay around and work a confidence game. But the longer I was here in the West, the better I liked it. Then I saw Molly, and after that I had to stay, whether I wanted to or not. But I was no Pendleton. I have no last name. I've worn a few, but I'm a guttersnipe, a foundling. That's the whole truth." He paused.

Molly Drayton dropped into a chair and sat with her head bowed, and her hands gripped together, hard, resting on her knees.

Suddenly Rory Pendleton said: "My friends, we can all see that the poor fellow is out of his wits and . . ."

But Paradise Al raised one finger and the tongue of the blackmailer was turned to stone.

"The rest of you know what happened, and how I got a start through you, Mister Pendleton. Then Molly . . . well, in the midst of everything, the man I called my father came out here and held me up. He wanted twenty thousand dollars for pretending that he was my father, and that everything would be all right."

"An infernal, audacious lie!" exclaimed Rory Pendleton.

"You have the money on you now," said Al.

"Not a penny that . . . ," began Rory Pendleton.

"Put it on that table," commanded Paradise Al. He raised and pointed like a gun the forefinger of his right hand. He spoke quietly enough, but something about him turned the courage of Rory Pendleton to melted butter. He took the fat wallet from his pocket and placed it on the table, where it fell open, showing the thickly compressed stacks of greenbacks.

"I cracked the Taggert safe," said Al, "and I took . . ."

"Be quiet, Al!" exclaimed Taggert. "You're committing yourself to . . ."

"And here's the rest of it," said Paradise Al. He swung forward the saddlebag that was slung over his left shoulder and threw it on the floor. "There's the rest of the loot. That squares me with you, Taggert, I hope."

He turned to Thomas Pendleton. "Uncle Tom," he said, noting the bent head of the big man. "I'm calling you that for the last time. It's to thank you for giving me my start. You get the place I started, of course, and the cows and everything on it. It was Pendleton land, and mostly Pendleton money that started me. I'm sorry it's ended, because being a Pendleton was the happiest experience of my life."

Thomas Pendleton lifted his big head and tried to speak, but failed. It was his son who cried out: "Why, Father, if I had the doing of it, I'd get hold of Al and adopt him! I'd get him into our crowd. He's better than the whole lot of us. I don't care what he's done. He's come clean in the wind-up."

Al heard nothing of this. He went to Molly Drayton, and, standing before her, said: "Sullivan and I are going farther west, Molly. I was all a pretense, but you'll forget me fast enough, and I won't hold any malice. I thought more of you than all the rest of the world. I only want you to know that. Are you saying good bye to me, Molly?"

She did not stir.

Suddenly Taggert turned on the others, and, with vague, scooping gestures of his hands, he brushed them from the room, as it were. Then, closing the door, he stood with them in the dingy hallway.

"They've got to be left alone for a while," he said.

No one answered except Rory Pendleton, to say: "I'll be going." With his head lowered, his eyes fixed on the floor, he opened the outer door and went down the steps. There he saw before him the figure of a man crawling away from the trees on hands and knees. It was Winchell, of course, and the dregs of decency and manhood left in the blackmailer compelled him to go slowly after the wounded man.

In the hall of the house Thomas Pendleton was able to say at last: "It is the worst blot that ever fell on the Pendleton name. As for Paradise Al, we need him, we want him to make us forget Rory."

"Hush," said Taggert. He looked down at the floor, smiling, but he raised one finger to caution the others to silence, his ugly head a little to the side as he himself listened intently.

They could hear, clearly enough, the voice of the girl, rising from instant to instant, as if hope had returned, and with it the promise of happier days.

THE QUEST

In addition to thirteen serials, in 1933, Faust published twenty-seven stories, which varied from short story to book length. One of the short novels was "The Quest" which appeared in the May issue of *West*. It appeared under Faust's Max Brand® pseudonym and is the first of a trio of stories about Barney Dwyer, a social outcast with more brawn than brain, who has yet to find a place in the world despite his efforts to do what is right. Another Dwyer story, "The Trail of the Eagle", which appeared in the July, 1933 issue of *West*, is collected in *Outlaws from Afar*.

I

A wind promising rain churned up little puffs of alkali dust and filled the air with a clean, pungent scent, but none of the cowpunchers outside the bunkhouse moved. They did not wish to be driven into the airless, stale heat of the room, so they remained sprawling, head and shoulders against the wall, and bodies stretched out limply while they stared gloomily toward the west. That half of the sky was all fire and smoke around a thunderhead larger than a mountain range and constantly rising. Sometimes lightning worked a vein of gold across the foundations of the cloud, while a gusty wind blew out of the sky and set wheels of dust spinning toward the ranch. Everything pointed to rain but the men continued to smoke their cigarettes in a gloomy silence, waiting for the boss to give commands for the covering of the load of hay that stood in front of the barn. Getting in winter feed is harder work than riding range, and they were all very tired.

Daniel Peary, who owned that stretch of sand and grama grass from the foothills to the river, had been studying the progress of that cloud even more intently than the rest, yet he delayed the order to pull a pair of big tarpaulins over the load of hay. He was a working boss, and his hands were sore from the haft of a pitchfork, and there was a quirk of pain in the muscles of his back. He understood the temper of his men, for his mind was as theirs, and he merely said banteringly: "The rest of us are all tuckered out, Barney, and you're as fresh as a daisy. Why don't you go and pitch that load of hay into the barn before the rain gets it wet?"

A reclining cowpuncher gets up very much like a horse, with a roll to the side and then a heave from hands and knees, but Barney Dwyer rose without effort as an Indian will rise, or a gymnast in the circus. He turned his good-humored face toward the coming of the storm and nodded in understanding.

"All right," he said. "I'll throw it off." He walked to the wagon, caught hold of the lofty edge of the hayrack, and drew himself up as though the body depending from his hands was not two hundred pounds of bone and solid muscle but a stuffing of dry straw.

He heard a mutter of laughter behind him. In a sudden flow of the wind he distinctly made out the voice of the boss saying: "He ain't a man, he's a horse!" Barney winced a little. He was accustomed to contempt, but he had never grown used to it. He rubbed his big hands together, and picked out the pitchfork that was stuck in the top of the load like an ornament on a great pale head of hair. The wild mare had come to the edge

242

of the corral. Sometimes she looked toward the storm cloud; sometimes she looked at Barney Dwyer with her mane and the silk of her tail rippling out to the wide in the wind. She seemed to be drawing a deduction from the cloud and the man with the cunning of her savage brain. And he stared back at her for an instant with admiration such as he always felt for creatures who are adequately pro-portioned brain and body. As for himself, he was all body and no brain. Many a time he had been told so, with curses.

He walked to the edge of the load, flashed the pitchfork, and leaned back, pulling a great roll of hay, a huge and increasing poundage, toward the door of the barn. As the weight increased, as the struggle became greater, a fervor came up in him and burned away the shame of his dullness of wits. For it was not often that he had a chance to fill those great hands of his with all that they could do, until his legs hardened to maximum iron and the cordage of muscle along his back began to creak with the strain. He began to pant, making a small, snarling sound of joy.

He was putting almost all his strength into the labor, but carefully, for he knew that when he was at full strain odd things happened to the tools he used. Axe handles, shovels, new leather reins burst apart. On this very ranch, in the short month of his employment there, he had broken two axes and a big-bladed cross-cut saw, meant for two men to sway, had snapped while he was using it alone. The temper had failed Daniel Peary on that occasion.

"You big flat-faced fool!" he had shouted. "You break anything more on this place, and you're fired. That cross-cut saw is worth more than you are. You're a dummy, is what you are!"

Barney Dwyer sighed as he remembered. People were always talking to him like that. And now he used all the care he could in tugging that monstrous roll of hay to the door of the barn, and pushing it through. It fell heavily, whipping an entangled train behind it, and he heard it land. The filling of the barn had barely commenced.

A damp wind struck his forehead. It made him hurry his work. Again and again he drove great weights of hay through the barn window.

"Good boy, Barney!" called the cowpunchers, lolling in the dust in front of the bunkhouse. They were all clever experts with rope and gun. When they saw a cow cutting up in the distance, they could tell by its actions what sort of flies were bothering it. They could doctor a sick horse, mend harness, build fence, weave horsehair into ropes and bridles. To see them work, to see what they accomplished with their puny hands, was always a wonder and a delight to him. Therefore, although they laughed as they praised him now, he forgave the laughter and reddened with joy because of the praise. He felt that they were good fellows, and someday, if the grace of chance ever came to him, he wanted to do one great thing in their behalf to gain their affection, even if he never could have their respect.

There was more than a ton of hay on that wagon; he cleared it off with the expedition of a Jackson fork until hardly a quarter of it was left. A volley of chill wind struck him and put twenty small cold fingertips upon his skin. He ran to complete his work, dipped the pitchfork deep, and heaved back. Alas, the handle of the fork shattered and broke off close to the tines.

Fear came over him. He saw the boss leap up and run toward the wagon; he dared not face Daniel Peary.

"Get off of that!" shouted Peary. "Get off of that wagon. Get off the ranch. Damn you . . . I'm through with you. I never saw such a fool. Get off that wagon!"

He climbed down to the ground. After the weight of exertion that he had laid upon himself, his body felt light. He was covered with sweat, and the wind blew him cold all over. But his heart was colder still. Night was coming on, but there was no shadow in night to compare with the darkness of his spirit. He looked down at the ground. All that he saw of Daniel Peary was the hand that he brandished under his nose.

"You're as worthless as that fool of a mustang mare. She's big, too. She's strong, too. And what's she worth? She ain't worth a damn! I'm through with you. I'm gonna pay you off. I owe you forty dollars and I'm gonna give it to you now. You take it and get out. I oughta take off the price of the things you've broke. You've eaten for three and you've broken for ten!"

That freckled fellow, Billy Murphy, sang out: "Give him the mare for part pay. Give him the mare for thirty dollars."

"I'll do it!" shouted Daniel Peary, his rage increasing as his injustice began. "I'll throw in the mare for thirty dollars. Take her. Take her and the old saddle and bridle in the barn. Take the bunch for thirty-five dollars. Take that, or you don't take nothing!"

Barney Dwyer looked sadly toward Murphy. Billy Murphy was clever at everything. He could sew like a woman, sing like a minstrel, do magic tricks with cards. And clever men were always the hardest on Barney Dwyer.

"What would I do with the mare, Mister Peary?" he asked.

"What would anybody do with a horse? Ride her, you half-wit!" shouted Daniel Peary.

Barney Dwyer shrank again. He could not argue, but he knew that the best horse wranglers in the outfit had been thrown by the wild horse. He knew that they had brought over the Mexican, Juan Martinez, to try his Spanish bit and cruel spurs on her, and she had thrown Martinez

246

twice, and tried to eat him after the second time.

"All right," said Barney. "That only leaves five dollars cash."

The cruelty of Daniel Peary waxed as he saw his victim submissive.

"You'll get that five dollars by walking for it," he said. "Walk up to that town of Timberline and find my son Leonard. Len owes me more'n five dollars. He can pay you five. Wait a minute. I'll give you an order for him."

He snatched out a little five-cent notebook with a sweat-stained red cover. With a pencil he scribbled a note. "Take that," he said, thrusting into the hands of Barney the page on which he had written.

Barney Dwyer went into the bunkhouse and rolled his pack. There was not enough of it to take long. He rolled the pack long and lean and hard and then walked out into the red of the sunset and the silence of the men. He was surprised to find that they were not laughing at him. Strange to say, they were all frowning at the ground, biting their lips. And Daniel Peary walked up and down in as black a rage as ever, never glancing at his hired hands.

Barney went along the line and shook hands. He was amazed again. They all stood up. They all gripped his hand heartily.

Billy Murphy said: "I'm sorry, kid. I've got a couple of bucks. Here, you take that along with you." He held it out.

Others were reaching for money, too, and Barney Dwyer backed away from them, overwhelmed with embarrassment, crushed by their kindness.

"I wouldn't be needing that," said Barney Dwyer. Tears came into his eyes. He choked, he felt that in all the world there were no men so noble, so good, so kind as these. "I'll be getting five dollars up there in Timberline," he said. "But I'll remember that you've offered it to me. I'll never forget *that*. I'll remember you all, because I see that you're my friends."

As the fullness of this delightful conviction came over him, it forced back his head a little, and the sunset flushed on his face as he smiled at them.

He offered his hand to Daniel Peary, saying: "I'm sorry that I've broken things. I guess I've broken about as much as my pay would come to. Maybe I'd better not take the mare?"

"Take the mare and be damned," said Peary, and turned his back.

To that lean back, somewhat bowed by riding and many labors, Barney said, with a sigh: "I wanted not to break things, and I'm sorry. If I had a chance to do anything to make up, I'd like to do it."

Suddenly Peary whirled around on him. "There's one thing you can do for me, and, if you break his neck handling him, I don't care. Take my son Len and drag him out of Timberline from that gang of crooks and put him back here on the ranch, where he belongs. Go on and do that for me . . . and I'll give you another horse as good as that."

He snapped his fingers at Barney Dwyer and strode off toward the ranch house, while Barney went into the barn and took the bridle, the old, battered rag of a saddle with the rope coiled on the horn of it, and went out into the corral.

He had to corner the mare half a dozen times, before he managed to rope her, for she dodged like a cat and made a game of it. However, she knew a rope, if she knew nothing else, and, once the noose was around her neck, she stood quietly and let him put on saddle and bridle. The cowpunchers stood along the corral fence, laughing, giving advice. He had no hope of being able to ride her when so many better men had failed, but nevertheless it was his duty to try. So he climbed into the saddle.

Sitting into that saddle was like sitting down on the end of a flying piston rod. With the power of his knees he crushed the big mustang till she grunted. Then he rose high in the air and came floundering down on hands and knees.

When he got up, the mare was standing in a corner of the corral, playing with her bit, cocking her ears at him.

"Next time you go up, bring us down a nice cool chunk of that cloud, Barney, will you?" called someone.

The men began to shout and laugh. They kept up that shouting and laughing while the red bay mare shed him six more times from her back, and finally slammed the length of his body against the wall of the barn.

He lay in the dust, stunned, till Billy Murphy and another man ran to pick him up. They thought he might have broken his back or fractured his skull, but he stood up and shrugged his shoulders as he started for the mare again.

"What's the use, Barney?" said Murphy. "She'll kill you, if you keep it up. What's the use?"

"Don't you think I'd better keep on trying?" asked Barney.

"Not unless you're made of India rubber."

"I guess I'll stop trying, then"—Barney Dwyer sighed—"because I'm not made of rubber."

They laughed loudest of all at that, but he forgave them easily. They had offered him their money, all of them, and he would never forget.

He led the mare out of the corral.

"Hey!" said Billy Murphy. "You come back and sleep here tonight. Not even a dog ought to be run off on a night like this, with a storm coming on."

"I can't stay," said Barney. "The boss wouldn't like it. He wouldn't like to have me stay around on the place. He doesn't like very well to have me around."

So he shook hands once more with Murphy, and headed straight into the foothills, toward the mountains. It would take him two days to get to Timberline, probably. His chances of eating along the way were very slender. And he had with him, for capital, exactly $5 in a note that had to be collected.

The night came down on him as he mounted through the hills, and the long-promised rain was on him with a rush and a roar, filling the darkness with sound as a river fills a narrow stone cañon. He thought of turning the mare loose, since she was useless to him. But as the thunder boomed over them and the lightning sprang, she pressed up to his shoulder for comfort. He stroked her face and went on, glad of that companion.

II

The world of dust and grama grass turned into a world of mud. He could not pause to rest unless he lay down in the wet, so he slopped on, stepping blindly most of the time. He would have lost the trail before long. It was the mare who kept to it, steadily, so he let her have her way.

Presently she began to act as though she were alone, not under the guidance and the chaperonage of the demigod man. If a strange scent reached to her down the wind, she paused, and Barney stopped beside her, admiring her manner of lifting her head and studying danger that was to him unguessed. Once or twice she stopped to sniff at the ground. Once she shied suddenly far to the left, and almost tore the lead rope from his hand. This wilderness of night was to her a hook in which she could read clearly and well, while to him it was a black wall that he leaned his head against, to no purpose.

But Barney had given over wondering why God had given to him nothing but the strength of his hands, and to all other creatures some special blessing of mind and spirit. He looked up to this wild, brave horse. She was all iron and fire. What was this night of storm to her, when she had known how to brave four or five lonely winters on the range, pawing away the snow to get at the grass, hunting out shelters before the hurricanes began?

The thought of this gave to Barney a sudden warmth of confidence. For if she could take such good care of herself, she was not apt to lead him into trouble. It was better, therefore, to let her go ahead on a loose rope.

They came to steeper hills and slopes where he could be glad that fatigue was such a stranger to him. Then they reached the lowest belt of the lodgepole pines and from these passed into a great forest. Here they had shelter from the edge of the wind, but the rain still found them, sluicing down among the trees in torrents, or again hail would crash among the branches. It seemed to Barney

Dwyer that many of those huge pine trees offered a perfect resting place for the remainder of the night, yet the mare went on with such eagerness that he kept expecting the trees to give back, at any moment, for a clearing with a house in it. So they continued through the forest on a trail that had grown into what could almost be called a road.

That road dipped out of the forest into a ravine that was filled with a sound of rushing like a great wind, but there was no stir of air through most of its length. It was merely the pouring of water that swept down the valley. The trail was looped along the rocky wall of the ravine. Sometimes it was safe enough. Sometimes horse and man had to go in single file. At those moments, Barney let the mare go first on a length of the rope, for her footing of the dangerous places held up a light for him to follow.

It was like passing through a storm inside of a storm. Sometimes at a bend of the stream he could hear the rush of water nearby, the booming of a waterfall in the distance, and over his head the lightning ripped from sky to earth, and the noise of the thunder beat incessantly on the base of his brain. That springing of the lightning sometimes lighted the whole range, and showed him down the narrow channel, framed between the glimmer-ing walls of stone, brief glimpses of the three mountains that he knew rose near the town of Timberline. By that he could be sure that they were on the right trail, although he never had traveled it before.

Those same lightning flashes always showed him the mare as she went busily up the trail, sometimes shaking her head at the peals of thunder, but never daunted, never hesitant, except when some narrowing of the trail threatened to leave no footing at all between the wall of the gorge and the water beneath. At those places, lowering her head, she would smell her way from step to step, as it were.

They came to the waterfall. The roar of it stunned the mind of Barney. Driftings of the spray blew into his face. And the lightning kept that bright downpouring of silver and white pulsing out of the darkness. All the rocks of the ravine wall and the trail were gilded with water, also, and it was a place to watch every step. Yet the mare went safely and steadily up the steepness of the way until they had gained the top. There was no longer a ravine, merely a valley with wooded hills rolling back on either side, and Barney heaved a sigh of relief. Exactly then luck failed them.

They had just passed the lip of the falls when the bank crumbled under the hoofs of the bay mare and she dropped into a current that was whipping toward the precipice like a flight of arrows. One instant she was before Barney, the next she was gone, and the rope burned through his hands to the final knot.

On that he glued the strength of his grip and was jerked into the margin of the stream, but on an elbow of rock he hooked his left arm, and endured the strain. By the lightning he saw the horse struggling at the end of the rope, her head lost to him in the flinging water, most of the time. But when he glimpsed it, he saw that the ears were still pricked. Just beyond her, the river bent down to make its long plunge.

Little by little she worked in toward the bank. It might be that she could reach it and clamber up. It might be that the bank was sheer. In that case it was merely a question of how soon Barney's endurance might give way. In the meantime, the snow-water froze him to numbness. There was no life in him below his straining shoulders. He dropped his chin on his chest and grinned with agony. Between his shoulder blades, the muscles seemed to be giving way. His shoulders ached with an increasing tension, but still his grip remained on the knot.

He told himself that he would count to ten, and then let go. He counted to ten, and hung on. He counted to ten again. He counted many times, but still he could not surrender that grasp that was the life of the mare. That was what he was doing, he told himself. He was holding a life in his hand. She was brave, she was wise, she was beautiful, she was strong, and all of her lay in the grip of his hand. It was like being God for one creature, but, ah, the agony of that being!

Then the rope jerked violently. The strain ceased. He thought that the strands must have parted, but, looking up, he saw the red mare on the ledge above him.

Slowly he clambered out. He sat for a time on the very edge of the bank, where it had crumbled, until by degrees the warmth of his strength returned to him. He rose. The mare was troubled with cold and exhaustion. Her head was hanging. Therefore Barney found a sheltered place among the pine trees. With twists of the pine needles he rubbed the horse dry, tethered her to a sapling, then wrung out his own clothes, which were soaking, pulled them on again, and into heaped up leaves and pine needles he crawled and slept.

The sense of the storm remained with him all night, but in the morning he found a brilliant sky with only enough white clouds steering through it to set off the blue. The world burned with life. Every rock glistened. The trees were a shimmering green. When Barney Dwyer walked up the valley from meadow to meadow and from grove to grove, it seemed to him that there was nothing ugly or dangerous on earth except the men who inhabit it.

The mare was quite herself again. She was gayer than the birds or the leaping of the water in the river. When they came to a green plateau of rolling ground, it seemed to Barney that no crime could be greater than to keep such a wild thing enslaved. So he stripped off saddle and bridle and rope. He swung the rope with a shout, and off she went, a red ray of speed that disappeared around the shoulder of the next hill.

He looked after her, long after she was gone, then settled saddle and bridle and rope in the fork of a tree before he went on. He was very hungry, by this time, so he paused to tighten his belt. He had heard in his boyhood that Indians found this a comfort in days of famine. It never had been a comfort to him, but he always followed the practice when he was starving. When at last he was ready to start up the valley toward the three mountains of Timberline, he saw the red mare not twenty yards away, cropping the grass.

Bewilderment made him take off his hat to the sun and the wind. She had returned. But perhaps it was merely as the wild hawk will dip down from the upper air in scorn of the hunter. He walked straight up to her, holding out his hand, and she, pretending not to see him, kept her head turned until the last instant. Then she was gone like quicksilver from the touch. She fled in a circle, brandishing her heels in the air, now and then tossing and shaking her head. He laughed with joy at her beauty and because of the circle in which she ran. At last she paused near him and, with legs well planted, ready to dodge him in any direction, dared him to come on. But still Barney laughed, for she had come back to him. Some gossamer thread of affection had drawn her back to him. If he had loved her beauty, her wisdom, and her courage, she had found something in him to love in turn. It was to Barney a benediction and a revelation.

She fell to cropping the grass. Without hesitation, with a strength of conviction, he walked straight up to her and put his hand on the gloss of her shoulder, but she merely lifted her head and turned fearless eyes on him, as one who might say: *Well, what of it?*

He took her by the mane, and led that red thunderbolt back to the tree, where he saddled and bridled her, put the rope on her neck, and then tied it to the horn of the saddle. After that, he walked straight up the valley with excitement bubbling like a fountain of wine in his heart.

Something linked him to her. Something would draw her after him. Once she was a mile behind. A little later she passed him with a rush, flourished her heels nearby, and fell to grazing well ahead of him. He laughed again, with tears in his eyes. Even far back into the dimness of childhood, the glances and the voices of men had been hard with scorn. Nothing about him had ever been desired, except the strength of his hands. But this was far otherwise.

He began to talk to her as he never had talked to a human being. In a short time, his whistle stopped her wherever she was running. When he spoke and held out his hand, she would come curiously up to him.

So he forgot the miles. He forgot his hunger. He could not stop smiling all the way through the uplands, while the three great mountains drew closer above him, their blue-white heads shining in the sky.

He reached Timberline, and, looking down into a great hollow where the trees began again and a stream angled through the midst, he saw a small village. On three sides of it the three mountains looked down, so that he knew he was at the town of Timberline at last. He took out the folded bit of paper torn from the notebook. Water had blurred the writing, but it was still decipherable. With that paper fluttering in his fingers, and with the red mare crowding close up to his heels, he came out of the happy wilderness and entered among men again.

III

It was a very small town, but complete after the Western fashion with general merchandise store, hotel, blacksmith shop, and three saloons.

Half a dozen boys playing in a vacant lot

pointed their fingers at the stranger and the red mare, and shouted, and laughed. No matter how accustomed he was to shouts and laughter, the iron entered freshly into the soul of Barney Dwyer; he had been free from pain so long that he had forgotten some of its quality, but the old ache began again in the familiar place.

On the verandah of the hotel sat one tall, stark man with his hands laid out on his knees, his eyes fixed far off on the darkness of his thoughts.

"Can you tell me where I can find Leonard Peary?" asked Barney. His hand made a slight upward movement. He always had an impulse to take off his hat when he spoke to a grown man, a stern man.

The other drew his glance away from the distance and examined Barney Dwyer without interest. Then he returned to his reflections.

"I said," repeated Barney more loudly, "can you tell me where I can find Leonard Peary?"

A faint smile of pleasure appeared at the corners of the lips of the man on the verandah. That was the only answer.

Barney broke into a sweat and turned helplessly away. The street was as empty as his heart. A gust of wind went by carrying a galloping phantom of dust, and the mare pressed close to him.

Through the storm and the wilderness she had been as carefree as an eagle in the sky, but now she was nervous with fear. The *creaking* of a shutter made her tremble. Down the street a yellow sign vibrated in the wind. It hung over a pair of saloon doors, and to that place went Barney Dwyer.

He tied the mare to the hitching rack and went inside. Half a dozen men were at the bar, talking quietly. Barney stepped up to the deserted end of the counter and faced his image in the mirror, the familiar gray flannel shirt unbuttoned at the throat —all collars choked him a little—his throat and face looking a little sleek, but not exactly boyish. Between his eyes there was one line of trouble, rather than of thought.

The bartender made a step toward him, leaned a little. "Yours, stranger?" he asked.

"I can't buy a drink. I . . . ," began Barney.

"No hand-outs here for bums," said the bartender.

"I only wanted to ask a question," said Barney.

"Shoot, then."

"I wanted to know if you can tell me where to find a man called Leonard Peary, in this town?"

The bartender elevated his brows, turned his head, and looked toward one of his customers. He was a darkly handsome fellow, young, with a continual glow of health in his cheeks, and a pair of those restless bright eyes that see everything at a glance.

He nodded toward Barney Dwyer.

"You want me?" he asked.

"I've got a note, here, from your father," said Barney. He came up and held out the scrap of paper.

Leonard Peary read it, reflected for an instant, and then drew out a wallet. He continued to talk to the others. And they hung upon his words, already smiling before they heard the point of the tale. They seemed to Barney a formidable lot of manhood, and yet it was plain that they were mere attendants upon this paladin. Everything set them apart. The very clothes he wore had a half Mexican dash and color about them. His peaked sombrero made him seem as foreign as his swarthy complexion; the flash of his smile was wholly Latin, too.

So, still talking, he drew out a bill, stiffened it with a jerk, and so extended it toward Barney without turning his head.

"Thanks," said Barney. "Thanks a lot! Sorry to bother you, but . . ."

Leonard Peary talked on carelessly. Not one of his auditors had so much as a glance to waste on the stranger. So Barney Dwyer went hastily out of the saloon. The mare danced and neighed impatiently as she saw him, but Barney stood overcome by a memory. Had not Daniel Peary told him to bring back his son to the ranch, even by the nape of the neck?

As well think of bringing a beautiful black

panther out of the woods with naked hands. Yet such a command had a weight with Barney. He always had tried to obey orders with a literal exactness. And now it seemed to him that, if he could do what Daniel Peary had bidden, he might win, as by a sudden stroke, the affection of those good fellows on the ranch, those who had been sorry to see him go, who had spoken to him with sympathy, who had offered him money out of their pockets. These were rascals who surrounded young Leonard Peary in Timberline. So his father had said. And if, on a day, Barney brought the son back to the ranch, would there not be a deathless rejoicing and gratitude?

So, on the instant, he fixed in his mind the great determination. He would have to eat, rest, and think over the project, first. It was so far the greatest action that ever had entered his mind that the might of it appalled him.

He untethered the mare and went down the street with her at his heels. He left her outside the general merchandise store, untied, while he went in to buy food. He found a counter running around three sides of the room to accommodate purchasers of hardware, or groceries, or of clothes. In the center of the open floor rose a big stove, the swelling iron sides of it discolored by the red heat that they often had endured. It was girt with a nickeled rail on which heels could be rested in winter, and half a dozen chairs were at hand, but they had been hitched around to face the central counter. There was the presiding clerk, a girl whose bare arms were folded as she chatted with the loiterers. She was so pretty that Barney, the instant he stood inside the door, dragged off his hat. He felt that the haste of the gesture had made his blond hair stand on end.

And one of the trio, half turning toward him, jerked a thumb over his shoulder to indicate the stranger. "Hey, look it," he said.

They chuckled, all of them. How strange, thought Barney, that they were able to see, with the first glance, that he was a fit subject for derision. Ah, the wisdom, the strange insight of all men.

As he approached the counter, slowly, the girl straightened.

"Why are you laughing, Riley?" she demanded briskly. "*You* wouldn't know enough to take off your hat, even if you were in church."

At this rebuke, they laughed all the more, and loudly.

And big Riley, lolling in the chair, exclaimed: "Is this a church, Sue?"

Barney waited for her to answer that question, but she kept her brown eyes fixed on him, expectantly, and took no more heed of the three, or of Riley's question.

"I'd like to get some flour and bacon," said Barney. "And some fish hooks and a line. And some salt and baking powder. And . . ."—he looked down to the torn left sleeve of his flannel shirt, where it had been ripped—"and a needle nd some thread," he concluded. He looked up at her from his sleeve. She was smiling, a twisted smile that made him blush.

"He's gonna set up housekeeping," said Riley. "That's like a married man, giving an order. That's what it is."

"Oh, no," said Barney, for he felt that the words should be answered. "I'm not married."

They crowed with delight. They smote one another on knee and shoulder. They leaned toward Barney and examined him with a bright pleasure, beginning to hope for more sport.

"You be quiet, all of you," said the girl. Yet Barney saw that she, also, would have liked to laugh. "How much of all these things do you want?"

Barney tried to think in pounds and numbers, but his mind was struck with confusion. He wanted only to get out into the street again as soon as possible.

"I don't know," he told her, making a vague gesture with both hands. "About three dollars' worth, if you don't mind."

He spread the $5 bill on the edge of the counter, and waited.

"Well," said the girl," if you don't know . . . oh, all right. I'll get everything together. Three dollars, eh?"

"Who's your father, boy?" asked Riley.

"My father is dead," said Barney.

The girl was busy, her brown hands flashing here and there. "Let him alone, Riley!" she exclaimed, but without turning from her rapid work. "Let him alone. It isn't fair."

"And a frying pan . . . not a big one," said Barney.

That seemed to amuse everyone more than all that had passed before. The girl was laughing, too, as Barney could tell from the movement of her shoulders. She struck that laughter from her face before she turned to the counter again, yet her eyes were still shining with it. She put all the desired articles in a heap, touching them with a slender brown forefinger as she named them to him.

"Is that all?" she asked.

"That's all," said Barney. "How much, please?"

"It's two dollars and eighty-five cents . . . if that's enough flour."

"That'll do fine," said Barney, and presented the bill.

She took it, opened the cash draw, and then paused. She frowned. Her head tilted a little to one side as she stared at Barney. "That money is no good. That's counterfeit," she said.

He, in a trance, saw the greenback being pushed across the counter toward him. He accepted it, raised it, turned it back and forth without understanding. "Counterfeit?" he said blankly.

"It's too bad," answered the girl. "I'm sorry. Who gave it to you?"

"Why, a man named Leonard Peary gave it to me," said Barney.

"He wouldn't do such a thing!" cried the girl.

"He's a liar!" exclaimed Riley, jumping up from his chair. "I've seen these simple-faced crooks working before today. They get away with a lot, but they're not going to get away with it here in Timberline! Len Peary never gave you that!" He advanced on Barney with arm outstretched, pointing. Behind him came his two companions, with happy looks, intent on mischief.

"I don't suppose Peary knew it was bad money," said Barney. "Only . . . it was he who gave it to me. I'm sorry."

"You'll be sorrier, when we throw you out of town. We're gonna give you a run, brother!" cried Riley.

Barney shrank back from that advance of the three. "Don't touch me!" he exclaimed. "Don't . . ."

"Let him alone!" cried out the girl. "He's not worth it . . . the great baby."

"Grab him, boys," said Riley. "We'll show him the rough side of Timberline."

They closed in on Barney with a sudden, happy shout, and a rush. This was what he dreaded more than all else in the world.

For if pitchfork handles of stoutest hickory will snap like straws, how can fragile bones of arms and legs be expected to endure a sudden wrench?

With a sweep of his arms he staggered two of them backward. The driving fist of Riley he picked out of the air, caught his other wrist, and crossed his arms across his breast.

"Help!" shouted Riley. "He's breaking my arms! He's . . . !"

"I don't want to hurt you," said Barney, instantly relaxing his grip. "I'm sorry I hurt you. Only, you all came at me. I sort of had to do something. I'm sorry."

One of them was rubbing the side of his cheek where the back of Barney's hand had landed in the first gesture. And big Riley was looking down at his wrists as though they were broken in fact. But all three of them began to back toward the door. Two went out first. Riley lingered to shout: "But I'm comin' back! I'm comin' back . . . and clean you up!" Then he vanished in turn.

Barney Dwyer, following toward the door, still held out a hand, as though in fact he were approaching a horse. He kept saying: "I didn't mean it. I didn't want to hurt you. . . ."

But when the door slammed hastily as he came closer, he turned back toward the girl, and made a helpless gesture.

"I'm afraid they went away because of me," said Barney. "I'm sorry."

"Don't be sorry," said the girl. "Sit down and tell me about yourself, will you?"

IV

To Barney, it was as though he had been chosen from multitudes, and by a queen, but he saw at once that there was no glow of pleasure in her. She had grown rather pale; there was a weariness about her eyes.

"Is it another of Leonard's little tricks?" she asked. "Did he send you here?"

"Leonard Peary?" he asked, amazed. "Why, no."

"He gave you the counterfeit money, you say?" she asked.

"Yes, but . . ."

"And you just *happened* to come straight here? It wasn't that he wanted to see if my eyes were really open so that I could tell good money from bad?"

"Oh, no," said Barney Dwyer, beginning to suffer in quite a new way.

"It was just by chance, then?" said the girl. "And I suppose it was just by chance that you sleight-handed those three big fellows into helplessness?"

"I have a lot of strength in my hands," he told her. "More than most people have, at least. That's all there was to it. I'm sorry that I hurt them."

She sighed, and shook her head, seeming to deny all that he said. "Will you tell me your name?" she asked.

"Barney Dwyer."

"Alias what?" she asked.

"I don't know what you mean," answered Barney. "You seem to think there's something strange about me. You seem to think that Leonard Peary sent me here. But I don't even know your name."

"It's as plain a name as yours. Susan Jones. But there's a difference. My name is real."

"But so is mine," said Barney.

She smiled at him, and shook her head again.

"What do you think I am?" cried Barney.

"I think you're a confidence man," said the girl. "And you've come up here to join Big Mack."

"Confidence man . . . Big Mack . . . I don't understand," he said.

Coldly her eyes examined him. "You keep your face well," she said. "It's all very cleverly done. But I'm not an admirer. I've seen too much crookedness since I came to Timberline."

Every word struck him to the heart. "You think that I'm clever? You think that I'm a crook?" Barney Dwyer said. "But I'm not! Everyone knows that I'm too simple. I'm only a ranch hand, and I came up here to collect some money from Leonard Peary. I came from his father's ranch to collect five dollars."

She started; her color grew brilliant for a moment. "You rode all the way from the Peary ranch?" she exclaimed. "And for five dollars?"

"No. I didn't ride. I walked."

She folded her arms and leaned against the shelves behind the counter. "Go on," she said. "I'll try to listen. I dare say that, since you're a friend of Len Peary's, you have something very deep behind it all. Only I don't see the point, so far. You say you walked . . . and yet I can see your horse in the street outside that window."

"Yes, that's my horse," he agreed. "But I can't ride her. Nobody can. She's wild, d'you see?" He came a little closer to her, trying desperately, pouring out his spirit to convince her.

"You can't ride her, so you brought her along, why?"

"Well, Daniel Peary gave her to me as part pay for my month's work."

"Just company for you, eh? And the saddle and the bridle you put on her for decoration, is that it?"

"Daniel Peary gave me the saddle and bridle with the horse. That may seem a lot to give, but the saddle is very old. So is the bridle. And the mare is so wild that no one can ride her. Not even a Mexican horse breaker. But I sort of had to bring her along. She'd been given to me, you see."

"What a fool you must think I am," said the girl. "And Leonard must think so, too, or he wouldn't have sent you here."

Barney, with his bandanna, mopped his face that was wet with the sweat of agony.

"Peary didn't send me here," he insisted. "It was

Daniel Peary who sent me up here to collect five dollars. He gave me a note, telling Leonard to pay me. So I came up. I brought the mare with me. Please believe what I say."

Coldly she eyed him. "Daniel Peary fired you, I suppose?"

"Yes," said Barney eagerly. "That's it. He fired me."

"Why?"

"Because I broke a pitchfork handle and . . ."

Something in her face stopped him. "You broke a pitchfork . . . you were fired . . . you were paid off with a wild mustang and a note . . . you walked clear through the mountains to collect five dollars . . . and the five dollars was paid you in counter-feit. It's quite a story," said the girl.

"You think I'm lying?" said Barney, gripping his hands together.

"Well," she said, "it's hardly a work of art, that story. But I suppose that every confidence man has to keep his hand in . . . he has to practice, though heaven alone knows what you can gain by telling me such yarns. Unless Leonard wants to prove that I'm really just half-witted."

"But it's all true!" cried Barney. He rose on tiptoe as he realized the vanity of his words. "And Daniel Peary told me to bring his son back from the mountains, if I could. If I did that, would you believe what I've told you?"

"Daniel Peary told you to take Len Peary out of

the mountains and back to the ranch? Oh, yes! If you manage that, I'll believe you. Certainly I'll believe you."

"Then I'll do it, somehow. Even if they kill me while I'm trying."

"How brave, how simple, how naïve," said the girl, sneering.

"I'd better go," said Barney feebly.

"Time like your time ought not to be wasted on such small games," said the girl. "When you see Leonard, tell him I've enjoyed your call. Good bye, Mister Barney Dwyer."

He got to the door and turned there to look back toward her. Indignation still flushed her face. Her silence was more terrible and wounding to Barney than all the words that men ever had laid upon him. More than ever before, he felt trapped and helpless. Something more had to be said, although what words he could use were not apparent to him.

"It's wrong," he managed to say, at last. "We ought to be friendly, and not hostile."

"We're going to see a good deal of one another, are we?" she asked.

"How can I tell that?" asked Barney.

"You know that Leonard Peary sees me nearly every day. If you're one of his companions, I suppose I'll have to be seeing you, too."

"Does he mean a lot to you?" asked Barney.

In her anger and disdain it seemed that she

would not even answer him, for a moment.

Then she broke out: "He means so much to me that I wish he were out of these mountains and away from every man like . . ." She paused there, frowning. *From every man like you* had been plainly in her mind, but she left the last accusing word unspoken.

Barney Dwyer sighed. "You want him away?" he repeated. "You really would like to have him away from Timberline . . . back on his father's ranch, say?"

"Yes!" she exclaimed. "Back on the ranch raising some honest calluses on his hands. I'd rather see him there than anything in the world. Go tell him that, and let him laugh and sneer with you. I don't care. It's what I mean."

Barney tried to speak again. He wanted to tell her that he would try with all the life and strength in him to accomplish what she wished. But words so failed him that he could only turn from her and stumble blindly out through the door and into the dazzle of the open daylight.

"There he is!" said half a dozen shrill voices.

A whole group of the bare-legged boys of the town had gathered. They fell back before the coming of Barney Dwyer. There was a dancing delight in their eyes, and he waited for their opening volley of mockery and baiting.

The mare came up to him at once. As he turned down the street, she followed. She even trotted half a length ahead as though to show him the way hastily out of this human habitation.

"Look it!" shouted the boys. "She follers him like a dog! I bet she can go, too!"

Barney, amazed, made out dimly that this was not mockery at all. He came to the saloon before which the sign swayed slowly back and forth in the wind, and there, as he paused, an eager youngster touched his elbow,

"Can I hold her, mister?" he asked.

"Thanks," said Barney. "Of course you can hold her."

"*I'll* take care of her," said the boy proudly.

"But don't try to ride her," said Barney. "Nobody can ride her. She's full of tricks."

"Nobody but you can sit her out, eh?" asked the happy boy. "Jiminy, wouldn't I like to have a horse like that, one day? Oh, but wouldn't I? She's a one-man horse."

Barney, at the swinging doors of the saloon, hesitated. He felt there was urgent need to admit that he was quite incapable of staying on the back of the red mare, but the last time he had said this, it had brought down the derision of Susan Jones. So he shook his head, sadly, more bewildered than ever, and, as he passed through the doors of the saloon, he heard the youngster crying out behind him: "Back up, all you gents! *I'm* watchin' after this mare!"

There was a clattering of many voices inside the

saloon, but, as he appeared, all of that noise ended.

"There he is now," said a whisper.

All faces turned toward him with a single white flash. Silently they regarded him. Neither head nor hand stirred. The bartender was transfixed, unable to move with the bottle that he held. His mouth had been open to laugh. It remained open. His eyes turned into round agates with spots of color in the center of them.

"I'm sorry to bother you," said Barney. "But do you know where Leonard Peary is?"

"It ain't any bother, sir," said the bartender. "I'd right sure tell you where he is, only I don't know. Maybe he'd be out at the Walsh place. He goes there a lot. You know where the Walsh place is?"

The grace of this extreme condescension and courtesy amazed Barney. He tried to look through it to find the ironical truth that must lie behind the words, but he was unable to discover a sham.

"I don't know where the Walsh place is," he said. "I'm a stranger here."

The bartender hurried from his place of business toward the door. "You ain't so strange to Timberline as you was a while ago," he said with a happy unction. "It takes us a while to get to know a man like you, sir. But after a coupla lessons we learn pretty fast."

He chuckled. Everybody in the room chuckled, also, softly.

"A feller like Riley Quintin, maybe he learned

all he wanted to know in one lesson," said a voice.

Subdued laughter welcomed the sally. All faces beamed upon Barney Dwyer. The bartender was ushering him through the swinging doors. He stood in the street, where his white apron flamed in the sun.

"There's the Walsh place, over yonder. Right toward Mount Baldy. That one with all the snow on it. You head toward Baldy. The Walsh place is about a mile out. It's got a lot of bushes around it. It's the only house in sight. You can't miss it."

Barney Dwyer thanked him, and started down the street, with the mare following at his heels.

"Hey, ain't you gonna ride her?" asked the lad who had watched her.

"No," said Barney.

"He ain't gonna ride her," said the lad to the others, explaining the mystery. "He's gotta save her. He's gotta save her for when he needs her, because when he needs her, I reckon that he needs her bad."

V

From the edge of the town, the boys watched him go up the winding trail. He turned a rocky corner that shut them from view. Still their shrill voices followed him for a moment, grew drowsily soft with distance, and at last left him alone. The sun had not set, but it was behind the western peaks and blackened them, particularly the great pyramid of Mount Baldy. The world was all dazzling light or deep shadow. And it seemed to Barney as though he were walking over the crown of the universe, held up where the truth could be seen clearly. Yet the truth about Barney Dwyer had not appeared, as yet, to the people of Timber-line. They had seen through him clearly enough when he had entered the place, but now all was changed. They regarded him with respect so profound that he could not think it hypocrisy. The very boys who had jeered at him when he entered the town had attended him in an honorable procession when he left it.

He shook his head over these facts. They had made him into a man of importance. A guilty tingle of pleasure passed through him. His face grew hot. It would be well for him to leave that community before they found him out. Even the girl, for all the clearness of her eyes, seemed to look upon him as a force, as a clever rogue playing a part too deep for her to comprehend entirely.

He was pondering over these things with trouble in his mind, when he heard the scattering of gravel under the hoofs of a trotting horse, and a rider loomed the next moment around the bend of the trail. He was a trim fellow of middle age with sandy mustaches cut short. The brim of his sombrero was stiff with newness. He sat as straight as a soldier and looked very much like one of those Englishmen who come West to raise cattle and lose money on a large scale.

He stopped his horse near Barney and waved his hand in a half military salute. Barney felt authority and halted at once.

"Where you bound, stranger?" asked the man of the mustache.

"Up yonder," said Barney. "The Walsh place."

"Ah," said the other. "You a friend of Bunny Walsh?"

"No, I've never seen him. I've never been in Timberline before. I'm a stranger here."

"I'm the sheriff. My name is Elder," said the other. "What do you want with Bunny Walsh?"

"Oh, are you the sheriff?" said Barney. He looked on Sheriff Elder with awe. People such as sheriffs do not ride into one's life every day. "I'm going up to ask about a man called Leonard Peary."

"Ah," said the sheriff. "You want to see Peary, do you? You want to see Big Mack, too, I suppose?"

It was not the first time that Barney had heard this name. He wondered at it. "Will you tell me who Big Mack is?"

"You never heard of John McGregor?" asked the sheriff.

"Just a moment," said Barney. He used that

279

moment to look with frowning intentness into his memory. John McGregor seemed a familiar name, yet he could not place it. "No, I don't remember hearing of him."

"You don't?"

"No, sir."

"Never heard of Adam, either, did you? Never heard of the devil, perhaps? What's your name?"

"Barney Dwyer. I've heard of the devil, of course, and Adam," said Barney. "Why do you ask?"

The sheriff grunted. "I see," he remarked. "You're the sort that plays the simple-minded part, and you do it damned well . . . though you'll probably be damned doing it."

"I don't understand," murmured Barney.

"You don't, don't you? But I tell you that you do understand. You want Peary, and you're going to the Bunny Walsh place. That's enough proof that you're one of 'em. Enough proof for a hanging, if I could have my way about it. And I'll tell you this . . . as I've told the rest of 'em . . . I'm going to wipe the lot of you off the face of the earth, one of these days. It's going to be your life or mine. You fellows murdered some of the people that went before me, and you've bought up the rest. But you won't buy me. And as for the killing, it's a game I know how to play. Good bye. But remember that I've got my eye on you."

He rode on down the trail, and Barney Dwyer

turned to watch him. Of all the strange encounters in his life, he felt that this was undoubtedly the strangest. And he was aggrieved. It was the duty of the law to stand by fellows like himself he thought—fellows who are not quite as clever and sharp as other men. The sheriff should be his friend, and the law should be his refuge. But now, with a sudden and brutal gesture, he was thrown out in the nakedness of his soul among the men of Timberline.

He could at least understand that Big Mack, or John McGregor, together with Leonard Peary and one Bunny Walsh were people who the sheriff detested. And since of course a sheriff must not hate any except offenders against the law, they were criminals, all those men.

Before Barney lay a sweep of Alpine meadow closely carpeted with low-growing furze, and misted over with the color of millions of obscure flowers. On those flowers the bees were at work, all their songs gathered into a voice like far-off violins. To Barney there was nothing soothing in the sound, but rather it worked on his nerves like an alarm.

Then he saw the house. It stood up like a gray fist in the midst of the furze with a cloud of big bushes rolling at its feet. When he came up to it, he saw that it was big enough to have served as an hotel, but time and rough weather had battered it, knocked in the windows, stripped patches of shingles off the roof, peeled and tarnished the paint. Some of the windows were boarded up against storms. In other places oiled silk would let in some light.

He stepped onto the verandah. Loose boards *rattled* under his feet. At the door, he rapped and heard the echo sound inside. While he waited, he turned. The red mare was in the middle of the path, sometimes stealing forward, sometimes shrinking back, trying to scan every inch of the face of the house at once, as though she were afraid that danger might leap out at her like a snake from any crevice.

After a time a step came slowly inside the building, the lock *clanked,* and the door was pulled open gradually, until Barney saw an old, bent Negro on the threshold. His head was covered with white wool; the many years had dusted over the black of his skin.

"Yes, sir?" he said.

"I want to see Leonard Peary," answered Barney. "Is he here?"

"Mister Peary ain't here, sir," said the Negro.

"You can't tell me where to find him?"

"No, sir."

A voice not far away said: "Bring him in, Wash."

Wash stepped back to show the way. "Mister McGregor says will you kindly come in, sir?" he invited.

Compared with the rosy brilliance of the outer day, the hall was as dark as the mouth of a trap, and inside it was the chief who the men of Timberline called Big Mack, the enemy called John McGregor by the sheriff. Barney thought of all this, looked down at his hands, and then promptly went inside.

There was still a gleam of varnish on the banisters that turned twice in climbing from the shadowy hall, and the masks of some old hunting trophies showed their teeth at Barney. That was all he saw before Wash took him through a pair of double doors into the next room. It surprised Barney with a look of useful cheerfulness. He saw a big open fireplace with a charred black log that had been eaten almost in two. There was no fire, but the acrid scent of wood smoke was still in the air. It made Barney remember many a campfire; his hunger took him by the throat and shook him.

For at a small table in the center of the room, eating a thick slab of steak from a platter piled with fried potatoes in the margins, sat the austere figure of the man he had seen before on the verandah of the Timberline hotel—that same fellow who had failed to answer his question. It was he who had just spoken to Wash. Therefore he must be Big Mack, that leader and focal head of crime in those mountains.

Eyeing Barney, McGregor placed a bit of meat

in his mouth and chewed it slowly. Big Mack would have been handsome, thought Barney, except for certain hard angles in his face and the grimness of his expression.

Now he nodded toward a chair. "Sit down," said McGregor.

Barney merely rested his hand on the back of the chair that had been indicated. He felt more nervous than ever. Somehow the loneliness of this meal and the unusual hour of it convinced him that Big Mack was capable of anything.

"Sit down." ordered McGregor again.

"I'm all right this way," said Barney.

McGregor continued to eat. "You know who I am?" he asked after a moment during which Barney did not dare to speak.

"I think that you're John McGregor," he said.

McGregor lifted dull eyes toward him. "What makes you think that?"

"After you spoke, a minute ago, Wash said that Mister McGregor wanted to see me."

"Wash is an old man. He's an old fool," said McGregor, without heat. "Wash!"

The Negro came through the door, bending forward in haste.

"More whiskey," said McGregor, instead of speaking the reproof that Barney expected. "And another glass."

"I don't drink whiskey," said Barney.

McGregor, at this, lifted his head and stared

calmly, coldly, curiously at Barney. From a stone jug, Wash poured three fingers of amber liquid into a tumbler. McGregor swallowed half of it, instantly. He asked for no chaser after it. The sting of that raw liquor brought not a tear into his eyes. His throat was unclouded with huskiness as he said: "You don't drink whiskey?"

"No," repeated Barney.

"Why not?" asked the unemotional voice.

"Well," said Barney," supposing that I liked it, I wouldn't be able to buy it, most of the time. And I get along with water or coffee, pretty well."

"You wouldn't be able to buy whiskey, eh?" said Big Mack, continuing to eat. He speared three slices of fried potato with his fork, salted the morsel, peppered it, dabbed it in the gravy at the edge of the platter, and lifted it to his mouth. All the while his dull eyes continued to examine Barney. "Why wouldn't you be able to buy whiskey?"

"I'm out of a job, a lot of the time," said Barney.

"So am I," said Big Mack with the smaller half of a smile. "But I can buy whiskey."

"You see," explained Barney," I don't often have a chance to work more than a month at a time."

"Neither do I," said Big Mack.

"And then I spend my money pretty fast between jobs."

"So do I," said Big Mack. "What's your game? And who are you?"

"My name is Barney Dwyer. I haven't any game."

"Look here, Dwyer. You do the trick very well. You could pass as the simple-minded fellow with most people. But I'm not such a fool. Don't take me for a fool. Take me for anything else you please, but don't take me for a fool."

"I won't," said Barney.

"Riley Quintin is a reasonably hardy lad," said Big Mack. "He talks too much, and he bawls out everything that's on his mind, but he's a good man with his hands. He had two others with him. You made one move, tied all three of 'em in knots, and threw them out of the store. And yet you come here and try to pretend . . ."

"I didn't throw them out of the store," protested Barney. "They walked out. I was sorry to hurt them. They sort of rushed at me, and I had to protect myself. I didn't want to do them any harm."

McGregor rolled the rest of the whiskey over his tongue, watching Barney constantly over the edge of the glass. Then he pointed, and Barney, looking through an open window at the end of the room, saw the red mare moving uneasily from side to side in front of the house.

"You can afford to buy a horse like that, but you can't afford whiskey, eh?"

"She was given to me," said Barney. "She was . . ."

"Ah? People will give you horses like that, will

286

they? Because they take a sudden liking to you, eh? They say . . . 'Dwyer, I never saw you before, but I like you. I want you to remember me. I want you to take a little souvenir away with you. I have a red bay mare in the barn. She cost me a couple of thousand dollars, but I want you to have her, because I can see that nothing but the best is fit for you. Take her, Barney Dwyer, and use her well, and think of me.' I suppose people talk to you like that, eh?"

"No, no," said Barney. "She's just a wild-caught mare, and she was given as part pay of my wages, the other day. She isn't worth much because nobody can ride her. She's really wild."

"Ah?" said Big Mack. "You keep her along for company, eh?"

"She's pretty good to have along," said Barney, "and . . ."

"That's going too far. You take me for a half-wit, do you?"

"No, no!" said Barney in a misery of confusion. "Only . . ."

"That horse can't be ridden, Dwyer?"

"I think not, but . . ."

"Would you give it to a man that could ride it?"

"I suppose so . . . ," began Barney, "but . . ."

"You wanted to see Len Peary. You'll have a chance. You'll have a chance to see him move, too. Peary!"

It was as though he had set a bugle to his lips

and blown a blast, so did his voice burst out resonantly, beating on the ears of Barney Dwyer, piercing through walls, ringing through the house until the entire place seemed to tremble a little with the vibration of the sound.

"Peary!" shouted Big Mack again.

And far away a door was heard to slam, and footfalls came racing—footfalls as soft as the padded step of a cat, and coming toward them as swiftly as a great cat can run.

VI

A door flashed open in the side of the room and that panther-like youth, Leonard Peary, sprang in with a revolver in his hand. He straightened from a crouching position, gradually.

"I thought you yelled . . . ," he said to Big Mack.

"I wanted you fast, but I don't need your gun," said McGregor. "Here's the fellow you handed five phony dollars to."

Young Peary put up his gun, strode to Barney, and stared him in the eye. "What have you got to say about it?" he demanded. "I've heard that you can break men in two. What have you got to say to me?"

His fearlessness and his contempt made him a fine picture that Barney was able to admire so heartily that he merely smiled and shook his head.

"I wouldn't fight you for five dollars," said Barney. "Fighting you would be a bad business, I think."

Big Mack began to laugh softly.

Peary, after staring at Barney for another instant, turned on his heel toward McGregor. "Is he trying to make a fool of me? Is he trying to talk down to me, Mack?" he demanded.

"If you owe him five dollars, give it to him," said McGregor.

Peary, without turning, flung a gold piece on the floor. It rolled into a corner, and Barney humbly pursued and captured it.

Peary was exclaiming: "You can't make a monkey out of me, Mack!"

"Don't be a fool," said McGregor. "You're wanting a real horse, you've said? Well, look at that red mare out the window. She's yours . . . if you can ride her. Go take a try. If you can't handle her, nobody can."

Peary went to the window and looked at the mare. He whistled. "I'll ride her or take the hide off her," he said, and was instantly outside the room.

Big Mack had finished his meal with expedition. Now he came to the window with another tumbler of whiskey and looked out on the contest, while Barney Dwyer stood at his side, feeling that he had been tricked into venturing the mare in such a chance, knowing that whether he could ride her or not, she had more value to him than any other horse in the world.

Leonard Peary went out and stood by the mare, while he tightened his belt. Then he whipped into the saddle with a yell, and threw the quirt into the horse. There was no second stroke of that whip. The mare rose like a cloud of fire; she dropped again like a thunderbolt. The earth was furnished with springs, casting her up higher and higher. At last she spun on the ground like a wheel and slung Len Peary skidding along the ground.

He was up at once.

"Thirty seconds, Len," said McGregor from the window.

Pure joy made Barney laugh, although he was sure that laughter was dangerous.

Peary was perfectly at ease, however. He dusted himself off, arranged his bandanna at his throat, and took note of a tear in his trousers.

"I know why you laugh," Len said, nodding at Barney. "You taught her to buck, eh?"

"No," said Barney. "I haven't taught her."

"You lie," stated Peary, although still without heat. "You trained her."

"Don't call people liars . . . not while they're in my house," said Big Mack coldly.

"It's not your house. It's Bunny Walsh's house. And this fellow trained her, all right. Did you see her start off fence-rowing? She switched to sunfishing, and finished me off with a spin. She's an educated devil, Mack. You could see for yourself."

"Going to try her again?" asked McGregor.

"Of course I am," said Peary. "I'll ride her, too."

The fear leaped up in the heart of Barney Dwyer. "No!" he called. "Once is enough. That's all I agreed to. One try is enough, and she won."

"You won't let me try her again?" asked Peary.

"Sorry," said Barney. "She means a lot to me. She's like a friend. Come here, girl." He held out his hand, but, as she started to come to him, Peary caught the rein and checked her.

"Let me see you try to stop me!" exclaimed Peary. "I'm going to ride her or bust. You stop me if you can!"

The mare pulled back on the reins, snorting, backing to reach her master at the window, and, at the sight of her effort to come to him, Barney felt a prickling of gooseflesh all over his skin, and a burning heat inside him. He laid his hand on the sill of the window ready to leap down on the outside.

"Let go of her, Peary!" he called.

"I'm damned if I do," answered Peary.

"Let her go," commanded Big Mack. "She belongs to Barney Dwyer, here . . . just now. Let her alone, Len!"

Peary, gradually relaxing his grip on the rein, obeyed that order, but his dark eyes were fixed not on McGregor, but on Barney Dwyer.

"We'll see some more of each other, Dwyer," he snarled.

"Of course you will, Len," declared Big Mack. "Come in here. We'll have a chat with Dwyer, the two of us."

Leonard Peary returned to the room, flung himself into a chair, and lounged back in it with his legs stretched out. He was scowling. His lips worked a little. A scratch like a pen stroke of red ink ran from his temple down one cheek.

"What's there to talk about?" asked Peary. "Doesn't seem to me that talking is in place now."

McGregor, carrying his half-finished whiskey back to the table, took his former place and sipped the drink. "I'll decide when it's time to stop talking," he declared. "Dwyer, come out with it. What's your game? What brought you up here? Who are you?"

Barney moistened his lips. He could feel that he had come to a crisis and his eyes ached, they were thrusting so far from his head. That slow brain of his refused to furnish him with words or an answer.

"I'm John McGregor. You know that. This is Len Peary. You know that, too. Now, we want to know who Barney Dwyer is. Let's have the news."

"I'm just a ranch hand," said Barney. "I came up here from the Peary Ranch to collect five dollars that Daniel Peary still owed me. He told me to get it from his son. He told me to bring his son back with me."

The two others stared at him.

"He's got a queer lingo, Mack," suggested Peary. "Is he a confidence man, or something?"

"He's something, all right," answered McGregor. "We'll dig down and get some information out of him, too. Listen to me, Dwyer."

"Yes?" murmured Barney.

"This stuff about taking Peary home to the ranch. What sort of rot is that?" He held the whiskey glass at his lips, waiting for the answer before he drank, and the light that strained through the amber liquid put a wavering flame on the chin of McGregor.

"You see how it is," explained Barney. "His father is getting older, I guess. He wants his son back home. He doesn't like having him in Timberline. He told me that he'd like it a lot if I brought him back home."

"How would you take him, Dwyer?" asked Big Mack.

Barney looked down at his hands. "Well, I'd just bring him along, I suppose," he said.

"Just tie you on behind his saddle, Len," said McGregor to Peary. "That's all he'd do. Take you along with him like a blanket roll." He smiled a little.

"Are you going to let him talk this sort of bunk and get away with it?" asked Peary.

"No," answered McGregor, "I won't let him get away with it. Dwyer, who have you talked to in Timberline?"

"Why, just to you two, and a bartender, and Riley Quintin, Susan Jones, and Wash, and a boy, and the sheriff," said Barney.

"You talked to the sheriff? What did he have to say?"

"He thought that I was one of you . . . one of your men, McGregor. He told me that he was going to clear up everything and everybody. He said that he'd do it, or die. He said that the men before him had been murdered or bought off, and that he wouldn't be bought, and that he would take a good deal of killing. That's about what he said."

McGregor studied him. Then he said: "Len, you may think that I'm a fool, but I've got half a mind to take Dwyer at face value, and call him a little bit simple."

"Come on, Mack," sneered Peary. "Can the old con game be worked on you like this?"

"Did the sheriff say anything particular about Peary?" asked McGregor.

"No."

"Didn't say that he specially wanted him?"

"No."

McGregor looked significantly toward Peary, and the latter nodded and smiled faintly with pleasure.

"You won't talk out to me, Dwyer?" asked McGregor. "You won't come clean with me?"

"I've said everything. I've told you the whole truth," said Barney Dwyer.

McGregor stood up and raised a finger. Len Peary unsheathed a pair of guns and directed the muzzles carelessly toward Barney, without rising from his chair.

"That's right, keep him covered," said McGregor. "Don't you know enough to hoist your hands, Dwyer?"

"Yes!" exclaimed Barney, and stretched his arms so violently above his head that the gesture brought him on tiptoe.

"He thinks he'll get a laugh with this low comedy work," said Peary. "Watch him, chief. I've got an idea that he's poison, and a new kind of poison, at that."

McGregor stepped back from searching Barney.

"He's a new kind, all right," he said, juggling a pocket knife that he had taken from Barney Dwyer. "No gun . . . only this to cut his way through the world. He just about beats me, Len. Get a pair of those handcuffs that Sheriff Cary loaned us last year. Maybe Dwyer's nerve will rust faster than the steel of those handcuffs. We'll make a try of it, and see."

VII

They took Barney Dwyer back through a kitchen where the smell of food was a torment to him. Old Wash, in the act of putting a big pan of bread into the oven, looked up at the three, saw the manacled hands of Barney Dwyer, and glanced hastily down again.

Peary opened in the floor a cellar door. McGregor took a lantern from the wall and went first, lighting the way down a flight of damp stone steps into a room piled with provisions. Beyond this he unlocked a door so massive that it groaned loudly on its hinges. Inside was a still larger room, three walls of which were living stone. The fourth wall, into which the door was set, was rough masonry—big, rounded stones having been cemented together to make the partition. One pillar of the natural rock had been left in the center of the room to uphold the floor of the house above. It was the storage place of wood. Some good-size pieces were corded along one side of the chamber.

"Think of Bunny going to all the trouble of having this place dug out," said Peary. "What did he think he'd put here? Treasure?"

"He's romantic," answered McGregor. "That's why I like him. Now look here, Dwyer, you can see that there's no way for you out of this room. You stay here and think things over. We'll look in on you tomorrow, maybe, and see if you feel more like talking."

"I'll talk now!" cried Barney desperately. "You wouldn't leave me here in the dark, would you? I'll talk now."

McGregor lifted the lantern until the light of it flashed in the eyes of Barney. "We've all got our little weaknesses," sneered McGregor. "What broke your nerve about darkness, Dwyer? Ever do a stretch of solitary in the pen? Well, if you'll talk, come out with it. I've guessed part of the truth already. I think Dutch Hendry is working with you. Dutch sent you up here to drop a monkey wrench into my machine, is that it?"

"No!" exclaimed Barney. "I've never even heard of Dutch Hendry. I've told you the whole truth. I'll tell you more of it. I'll tell you everything that ever happened in my life and . . ."

"You've been telling me the truth, have you?" said McGregor. "Well, then you stay here till you can think up some interesting lies, then. Sorry the floor's a little wet. But you can sleep dry enough on that woodpile. So long."

He went out—the door slammed—the lock turned with a grinding and a rusty *clank* of iron against iron—then the terrible velvet blackness fell upon the eyes and across the brain of Barney Dwyer.

The strength went out of him. He dropped to his knees and gripped his hair with both hands. The darkness of a shut room had been a horror to him since his childhood. The black of open night, no matter how storms curtained it in, was nothing to him, but in the stifling shadow of a closed room he could not breathe and the light went out of his mind.

They would look in tomorrow—perhaps. Twenty-four hours of this would bring madness to him, he thought.

He found the woodpile and leaned against it, gripping the rough wood, breathing the resinous fragrance of the pine. And that restored him, somewhat, for it set him thinking of the great, gallant forests that go up the sides of the mountains. It made him think of the winds that beat the branches, of the squirrels, of the woodpeckers chiseling tunnels under the bark. So many pictures of life helped to ease his mind. But still he was desperate.

He found the door, and leaned his weight against it, braced his feet, gradually gave his whole strength, not in a sudden effort, but little by little, until the mighty stress made him rigid as a vibrating steel beam of a bridge. But the door held. He had known it would hold. The ponderous *clang* of it in shutting had told him that he would not be able to break the lock.

He went to the corner of the room and fumbled

until he found a stone much larger than its neighbors in the wall. He scratched the cement and felt it come away in small flakes under the tips of his fingers. So, not with hope but because he felt that inaction would drive him insane, he wedged his shoulders against the corner of adjoining walls and stamped his feet against the face of that larger stone in the masonry. With pulsing efforts, he thrust out.

He thought his feet had merely slipped on the smooth surface, at first, but then he heard a faint noise of something falling. He thrust again, and there the stone was quite dislodged. He heard it bump heavily on the other side of the wall, against the floor of the provision room. The hole was large, and he quickly made it larger, pulling out adjoining bits of rocks from the mortar that embedded them, until he was able to wriggle through the opening. He lay still for a moment, panting, incredulous of this escape. He stood up to fumble for the stairs, and, as he felt his way through the darkness, he heard a rasping noise.

A wedge of light drove from the stairs, striking his feet, spilling across the floor. It jerked upward and steadied on his face, and struck him to the heart like a flight of arrows. It was a dark lantern that had just been unshuttered.

The voice of Len Peary said: "You were right, chief. I don't know how he managed it, but there he is. Look at that hole in the wall."

"He's silent dynamite," said Big Mack. "He explodes but he doesn't make a noise. Bring in a fifth-chain from the wagon shed, will you?"

"I'll have it here in a jiffy," said Peary, running up the stairs. "But how did he get through that wall? Did he gnaw it open?"

The door opened and slammed at the head of the stairs.

"Well done, Dwyer," said McGregor, having come down to the foot of the steps. "How did you get through that wall?" He used the lantern to examine the breach.

"I pushed through," said Barney rather feebly. "I wedged my back against the other wall, in the corner, and I pushed through."

"I believe it," said McGregor. He came up to Barney, put the muzzle of a revolver against the breast of his prisoner, and then, with the hand that also held the lantern, fingered the shoulder of Barney, working the tips of his fingers among the big rubbery fibers. "You're not so big, Dwyer," he said. "Not more than two hundred pounds, I'd say. But strength isn't a matter of poundage, with some people. Two hundred pounds of wildcat, for instance, would go a long way." He had the air of a jockey, looking over a fine horse.

"I could use you, Dwyer. The way you keep your face is a charm, to me. I'll tell you what . . . for a time I was on the verge of breaking down.

For a while I was about ready to believe that you were actually no more than a simple ranch hand . . . an extra simple one with simply an extra share of strength in your hands. But there was a flicker of something else in you. I could feel the heat even when I couldn't see the flames. I knew that there was a fire in you, somehow. That was why we came back here to watch for a little while. I heard the door groan and shudder, and knew you were at it. And it gave me a groan and a shudder, too, Dwyer, to think what would happen if you got those paws of yours on me."

He stepped back a little, and again threw the flare of the lantern's light straight against the eyes of Barney Dwyer, who steadied his glance a little, seeing the wavering image of the flame in the intolerable brightness of the polished reflector, inside.

This seemed to be of importance to Big Mack, who muttered, partly to himself: "You could look right into the eye of the sun, too, I suppose?"

Still Barney Dwyer did not speak. Words were evolving slowly in the back of his mind, but they would not reach his lips. He felt that a steer might wait in this manner for the butcher's mallet to fall.

Young Leonard Peary returned, carrying a heavy weight of chain on which eight horses could safely pull. The door was unlocked once more. McGregor passed the big fifth-chain inside of the slender steel links that bound the wrists of Barney together. He padlocked the wagon chain together. Then he stepped back and played the light of the lantern over the picture before he left it.

He said: "How does it look to you, Len?"

"That'll hold a plow team. It ought to hold a man," said Peary.

"Yes, it ought to hold him," agreed McGregor. He stepped up to his prisoner, saying: "Wait outside for me, Len."

Peary passed into the provision room, and McGregor said very quietly: "Now, Dwyer, you see how it is. You have no chance. I've got you, and I'm going to keep you. However, I'm not a fool. I know how to value a man when I find one. Talk straight to me and you'll find that I'm open to reason. Probably you could make more, working for me, than you ever have made working alone. Perhaps Dutch Hendry isn't behind you. Perhaps you're working your game alone. But whatever it is, you can understand that I'd be committing suicide if I let a fellow like you run loose in my part of the country. There isn't room in the whole of the Rocky Mountains for two men like you and me. Come, now. Will you talk?" And he flashed his lantern again into the eyes of Barney Dwyer.

Desperately Barney strove to bring some rich invention to birth, some sounding lie that would fill the imagination of even a McGregor. He could say that he was a bank robber, or a train robber. He could say that a life of crime stretched behind him, but how could he convince McGregor without sufficient details? How could he really offer an explanation of a purpose sufficient to bring him into these mountains?

Before he was half ready to speak, McGregor snarled: "All right, Dwyer. It's to be a contest of strength, eh? Well, man, I tell you I'll keep you here till those handcuffs rust off your wrists. I'll starve you, damn you, or else I'll get words out of you."

He left, slammed the door, and the darkness swallowed Barney again. He heard the footfalls go up the stairs. He heard the sharp, rapid voice of McGregor speaking to Peary until the second door shut this noise away.

Then, at last, a sound bubbled up in the throat of Barney Dwyer. Even that groan died before it reached his teeth. He leaned his forehead against the damp coldness of a stone. There was no hope. There was no thought of hope, unless he could break the chain that bound his wrists together. He put his feet against the base of the column, swayed back, and gave his mighty strength to the pull. The handcuffs turned into collars of fire on his wrists, but the chain held.

A pull would not turn the trick. A sudden wrench with all his force might give him a better chance. It might also crush all the bones in his wrists and hands. But even to be a handless cripple for life would be better than to die here, in the grave-like darkness of the cellar.

He turned his hands into two bulging fists the better to cushion the shock. He replanted his feet at the base of the pillar. Then he swayed his weight far back, thrusting with the power of his legs, jerking with the strength of back and shoulders and arms. The chain parted. The impetus of his lunge skated him far off along the cellar floor. He got to his knees and remained there a moment with his head thrown back, trying to give thanks. But not a word entered his mind. Blood dripped from the fingers of his left hand. While the red was still running, he wanted to fasten his clutch on the throat of McGregor. That was the image that filled his mind, instead of prayer—his grip on the throat of McGregor, and Big Mack on his knees, biting like a frantic, helpless dog at the wrists that still wore the steel bracelets.

Then Barney stood up, found the hole in the wall, and squirmed through it a second time. There would be no third imprisonment. He knew that. If he had to use his naked hands against guns, still he would not surrender to them again.

He stole noiselessly up the stairs.

VIII

At the door above, he bowed and listened for his life. Hearing had to be to him then like sight, piercing the walls and seeing the dangers that were still ahead. He heard a *clanging,* as though

304

the oven door in the kitchen had been shut suddenly, with force. Footfalls crossed the kitchen, treading on the cellar trap door and knocking dust into the face of Barney. The step went on. Another door closed lightly. Might it not mean that Wash had left the kitchen?

No better chance seemed likely to come, at any rate. So Barney lifted one wing of the trap door and looked cautiously out. The room was empty.

Stealthily he crawled out. The back door was open on the dark of the night. Beyond the other door he could hear the voice of McGregor saying: "If you want the girl, Peary, you don't want your place with me. I won't give my confidence to any man who's tied to apron strings."

"Then sooner or later I'll have to break with you. I'll have to break anyway, if I hope to get her. She's told me that," said the voice of Peary. "She knew that I'm hand in glove with you, Mack. And she hates the idea. Stolen money is poison to her."

"All right," said McGregor. "Do as you please and when you please. Only give me warning. And this is the last that I want to hear about Sue Jones or any other girl that comes into your life. Women are a waste of time."

The voice of Peary began to answer, but the words had no meaning to Barney. He was too occupied with stealing across that floor without permitting the boards to *creak,* putting down his feet cautiously, the outer edge first. Yet, reaching the table, he could not avoid stretching out his hand and passing a package of raisins into his pocket.

As he did so, a door *creaked,* the voice of Peary entered suddenly into the room, saying: ". . . Wilson told me about the tunnel that they cut under the wall. Wait a minute and I'll tell you what he said . . ."

For at the door between the kitchen and the dining room stood Leonard Peary, pushing it open, still talking with his head turned toward McGregor.

But in another instant that head of his would be facing straight toward Barney, and it was impossible for Barney to get suddenly from the room without betraying himself with the noise he would make.

Therefore he stole straight at Peary, and, as the latter stepped on into the kitchen, he turned his head just in time to have a bleeding fist clip him on the chin. It was only a grazing blow, but it was like being grazed by the great steel knuckle of a walking beam.

With wide open eyes, Peary stared before him at Barney, but they were the eyes of a sleepwalker. The second blow that Barney had started, he checked in mid-air, and instead caught up the sagging body lest it should slump noisily to the floor.

Not till he had the weight of Peary in his arms did he remember the greater purpose that had been in his mind when he came to Timberline. So, holding his breath, the head, the arms, and the legs of Peary trailing down from his grasp, he crossed the kitchen floor.

"Hurry it up, Peary!" called the loud voice of McGregor. "Bring the coffee with you, too."

Barney with his burden reached the outer door. The boards of the verandah *creaked* ominously under his tread. He got to the ground with a leap, and then ran hard toward the barn that stood behind the house.

There was only the dimmest twilight to show it to him, but there he would have to get transportation for Peary and himself. There, surely, they must have placed the red mare.

As he pulled open the nearest door of the barn, Peary stirred, groaned, began to struggle. That meant further delay when every moment was a breath of life to him. At least, in fanning him, McGregor had not taken the twine from his pocket. He used a length of it now to tie the hands of Peary behind his back.

One of the rows of stalled horses began to whinny loudly, and Barney knew that sound as well as though it were a human voice. It was the red mare, calling to him, betraying him with her love, summoning danger on his head.

He groaned at the ear of Peary: "Stop trying to

break away. I've got you. Keep in front of me. If you yell . . . I'll strangle you, Peary!"

In the meantime, he was picking saddle, bridle, and blanket from the peg on which they hung. And Peary obediently stood close by while the first horse was saddled. It was a gray whose bright color made it easier to work on her in the almost total darkness of the barn. The next in order was a taller horse; he jerked saddle and bridle on this one, also.

The voice of Peary kept gasping and muttering: "Dwyer, don't do it. Don't take me away like a chicken picked out of a hen house. I'd rather be murdered. The whole range will start laughing at me. I'll be shamed, Dwyer, more than if I took water from a Chinaman. For God's sake, give me a fair chance. I'll do anything you want. I don't care what your game is, I'll play into your hands. But to be kidnapped like a baby . . ."

"Be still," hissed Barney Dwyer. "Come with me down here while I get the mare."

She was in a frenzy of excitement, rearing, stamping, pulling back on the rope that tethered her to the manger. But when Barney came near, she was quiet at once, her whinny no more than a whisper of greeting.

He sighed with happiness as his hand touched the silk of her flank. That battered saddle that Daniel Peary had given with her he recognized by the rough tatters of leather. It hung almost directly behind her, and quickly it was on her back, and the bridle over her head. He led her to the first two, and untied their lead ropes. He was at the door of the barn, with Peary beside him, when the great voice of McGregor rang through the night.

"Peary! Len Peary! What's come of you, man?"

Instantly the cry of Peary answered, pitched wild and high by desperation: "Here! Quick . . . the devil's got me helpless in his hands. Dwyer . . ."

The grip of Barney strangled that shouting voice. He picked up the struggling bulk of Peary like a sack of bran, threw it across the saddle of the gray horse, and himself sprang onto the back of the tall gelding that had been second in the line.

With the grip of his knees he had to hold his place. With one hand he guided the gray. With the other hand, he mastered Peary and kept him in place, while the horses broke into a trot. A glance to the side showed a dim figure racing from the house. A gun spoke, sending the *whir* of a bullet high above his head.

"He's on the left horse!" yelled the voice of Peary. "Stop him, Mack! I'm tied! I'm tied!"

The gun spoke again, and this time the shot cut close to Barney's head. He swung the horses clumsily around the end of a haystack and brought them to a gallop, while the red mare ranged ahead, dancing, leaping, pitching in her joy of freedom and of motion.

Side-by-side the horses cantered.

"You'll have no good of it in the end," groaned Peary. "You may win today, but, before the finish, you'll be cursing. I'm going to kill you for this, Dwyer. I'm going to kill you inch by inch."

But Barney was too busy to answer. He was tying another length of twine that passed from the wrists of Leonard Peary across his body and was fastened at the other end to the horn of the saddle. After that, and only now, he remembered weapons. Under each of Peary's armpits he fumbled for and found a revolver held by a spring holster. These he transferred to the two empty holsters that were attached to the saddle in which he was himself sitting. Lastly he fastened the reins to the pommel of his saddle, and now he was ready for riding at full speed.

The horses, unguided, had slanted across to the trail that pointed toward the town of Timberline, whose lights were scattered in irregular groupings before them; now Barney urged them to a full gallop down that road. For behind him he knew that the swift hands of McGregor must by this time be whipping saddle and bridle onto the fastest horse in the barn. And perhaps already Big Mack was on the road, and rushing in pursuit.

"D'you hear me?" shouted Peary. "If you try to take me into Timberline, if you let the people see me tied up like a bundle of laundry, I'll throw myself off the horse. There'll be nothing but a dead rag of me, and be damned to you!"

"Where else can I take you?" called Barney in answer.

"There's a draw to the left that you can ride down. D'you see it now?" urged Peary. "Turn down it. He'll never guess you've gone that way around the town."

It opened like a wide shallow trench, and into it rode Barney, for he knew that his captive was desperate enough to commit suicide rather than allow himself to be made into a public spectacle.

Thick turf muffled the beating hoofs of their horses, instantly, and so he was able to hear the ringing gallop of the pursuer, flying straight down the trail toward Timberline.

IX

If that were Big Mack, his horse kept on raising the echoes all the way into Timberline, while Barney, beginning to breathe again, put the horses into a trot.

They went steadily on out of the big hollow in which the town stood. From the brim of the slope, Barney looked back on the keen lights of Timberline, and so passed on among the hills until the darkness of the forest began around him. He had not the slightest idea of his place or of the proper direction.

So at last he said to his companion: "Peary, can

311

you tell me the way back to your father's ranch?"

"You mean that you'd really take me there?" demanded Peary.

"Yes," answered Barney.

A rage of groaning and of curses broke from the lips of Peary. "What'll you gain by that?" he demanded. "You mean to say that my father offered you enough coin to make it worth your while to risk your neck, taking me back home?"

"No, not for your father, so much."

"For what, then?"

"Sue Jones thinks you ought to go home," said Barney.

"I'm going crazy!" exclaimed Len Peary. "*She* thinks that I ought to go home? By God, Dwyer, is she the one that persuaded you?"

"She didn't persuade me. But she seemed to think that it would be best."

"I see it all, now," said young Peary. "You want her. She says that you can have her, once I'm brushed out of the way. So you cart me away like a watch dog that's a nuisance . . . Dwyer, when I first saw your smooth mug and your round eyes, I thought that I'd have the killing of you, someday, and enjoy it. Now I *know* that I will."

"Have her?" cried Barney. "D'you think that she'd so much as look at a simple fellow like me?"

"A simple fellow like you, eh? So simple that you make a fool of McGregor and take me off under your arm like a bit of firewood? So simple that you walk through Timberline scaring the town to death? You are a fool, though, if you think that other people can't see through all your pretending. But Sue . . . oh, God . . . she's through with me and she's told you to get me out of the way . . ."

Such a helpless fury came over Barney that, seeing the uselessness of explanations, he leaned from his a saddle and struck Peary across the mouth with the back of his hand.

Peary gasped and reeled.

"Keep the dirty talk off your tongue and out of your throat," said Barney in such a voice as never had issued before from his lips. "Or else I'll . . ." He stopped himself before the last words were spoken. But he knew what he had intended to say, and that intention amazed and shocked him. He was ashamed of the blow he had struck a helpless man. Yet he could not apologize. He felt, in fact, that, if he so much as spoke another word to Leonard Peary, he might lose control of himself and finish with the terrible strength of his hands what he could not put into speech—a vast loathing for this youth who was, he knew, the chosen man, the hero of Sue.

In the meantime, he could not ride on blindly, perhaps going in exactly the wrong direction. So he made a halt in a glade beneath the trees that was like a great hall, with the brown trunks for pillars, and the green of the spreading branches for a roof.

There he unsaddled and tethered the two horses, lashed the right arm of Peary to his left arm, kicked the pine needles into a deep bed, and lay down.

He had not spoken to Peary since the blow he struck. And Peary attempted no speech on his side. In silence, Barney lay for a moment, staring up at the darkness. A single star of the first magnitude gleamed down at him for a time. Then this moved eastward and was lost. He fell asleep.

The squirrels wakened him. Profound gloom covered the lower stretches of the forest, still, but the gray of the morning had reached the higher branches, and the nut gatherers were chattering. Barney turned his head, and looked into the dark eyes of young Peary, brilliant with hatred. That was the way they began the second day.

He shared the last of the raisins with his captive, then saddled and bridled the horses and took an upward slope that brought them out of the trees on the high shoulder of a mountain. From that point he took his bearings, located in the distance the flashing face of the water that had been his guide toward Timberline, and struck out in this direction.

The mare still followed, or ran ahead, or came back to prance at the side of her master, or raced off until trees or hummocks concealed her. She was such a beauty as she frolicked, that Peary seemed to forget his own gloomy thoughts; with a hungry eye he watched her come and go.

"She's better than a passport to get a man across danger lines!" exclaimed Peary, at last, as they came out from the thick of the trees into that open, pleasant valley where Barney had ridden before. "No wonder you save her up for the pinches."

Barney looked calmly on his companion. "I'll tell you one thing . . . you try to believe it. I never rode her half a mile in my life."

"You keep her for company, eh?" said Peary.

"That's all," said Barney. "I don't expect you to believe it. The truth about me is something that nobody is willing to believe, just now . . . nobody that I've met in Timberline. The rest of the world knows the facts well enough, though."

Peary stared back at him. For the first time a doubt, a new inquiry was in his eye. And now the red mare, which had disappeared around the edge of a dark grove of trees, flashed back into view with a loud neigh, and fled as if for her life toward them. She had come in this manner before, how-ever, except that her ears had never been flattened quite so close to her neck.

"Is there something in that wood?" asked Barney only half aloud.

"She saw a shadow, that's all," answered Peary. "When a horse or a man starts in making a fool of itself, it enjoys jumping when it sees even the wind in the grass."

The mare cast a rapid loop around them and halted in the rear, whinnying again, like a trumpet call.

"There's something wrong," said Barney. "She means something by that."

"You know horse language, eh?" sneered Peary. His upper lip was swollen and purpled by the blow that he had received the night before; his whole mouth twisted a little to the side as he stared in contempt and disgust at Barney.

"She's calling us back," insisted Barney, staring at the green shadows of the woods as he came up to it. They were close to it, now, and he drew rein, halting both horses.

"Maybe she sees a ghost," said Peary in scorn.

And as he spoke, out from under the branches of the trees rode four men, each with a rifle balanced across the pommel of the saddle. And he who was in the lead was none other than the sheriff who had spoken to Barney the evening before.

It was far too late to cut the twine that tied Peary and Barney Dwyer together, and then to flee. With a twitch of his fingers, Barney snapped that tough, hard-twisted cord, but the four, fanning out into a wide semicircle, were close on them.

"It's Jim Elder," groaned Peary. "Don't try to run. He doesn't know how to miss with a rifle. I don't know what game you were trying to play,

Dwyer, but he's going to finish it for you. Damn you, you've sewed me up in a sack, and made me a present to him. You knew he wanted me."

The sheriff shifted his rifle until he was carrying it at the ready. Close by, he spoke to his horse, and halted it. "Something told me that I'd find you again, Dwyer," he said. "And I even guessed the sort of company that you'd be in. But how do your hands happen to be tied, Peary?"

Peary took a great breath, and said nothing. He was white with shame.

"Get behind 'em, Mike," said the sheriff to one of his men. "Mind you, if you see any queer moves, don't stop to ask for orders, but shoot, and shoot to kill."

"I'm only aching for the chance," answered Mike. "I won't need telling to take my share out of 'em."

"Get off those horses!" commanded the sheriff. "Pete and Harry, fan 'em. Get everything down to the skin."

"Are you aiming to arrest me, Sheriff Elder?" asked Peary.

"I'm aiming to arrest you, and I'm aiming to hang you, too, when the time comes," said the sheriff.

Peary, dismounting clumsily because of his tied hands, answered: "You can't arrest me without a charge."

"I would have arrested you any time the last

three months, without a charge," declared the sheriff. "I would have arrested you and taken my chance of digging up the right sort of evidence, once I had a grip on you. But now I've got you and the evidence, all at once. You're a slippery lad, Peary, but I think that a good hemp rope could be fitted to your neck tight enough to stay."

"What's the charge?" asked Peary firmly enough.

"Robbery, and murder," said the sheriff.

"It's a faked lot of evidence that you have, then," said Peary.

"You never killed a man, eh, boy?" asked the sheriff.

"Not unless it was self-defense."

"You stuck up the Coffeeville stage, last week, and you killed Buddy Marsh on the driver's seat," said the sheriff.

At that, a big fellow, who was searching Peary, grabbed him suddenly by the lapels of the coat and shook him violently, while he yelled at the top of his voice: "And you're gonna hang for it, you snake! You're gonna hang for it by the law, or by me!"

"Steady, Pete, steady," said the sheriff. "He'll hang for it, all right, without any help from you. We've got the evidence on you, Peary."

"You bought it, and you bought a lie, then!" cried Peary.

"That may all be true," said the sheriff. "We have judges and juries to find out the truth of things. Our job is just to find the bloodsuckers and bring them in when we can." He turned on Dwyer. "Now, who are you?" he asked.

"I'm Barney Dwyer. I was working on the Peary Ranch. I was fired. But Daniel Peary told me that, if I could bring back his son, he'd be glad to see me again. I came up here. I found Peary. He and McGregor thought there was something strange about me. They shut me into the cellar and put handcuffs on me. They were going to starve me until I confessed what had brought me up to Timberline. I managed to get away, took Peary and a couple of horses from the barn, and got this far, when I met you."

Mike, who held a rifle and kept surveillance over the entire group, began to chuckle softly. "I've heard my share of lies, soft and loud," he said," but a more fool lie than that, I never did hear in all my days."

"They put you in handcuffs in the cellar, eh?" said the sheriff. "How did you get away?"

"First I kicked a hole in the wall and got out, but they put me back in again. . . ."

"That's a heavy stone wall, up yonder, in the cellar of Bunny's house," put in Mike.

"I don't expect anyone to believe me," said Barney. "But I'm telling you because you asked. The second time, they chained me to the stone post in the center of the room, so I broke the chain off the handcuffs and crawled out, and got Peary, and came away, just as I've told you."

The sheriff smiled, and touched both sides of his short-clipped mustache. He looked toward his men, and they grinned in turn. "I think you can rest in jail with the story for a while," he said. "Any proofs of that yarn?"

"The hole is still there in the cellar wall, I suppose," said Barney. "And here are the handcuffs, still on my wrists."

The sheriff gave a faint grunt of surprise. He stepped forward and examined the steel bracelet that still covered the wrist of Barney, the dangling links of the steel chain being tucked inside the metal circlet. The mere stretching forward of Barney's arms caused the cuffs of his sleeves to rise and expose the handcuffs. The wrists were chafed. The backs of the hands were swollen and discolored.

The sheriff stepped back again, and shook his head. "That pair of hands looks as though you were telling the truth," he said. "But that's a new steel chain. No man could snap it the way you say you have. It would hold a horse. Besides, your whole story is a funny thing to listen to. Is Daniel Peary an old friend of yours?"

"No," said Barney.

"Did he offer you a lot of money to bring back Len Peary?"

"No," said Barney.

"Do you expect me to believe you?"

"No," repeated Barney. "It's the truth, but nobody would believe it, I suppose."

Two or three of the men guffawed at this, but the sheriff stepped a little closer.

"It's a queer tale, Dwyer," he said. "Down in my heart, I think that you're a thug. But you brought me Len Peary with his hands tied, and that may have saved some bloodletting all around. Besides, I haven't anything against you. To do what you've done, you'd have to have the strength of a horse. Can you show me some of that strength, Dwyer?"

"I've heard a strong man that could bend a horseshoe," said Mike. "Wait a minute. I've got the shoe that my horse cast this mornin'. Let him try to bend *that* one." He chuckled as he spoke, and, hurrying to his horse, he brought from the saddlebag a quite new horseshoe, the iron thick for wear on the mountain rocks.

Barney took it in his hands and made an effort. He merely hurt his fingers, and stopped a moment to look down at the insides of the where the flesh was bruised.

"He's a fake," said Mike. "You bring him along, Elder."

Once more Barney put his hands on the heavy semicircle. All the twisting strength of his hands came into play. His forearms swelled until the sleeves of his shirt were filled solidly. There was a faint *cracking* sound, then a distinct *snap*.

"I'm sorry," said Barney. "I guess I've spoiled

that horseshoe." And he held out the two broken fragments to Mike.

A more than churchly silence fell over that group. Mike received the broken horseshoe with both hands reverently.

"It must've had a flaw," said Pete, leaning nearer.

"No," muttered Mike. "Look for yourself. That's a clean break in good iron. Dog-gone my eyes!" He lifted those eyes toward Barney, slowly shaking his head.

As for the sheriff, he was supporting his chin with one hand while he considered Barney Dwyer, but finally he said: "Perhaps I'm wrong. But I'm going to believe you, Dwyer. Let me try my keys on those handcuffs, if you wish." He took out a small batch of them, studied the locks of the manacles, and at the second try he made the wrists of Barney free. After that, he mounted his men, with Leonard Peary among them. And he said briefly: "Perhaps I ought to pick you up as a horse thief, Dwyer, because you've admitted taking two horses from McGregor. But things taken from McGregor don't seem exactly stolen to me. Besides, that red mare ought to do you for any riding you have ahead. So long . . . and all the luck you deserve."

But Peary, as they rode off together, turned his head and looked with fixed, bright hatred toward Barney Dwyer. A dip of the ground and a bending of the trail took them presently out of sight.

X

Barney Dwyer sat on a rock by the edge of the bright, flowing water, and he pulled up his belt another notch. The raisins had restored his strength, somewhat, for hardly a food in the world contains such nourishment in such small bulk, but still hunger worked in him like a mine of fire. Yet hunger was nothing, compared to the pain of his failure. Success had been just before him. Would not the girl have opened the eyes of her mind, if he had done the thing she wished so bitterly? Would not Daniel Peary have banished all bitter-ness and contempt from his face? Would not those good fellows, those generous cow-punchers on the Peary Ranch, have made much of him?

But he had failed, and now his heart was empty, and all the bright beauty of that mountain valley seemed to him an empty thing, also.

He had failed, and yet if he had trusted to the red mare and to his own instincts, he would not have allowed Peary to fall into the sheriff's hands. He would have been warned in time to turn far aside and flee from that danger.

It was Leonard Peary who had laughed him out of his proper intention. They were wise, all these other people, all these other cunning, tricky men. And yet sometimes they made mistakes. Sometimes simplicity could see deeper and farther into the truth, it appeared.

He was brooding on this, when he heard the *rattling* of hoofs coming down the trail. He remembered Big Mack, as he heard the sound, and suddenly was aware that once more he was unarmed.

So he started up, and the red mare came to him as though she, also, knew the danger was rushing toward them. Beside him, she faced about, snorting and stamping. Oh, if he could sit the saddle on her, he could laugh at all riders in the world, he felt. He could leave them as though he wore wings that could carry him smoothly and swiftly over the mountains.

The approaching horseman was out of sight beyond the trees, the hoof beats grew louder, and suddenly it was Susan Jones on a racing pinto pony that swept down on Barney. The tan collar of her blouse flew in her face; the brim of her sombrero curled with the speed of her going.

When she saw Barney, she turned suddenly aside, and drew rein. The pebbles scattered and *rattled* far before her as the hoofs of the mustang slid to a halt.

"Have you seen Len Peary? Has he been down this trail?" she called out.

"Yes," said Barney sadly.

"Which way?" she exclaimed. She was wild with excitement. Her face was flushed. The bigness of her eyes made her look like a child. "Did he go down the trail, or up? Did he . . . ?"

"That way," said Barney, pointing across country. And all the time his heart was aching. For how many men have such women been in such agonies of fear? But there was no other woman like her, and there never would be. She was made to fill the eye and the soul and all the aspiration of a man at a glance, thought Barney.

"That way? That side trail?" she repeated eagerly. "Thank heavens! The sheriff . . . he was going to block this trail . . . I couldn't find Len to warn him that, if he happened to come down this way . . . oh, I'm glad." Suddenly she was grave again, staring into the upturned misery of his face. "What's the matter?" she asked.

He pointed toward the empty side trail for a moment before he could speak. "The sheriff has him," he said.

She slid from the horse as though all the strength had run out of her body.

He looked at her pale, compressed lips, and tried to turn himself into steel, so that he could speak. "We ran straight into them. Right straight into them," he said.

"Were you with him, then?" cried the girl. "Is Len hurt?"

"There wasn't any fighting . . . Peary's hands were tied," said Barney. "I . . . I tied them," he ended feebly, explaining: "There wasn't any other way to bring him from Timberline. He's too dangerous to leave with his hands free. He didn't want to come away with me, you see."

She struck both her hands against her face, then jerked them down as far as her chin and cried: "What happened? *What* happened?"

"I got him at McGregor's house and carried him away, with a pair of McGregor's horses. I lost the way and had to sleep in the woods, with Peary tied to me. Then we came down here . . . and the sheriff and some other men came suddenly out at us, with rifles. And Peary's hands were tied, you see?"

"Are you telling me that you, alone, were taking him away?" she asked.

"You wanted him gone. You told me you wanted him away from Timberline and back on his ranch," said Barney. "I don't think that I ever would have touched him, except that you said that."

"And the sheriff . . . ?" groaned the girl. "God help me. Poor Len. You . . . you . . . you took him away with his hands tied? Are you mad? Are you a half-wit? Are you a simpleton? Why do you stand there speechless and goggle at me?"

Every word struck Barney to the heart. "I'm not very clever," he said. "I was trying to do what you wanted me to do."

She caught him by the thick round of his wrists, and shook his arms. "Is this still the same playacting? Are you still trying to play your insane game with me?" she demanded. "Have you told me the truth? What . . . ?"

She seemed to feel for the first time the heat of his swollen wrists, and, snatching away her hands, she looked at the bruised hands that had seemed so helpless in her grasp. From them she looked up into that frightened, grief-stricken face.

"I'm going to be patient," said the girl. "Will you tell me what happened, all of it?"

"I've told you. They had me in handcuffs, Peary and McGregor. They thought that I was something important. They were going to starve me into saying what I was. But I'm nothing. There was nothing to confess, except what you've seen, just now . . . that I'm not very clever. I'm not as bright as other people." He flushed miserably. "I managed to get away and take Peary with me," he said. "That was what you wanted. I was trying to please you . . . I didn't know that the sheriff would be here . . ."

His voice trailed away. He seemed to be waiting for her to strike him. And into her bright eyes, full of grief and terror for what she had heard, there rushed a sudden understanding that was like a shadow. She drew back from him a little, murmuring: "Oh . . . It's really that."

He felt her judging him, pitying him; he felt scorn and anger and disgust, all combined. And this, he was sure, was all that he deserved from her. This was the way that most men and women looked upon him. When she poured anger and suspicion on him in Timberline, he had been closer to her than he was now, far closer. But he must give to her the entire bitterness of the truth.

He said: "The sheriff charged Peary with holding up the Coffeeville stage and killing Buddy Marsh, the driver."

She got hold of the reins of her pinto, close to the bit, and steadied herself with that support.

"I'd rather be dead than see you look all white and sick!" cried Barney suddenly. "I'll tell you what I'll do . . . I'll go after them . . . try to get Peary free again."

"Hush," said the girl. "Do you think that I can let you throw yourself away? You've tried to do what's best. You've done all you could . . . for me." One sob rippled up her throat and broke from her lips. But not a tear fell. She mastered herself at once.

"What could *you* do against all of them? No, no, I've got to find Big Mack. *He'll* manage something. But, oh, the life of a Leonard Peary thrown away by the blundering of a . . ." Fury sparkled in her eyes for an instant. Then she swung lightly into the saddle and darted back up the trail.

She left Barney standing with his head bent, his arms swinging a little forward, helplessly, like those of a man exhausted by the lifting of great burdens.

She had said in effect: *Oh, to think of the life of a man like Leonard Peary thrown away by a half-wit, a simpleton, a worthless fool!*

He looked down the trail along which the sheriff had disappeared with his men. He glanced wistfully at the mare. If he could only use her speed, he would soon be at the heels of the men of the law. As it was, all her strength was useless to him, and all he could do was to swing down that trail at an Indian's dog-trot.

The mare followed him, as usual, but, for once, he would almost rather have been alone. For he felt that he was running toward his doom, and that he was hurrying like water down a gorge toward the plunge of a waterfall.

XI

The sign of the six horses, that Barney followed, led straight away through the mountains and soon left the faint trail to blaze a more direct path. A mighty respect arose in Barney for both the sheriff and his men, and that respect grew as he saw the manner in which they slid their horses down great angling slopes, and toiled up the almost perpendicular sides of ravines. But over such terrain, a man like Barney Dwyer could more than keep pace with them on foot.

In four hours he had sight of them. A wisp of

dust was blowing on a mountain shoulder two miles away, and through the dust he saw the small forms of the riders.

After that he went on more carefully through the day, afraid to get too close, afraid to stay far off lest he should lose all sign of the party when it turned down some naked, rocky ravine. And all this while the red mare followed him like a mountain goat over rough and smooth.

The sheriff's party halted for lunch. Barney Dwyer, from the top of a great slope, looked down through the trees and saw the party halted at the side of a glacial lake as blue as a bit of ocean. He saw their fire smoke, and hunger stabbed him through the midst of the body. He drew still nearer. Others had apparently camped there, and in a big tin boiler that had been blackened by many fires, the posse was cooking a stew, perhaps. Whatever they had managed to shoot on the way, rabbits or squirrels, would be cut up and mixed with chopped bacon, flavored with roots and herbs—if any of the party knew enough Indian lore to select the correct plants—and thickened with bits of hardtack or eaten with pone. Starvation searched Barney with many pains when he saw the party being served from that old boiler.

Afterward, the group lolled about to complete an hour's rest for man and horse, but finally they moved on into the opposite woods, and Barney came down like a ravening wolf on the camp. He had no hope—but when he looked into the boiler, he found that the sheriff's party had actually left at least two quarts of a most delicious mulligan at the bottom of the boiler. That he ate with more infinite relish than anything he ever had tasted, and then, abandoning all precautions, he lay flat on his back beside the lake and slept for fifteen minutes.

When he stood up, he was a man re-made. The absorbing hunger was pacified. He drank a final time from the lake, sparingly, and continued with the labor of that trail all through the afternoon until the evening descended, until the darkness came, until, finally, he had to keep close up and be guided more by the noise the posse made than by the starlight glimpses he could catch of them.

A slender sickle of a moon rose in the east through a clear sky, and by that light, as he issued from the forest onto a bald, level, upland plateau, he now saw the procession winding before him. It seemed that the group intended to journey all through the night, although the slowness of their movements proved that their horses were utterly beaten. They dipped out of view over the edge of a ravine. Barney, coming to the edge of the rock, saw them descending far beneath him down the jags of a trail that hugged the precipitous face of the cliff. Below them ran a straight, narrow flume of water, sweeping fast, but through a channel so smooth that hardly a sound of rushing came up to the keen ear of Barney.

At the bottom of the trail, the cliff gave back and afforded room between its foot and the edge of the water for a beach covered with shrubs and with big stones. There the posse halted, at last. There a fire was kindled, and the sight of it made Barney suddenly aware that the air of that moun-tain night was very cold.

The red mare, at this moment, snorted and ran to him. Something had startled her. Now he saw the nature of the alarm, for close behind him came half a dozen riders whose approach had been muffled to silence by the noise of the wind. They were spread out in a line that permitted no escape to Barney. For that matter, they could hardly be enemies who would offer him any danger.

One man rode a little from the rest, demanding calmly: "Who's there?"

"My name is Barney Dwyer," he answered. "And I am . . ."

"Dwyer!" suddenly exclaimed the familiar deep, ringing voice of McGregor. "It's Barney Dwyer, for a fact. Close in on him, boys. Dwyer, don't budge!"

And the quick, frightened voice of Sue Jones added in haste: "Don't harm him. I've told you what he is! Don't hurt him, Mack!"

They stood about Barney with their guns, and the moonlight slanted into savage faces, as naturally unkempt with unshaven beards as mountains with forests.

McGregor stood among the rest. By his mere vague silhouette Barney could recognize him. He was saying: "Maybe you're right, Sue. I'll do him no harm, if he's as simple as you say. Look here, Dwyer, what's the game you're up to now?"

"It was account of me," said Barney, "that poor Peary was caught by the sheriff. And so I'm following along. I'm hoping for a chance to get him free again."

"One to four . . . you'd try that, would you?" muttered McGregor. "You've been riding all day after 'em?"

"I've been walking. Didn't I tell you before that I can't ride the mare?"

"Wait a moment," said McGregor. He leaned and felt the inside of Barney's trousers from the calf of the leg to the heel. There was not a trace of perspiration from the horse. McGregor, straightening again, exclaimed "Sue, you're right! The poor devil keeps the horse with him for a mascot, or something . . . not to use. He is a half-wit, and I've been a fool about him. Dwyer, you really mean that you'd try to tackle the four of 'em? How?" He asked it with a mild derision, pointing down toward the dim forms that, at the bottom of the cliff, were moving about the fire.

"One man," said McGregor, "can hold the narrowness of that trail. How would you get at

Peary, for instance, through those four men tonight?"

Barney answered instantly, for the thought had come to him at the very first, making him shiver: "I'd try to get down to that run of water, above the camp, and then float with it down to the fire. They wouldn't likely expect anyone to come in water as fast as that. I'd lie at the edge of the camp and wait for a chance to help Peary. That's all."

"Yeah," drawled McGregor, stooping back. "He's only got a piece of a mind, not a whole one. But let me see you start the job, Dwyer. Boys, the rest of you scatter ahead. Ride straight on. You know where to cut through to the pass toward Coffeeville. We'll lie for the sheriff there and give him hell, and get Peary away. Hurry on. I'll stay here a minute to see what poor Dwyer is going to try."

Barney was already working down the dangerous face of the rock, and studying the narrow ledges that extended beneath him. He heard the voice of Susan Jones calling eagerly above him: "Come back, Barney! Please come back! This is only a way to kill yourself, not to do anything for Len Peary!"

He answered briefly: "What does it matter? The life of a half-wit isn't worth anything. There's no man or woman or child in the world that would miss me. There's only the mare, poor thing." For he could see the head of the red mare as she ventured to the very verge of the cliff to look down after her master. Something choked in the throat of Barney as he saw her, then down he went again.

He heard the girl cry out, pursuing him with anxious words.

"*I* care about you, Barney. I know you're honest and kind. You can't help the harm that you've done. Come back while you still can."

But he climbed down rapidly, hurrying his descent for fear that voice should overmaster his courage and charm him to a standstill, and then draw him back to that world where he was no more than a chopping block for the scorn of every jester.

The wind, its strength gathered like liquid in a funnel, struck at him. He lost one handhold and swung like a pendulum over a sheer drop of a hundred feet, but, recovering his grip, he went on with the descent.

The voice, above him, had ended. He could hear nothing, see nothing over his head except the sky, a few pale stars, and the gilded arc of the moon among them. Below him, the river shot by with a whisper. He clung to a rock on the verge of it, now, and saw it hurling past. In spite of its speed, in places it was so smooth that the shattered images of the stars appeared; again a riffle of foam whipped down the stream to mark the rate of its progress.

He tried it with his hands. It was snow water fresh from the summits and of a power to spread numbness with electric speed through the body. But it seemed to Barney, as he leaned over the cold rush of the creek, that this was an easy way for a poor half-wit to pass out of this life into whatever nebulous region of bewilderment and sorrow is reserved for the souls of those who are not quick of mind.

So he lowered himself into the stream, and was flung like a dry stick down the current. With hands stretched before him, he warded off a dozen times the dangers from sharp, reaching points of stone that leveled like bayonets at his breast. Then he saw the yellow gleam of firelight, the black shadows of stone and of human forms. So he caught one of those projecting points that threatened him. His grip held. His body streamed out with the force of the water for an instant, and then he drew himself, shuddering, out on the beach.

In a narrow path of firelight that streamed between two of the boulders, he saw a man walk past him. He dared look no higher than the knees. He saw the gleam of the spoon-handled spurs, brightly gilded. And at the edge of the water that figure paused, looking down, gun in hand, no doubt, at the outstretched body of Barney.

No, the fellow merely stooped, filled a canteen with water, and returned toward the fire.

Barney, breathing again, took heed of his surroundings. It was the deep, black shadow of a large rock that had blanketed him away from the unsuspecting gaze of that water carrier. In that same shadow he could rise to his knees and peek from side to side and over the top securely.

To his left was Len Peary seated against a narrow projection of rock. In his hands, which were free, was a tin of coffee, that he sipped comfortably, while smoking a cigarette. They had secured him, simply, by passing the length of a lariat around and around his body, then knotting it behind the rock.

Two men had lain down, wrapped in their blankets, their faces turned from the fire toward the cliff. Another sat on a boulder with his back to the fire, a rifle across his knees, while he kept watch on the trail that came down the face of the cliff, the one apparent direction from which danger could come at the party. The fourth man, now tending the coffee pot at the fire, was the sheriff himself. He was humming a tune, contentedly, the short-stemmed pipe working up and down between his teeth, now and then.

Barney worked snake-like to the rear of Peary's stone and rapidly unfastened the knot that held the rope. Off to his left the well of the ravine was no longer a sheer face of rock, but a steep slant of boulders of all sizes. Once he had Peary free, perhaps they could dodge away to safety among those stones, and so climb up to the top of the bank. But the shudder of cold that was in the body of Barney Dwyer was not in his mind. Whatever happened, his life was not a thing of importance. He would never find, he was sure, a soul more tender and sympathetic than that of the girl, and to her he was a mere object of pitying contempt.

A sudden start that tugged on the coils of the rope, as the knot came free in his fingers, told him that Len Peary was aware of what was happening. He had to whisper: "Steady . . . and watch your chances."

He could see the sombrero of Len Peary nod in understanding above the top of the rock.

But now the sheriff came straight from the fire and sat down, cross-legged, beside his prisoner. "I can tell you this, Peary," he said gravely. "If you make a confession, you'll probably get your life. And life in a prison is better than a broken neck and the long night."

"I know." Peary nodded. "But the fact is that I didn't kill Buddy Marsh."

"You weren't even at the hold-up, I suppose?" sneered the sheriff.

"I'm saying nothing about that," answered Peary. "But I'm telling you that I didn't kill Marsh. I've never pulled a trigger in my life until the other fellow was going for his gun with a clean, clear break for both of us."

"Do you stick on that?"

"I stick on that, because it's true," said Peary.

"Well," said the sheriff, "whatever the truth is, they have enough to hang you. And they'll do it. I don't pity you. It's what you have coming to you . . . you and all your kind. But because you're young, I was trying to show you the easiest way out."

"Thanks," said Peary. "But I still keep hoping."

"What sort of hope have you got?" asked Sheriff Elder. "The only thing that could get at us here would be a bird. And tomorrow we only have a few miles to get you into Coffeeville. Where's your hope, Peary?"

"I was born hoping, I'll keep on hoping till I die," said Peary carelessly.

And that was the moment that Barney chose. He rose from hands and knees. The sheriff, as though a shadow of peril whipped across his quick mind, jerked his head around over one shoulder, but Barney already had him by the arms, and so jerked him to his feet, and held him helpless.

Len Peary was up, also, shaking off the limp coils of the rope, and into the shout of the sheriff went the Indian yell of Peary as he snatched the revolver from the sheriff's holster.

The sentinel at the foot of the trail had leaped and whirled toward the noise. The pair who was wrapped in blankets rolled out again, reaching for their guns, but they saw their targets retreating with the sheriff held as a protection before them. Back among the boulders they went, while Sheriff Jim Elder, maddened with shame and disappointment, called out to his men to fire, regardless of his safety. But they would not shoot through him to get at the other pair.

All was confusion. One yelled one bit of advice, and one another, until, when they were high up the boulder-strewn slope, big Barney Dwyer released the sheriff.

The man ran down the way toward the frantic confusion of the forms around the fire, shouting orders as he went. But Dwyer and Leonard Peary were already on the level of the upper trail. The grip of Peary bit into the arm of Barney Dwyer.

"Someday, old-timer . . . ," said Peary. "Someday . . ."

He could not finish the remark. There was no need of finishing it. The tremor of his voice was enough.

Big Mack and the girl were on them, and the red mare came at Barney, sniffing him curiously, snorting, and then pawing at the ground.

"We saw that by the firelight," said McGregor. "We saw the shadow of you all the time, and of all the cool bits of deviltry that I ever saw . . . well, you're alive, Peary, and that's more than you have a right to be."

"He ought not to have turned the sheriff loose," complained Len Peary. "We all could have said a few things to that fellow Elder. What's the matter, Sue? What are you crying about? Let's get out of here."

"I'm crying because I've found out what a hero is," said the girl.

"They're coming pretty fast!" exclaimed McGregor. "They're coming up the trail fast, and they're well mounted, the lot of 'em. Len, pop into the saddle on the pinto!"

"It's the horse of Sue," said Peary.

"I'm talking about the saving of your neck, man!" cried McGregor. "They won't hurt a woman . . . or a dunce that happens to be a hero. Len, jump on that horse and come with me!"

And Peary, to the bewilderment of Barney, actually sprang on the pinto and galloped away with McGregor.

XII

They had reason for their going that beat louder and louder in their ears as the posse men drove their horses as hard as possible up the steep slope of the cliff trail. The sheriff had straightened out all the confusion of his men and now he brought them on with a savage rush, eager for revenge, eager to make atonement.

From his horse, Peary had cried out: "Scatter, Sue and Barney! They won't bother you. They'll tackle us. Scatter and lie low! They've left us . . .

they've left you, Barney. I won't believe it. Try the mare . . . try the mare and ride for your life, if you can! Oh, Barney . . . the traitors!"

As for Barney, he moved in a dream, dimly. The thing was beyond his comprehension. They might have shared the horses. They might have stayed to fight. Perhaps they would have done this except that McGregor realized that his was the only rifle in his party, and revolvers are poor things for moonlight shooting.

But they had fled with hardly a word.

Barney went to the mare and fitted his foot into the stirrup, not because he had hope, but because his back was so against the wall. Then he swung into the saddle and sat loosely, waiting for the explosion that would hurl him into the air.

Instead, the mare merely lifted her head and turned it, looking back at him with ears pricked. There was not a tremor in her powerful body. She was still as a stone.

In the meantime, the posse men were near. Their voices seemed already to have topped the rimrock and to be rushing at the fugitives. Far away, the forms of McGregor and Len Peary were dwindling in the moonshine, but Barney Dwyer would be in the very jaws of danger. That moon that had given him so ineffectual a light when he needed it, now seemed to be a blazing sun.

He reined the mare across the neck. At the first touch of pressure, she turned readily, and the heart of Barney leaped. She was his, and it was not strength that had conquered her. Even in the terror of that moment and the haste, he had time to realize that there is a force of beauty and mystery in life far different from the brutal ways of most men.

He stretched his hand to the girl. "She's tamed, Sue!" he called to her. "And she's strong enough to carry us both. Get up behind me. . . ."

She waved him frantically away with both hands. "Go on!" she shouted. "They won't hurt me. I'm only a woman. Save yourself, Barney. Don't . . ."

"I'll stay here, then," said Barney simply.

When she saw him so calmly immoveable, she ran suddenly, put her foot on the stirrup, and was instantly up behind him.

And as Barney patted the shoulder of the red mare, she broke into a gallop as long, as free, as swift as though there were not a feather's weight upon her back.

Every stride was a long step toward safety, but the mare was hardly in motion before Elder and his men were on the upper plateau. They could hear his voice, shouting: "Mike, Pete! Take the girl and Dwyer, yonder. I'm going after Peary and the other. Ride like the devil, and then come back on my trail. . . ."

So, while two riders swept off after McGregor and Peary, two more came like yelling Indians after Barney and the girl.

When Barney looked back, it seemed to him that those flying mustangs must surely overtake him in an instant, but still the long stroke of the mare's gallop kept them at their distance. How she could have swept away from them with only a single burden on her back! If she could last until they reached the dark cloud of trees that rolled up on the other side of the little plateau—then there might be a chance to dodge away to safety. Toward that goal, Barney directed her. Gallantly she ran, but almost instantly the immense strain began to tell. Her ears flattened; a shudder of effort came in every stride.

And the girl cried, close to the ear of Barney Dwyer: "Let me drop off, Barney! Then you'll be off like a bird. Let me drop here, or I'll throw myself down to the ground . . . they won't bother about me . . . they'll go on after you and . . ."

Her right arm was firmly about him. He caught that arm and held it in a vise. "When you have to stop, I have to stop with you," he said quietly. "We've still got a ghost of a chance."

He heard her groan with despair, but the grip of her arm tightened around him. Joy came over him like a light, like a madness. To her, he might be no more than a dolt, a half-wit, but for this moment they were sweeping on to a single destiny.

Behind them, he heard the pounding of hoofs that seemed to make the earth beneath them tremble. But here were the woods, a pale glistening front of trees and black caverns of shadow.

Under those shadows he swept. The beds of pine needles almost silenced the noise of hoofs, yet the pair was so close behind that he could feel the beating of the hoofs. He crashed the mare through a tangle of shrubbery, dodged into a region of vast shadow under the pine trees, and suddenly halted the mare beside a great trunk. Both of them slid to the ground, and waited. Straight toward them came the noise of the pursuers, the pounding hoofs, the *creaking* of the stirrup leathers. Two dim shapes drew into view, pressed nearer—and went by! They passed through a little silver streak of moonlight, and were gone.

So the two stood in a silence. Barney heard the labored breathing of the mare. With every inhalation the cinch straps *creaked* a little.

"We'd better go on," said Barney. "They might stop going ahead and begin to hunt for us on the back trail."

He walked slowly on, at right angles to the direction in which they had fled. The girl hurried to get into step with him. She was on one side. On the other, his hand rested affectionately on the mane of the red mare. And so they went by the big trees, quietly, never speaking, until they came to a point where the trees left off for a moment, and the shoulder of the mountain dropped swiftly away before them. Through the moon haze they looked far off at mountain shapes, only real and clear where the light glistened on the upper reaches of snow and of ice. Out of the black of the cañon below them a voice of water kept booming softly, like the beating of great kettle drums and the blowing of distant horns.

She stretched an arm out, pointing. "You're like that, Barney," she said. "There's more scope to you than to millions of the men I've known. If ever I've hurt you . . ."

"I'm used to pain," said Barney earnestly. "It doesn't matter. And I'm so happy now that I want to shout. Only, shouting wouldn't say it at all."

"You're happy because you've saved the life of one man . . . a man you didn't like . . . a man who'd wronged you . . . but you saved him. And then you saved me from being paraded in front of people, and shamed and disgraced. That's why you're happy."

"I wasn't thinking of anything but this," said Barney. "I mean, being here . . . with you."

She began to laugh a little, but there was an amazing tenderness in the sound.

He said: "Why are you laughing? I don't understand, but I suppose that's because I'm not very bright or . . ."

"No, you're not bright," said the girl, facing suddenly toward him. "The bright things are often the small things . . . the rats and the squirrels. And small minds are often bright ones. Always fighting for themselves. Thinking of nothing but them-selves. Hungry for money and praise, and glory. Never seeing the truth. Never giving up heart or soul to anyone. But no one has the strength of your hands and no one has the strength of your soul."

"Hush," said Barney, shocked with amazement. "You mustn't say things just to make me happy. I know how simple I am. There's very little that I really know."

"You know all that God wants a man to know!" cried the girl. "I'd go on my knees and pray, if praying would make me like you. But how could I ever be gentle or true or brave or noble like you, Barney? How could I ever be anything more than the dust under your feet?"

He saw that tears were running down her face. He put out both his hands, but, in his awe, he dared not touch her.

"I've made you cry," said Barney. "I'm always doing what's wrong. Forgive me, Sue. I wouldn't hurt you. I'm just a blunderer. You're the only person I've ever been happy with."

She got hold of those hands that were clumsily, helplessly extended toward her, and, drawing them over her shoulders, she said: "It's pity for all the pain you've suffered that makes me cry. And I'm crying because I've been such a wretched thing, such a small, vain, silly, worthless, selfish nothing. But I'll never have tears in my eyes again, if you mean what you

347

say about being happy with me. Do you mean it?"

"Mean it?" said Barney. He took a great breath. "Yes," he said, "I mean it so much that there's an ache in my heart."

"Barney, Barney, Barney," said the girl.

"You're still crying," said Barney Dwyer. "What have I done now?"

She came closer to him. She drew one of his arms about her neck, and leaned her head back against it, watching his face. "If you're the least whit happy with me now," she said, "do you think that you could go on being happy if I try to make myself over and work with all my might to be better, and be more like you?"

"You're not laughing at me," said Barney. "Why do you talk that way?"

"Because, Barney, everything has gone out of my life. Everything else is something I dreamed, but now I'm awake. I'm saying that I love you, Barney."

"Don't," he begged her. "You can't be saying that. I'm only Barney Dwyer . . . who everyone laughs at."

"Then I want to be laughed at, too," said the girl.

With his hands on her shoulders, gently he pushed her back so that he could see her face, and consider it. In his eyes there was no more joy than there was fear and reverence.

"It's like praying, and being answered," said Barney. "Only, I never would have dared even to pray for this."

ABOUT THE AUTHOR

Max Brand® is the best-known pen name of Frederick Faust, creator of Dr. Kildare, Destry, and many other fictional characters popular with readers and viewers worldwide. Faust wrote for a variety of audiences in many genres. His enormous output, totaling approximately 30,000,000 words or the equivalent of 530 ordinary books, covered nearly every field: crime, fantasy, historical romance, espionage, Westerns, science fiction, adventure, animal stories, love, war, and fashionable society, big business and big medicine. Eighty motion pictures have been based on his work along with many radio and television programs. For good measure he also published four volumes of poetry. Perhaps no other author has reached more people in more different ways.

Born in Seattle in 1892, orphaned early, Faust grew up in the rural San Joaquin Valley of California. At Berkeley he became a student rebel and one-man literary movement, contributing prodigiously to all campus publications. Denied a degree because of unconventional conduct, he embarked on a series of adventures culminating in New York City where, after a period of near starvation, he received simultaneous recognition as a serious poet and successful author of fiction. Later, he traveled widely, making his home in New York, then in Florence, and finally in Los Angeles.

Once the United States entered the Second World War, Faust abandoned his lucrative writing career and his work as a screenwriter to serve as a war correspondent with the infantry in Italy, despite his fifty-one years and a bad heart. He was killed during a night attack on a hilltop village held by the German army. New books based on magazine serials or unpublished manuscripts or restored versions continue to appear so that, alive or dead, he has averaged a new book every four months for seventy-five years. Beyond this, some work by him is newly reprinted every week of every year in one or another format somewhere in the world. A great deal more about this author and his work can be found in *The Max Brand Companion* (Greenwood Press, 1997) edited by Jon Tuska and Vicki Piekarski.

Additional copyright information:

Center Point Large Print
600 Brooks Road / PO Box 1
Thorndike, ME 04986-0001 USA

(207) 568-3717

US & Canada:
1 800 929-9108
www.centerpointlargeprint.com